THE BRUISER

by Jo Milanne

THE BRUISER

Paperback ISBN 978-1-7637284-2-4

Contents

1

The Man

The tall man, wearing a wide brimmed hat, drifted in with the burning desert wind, amid a billowing cloud of red dust.

He paused at a garden gate fronting an old house. It was the first dwelling he had come across after trudging through the hot dry Australian terrain for hours.

The man noted only a single name on the letterbox: Alba Jenkins.

An aroma of baking flavoured the air. The homely promise of food wafted from an open window of the rambling weatherboard homestead. The traveller felt his stomach constrict and grumble with hunger pangs.

Above a wide verandah that hugged the house, a small dormer window, set in the high peaked roof, reflected an orange sun, red-hazed by dust and low in the western sky.

Alba Jenkins first perceived the man from her kitchen window as she washed and dried the basins and utensils from her baking session. The woman stopped humming to herself and stared in surprise. The figure seemed to materialise out of nowhere.

The man dropped his swag and wiped his sweating brow as four bitsa dogs ran out barking and snarling. As always, Alba was glad of the dogs. They gave her confidence and company.

When the man stopped at the front yard gate of her lonely outback residence, Alba walked outside, hands on her wide hips. The woman took stock of the man while wiping her gnarly work worn hands on the floury apron she wore.

"Who are you? Where did you come from? Are you lost?"

The buxom property owner jumbled her questions together out of anxious curiosity for having a visitor turn up without any vehicle or horse in sight.

Alba Jenkins lived alone apart from the dogs but did not fear the unexpected visitor. As the landed householder in the remote area, she felt a certain responsibility to offer aid to any traveller seeking help, as her parents had always done.

Alba Jenkins inherited the place from her elderly parents who had been completely amazed to produce their only child late in life. The old couple cherished their daughter and taught the girl everything they knew, albeit rather sadly limited to their own knowledge, beliefs and misconceptions.

When it seemed that Alba had literacy difficulties, her parents weren't worried as she would be getting the property in the long run. So lessons focused on domestic issues and farm work. There had been no school bus in those days and the older Jenkins saw no advantage in sending Alba where the kids they observed in the town schoolyard sounded unruly and rowdy. It could only lead to no good, they said.

Every day and at bedtime Alba's parents read aloud to her from old books and magazines. Alba loved the story times and much preferred to listen with her eyes closed, rather than make any attempt to decipher the words by herself. The old classics served to build the girl's vocabulary and she became quite well spoken, considering her slow wit and lack of formal education.

The broad rather barren acres of the Jenkins spread had never been very productive but Alba leased the land to an old cattleman who kept her in meat. She went into town fortnightly but mostly thrived by running some poultry and keeping her kitchen garden well fed with cow and chook manures.

Every drop of waste water was drained towards the food plants by a series of shallow channels. Alba kept the irrigation channels dug out as drifting sands blew in, just as her parents had taught her.

The unexpected visitor who'd turned up at Alba's gate, out of a red dust haze, politely doffed his wide brimmed hat, said his name was Kirk and asked for a drink of water.

"Don't tell me you're travelling without water!" Alba exclaimed.

To go anywhere without water went against the strictest rule drummed into Alba's head since early childhood. The traveller adopted a suitably downcast and chastened expression.

"No. I had some but I drank it all. I've been walking since sunrise." He replied.

Alba opened her front gate and ordered her dogs to desist with just a hand signal. The crossbred mixes of cattle dog, kelpie and greyhound obeyed although they remained on high alert to any trouble.

Invited to sit in the shade, the man gratefully stepped up the four broad stairs, put his dusty hat on the floor and removed his dark sunglasses. Mesmerised by his cat-like eyes Alba felt momentarily hypnotised. Shaking herself to focus, she indicated he should sit in a wicker chair beside a wooden table on the wide front verandah. Her guest, Kirk, sat under the cover of the bull nose iron roof while his hostess fetched a jug of cold water and a glass.

Alba watched as he drank, fascinated by the movement of the Adams Apple in his throat as he swallowed. The handsome stranger had a shadow of whiskers but his throat was smooth and tanned. The woman thought he could not be very old, maybe late twenties, early thirties. That made him about her own age. She had reached her thirtieth year but outdoor work in the unrelenting harsh climate had done her no favours.

Kirk, if that was his name, knew himself to possess a good body and handsome face. He also knew the woman admired him as he drank. Letting a dribble of cool water spill down his chin, he noticed her eyes follow the trickle and dwell on his muscular chest.

The man chuckled knowingly to himself as Alba pushed some stray hairs behind her ears and licked her lips.

Once the man quenched his initial thirst, Alba made him a cup of tea and a sandwich, which he wolfed down. She thought: *The poor bugger is starving.* A second cup of tea and a plate of fresh baked scones were also gladly accepted.

At last the man sat back and sighed with satisfaction, prepared to offer an explanation for his uninvited presence.

"Thank you for you kindness. I am so sorry to intrude on you like this. I'm not usually this useless. But I hitched a ride a long way back and the bloke tried to rob me. Anyway, I got away with my swag at least. But he left me stranded. All I could do was keep walking...just following the road."

He said it in a tired voice and truthfully, he had undergone a long arduous walk under the hot sun. Alba took his story for granted. It sounded plausible and he certainly appeared to be weary.

"You're still ten miles out of town." She told him.

Alba measured distance in miles as her parents had taught her. They had no use for all the modern malarkey about kilometres and litres and suchlike which they thought to be a political fad that would never last. They would never have voted for it, given any choice, they had declared. Decimal currency was bad enough and now they were stuck with it. The older Jenkins were adamant: Bloody government pen pushers were to blame.

Right or wrong, Alba had complete faith in her parents, having never known them to be mistaken. Nor had she ever known her parents to turn away a stranger who needed a hand.

The man calling himself Kirk, summed up the situation and the simple woman. He used reverse psychology to gain an overnight stay:

"I've taken enough of your time. I'll be on my way. Could I possibly trouble you to fill my water canteen?"

He opened his zippered swag bag and took out an empty flask, placed it on the table and left the knapsack open on the timber floorboards of the verandah.

Alba knew it was too late to begin a walk into town and she did not like driving in the dark. Just the thought of arriving back to her lonely house at night sent shivers down her spine. She would have to let the dogs inside and check every room and cupboard for spooks.

As Alba sat contemplating what to say to the man, hundreds of yellow-headed green budgerigars flew in and mobbed the cattle troughs to drink, as they always did before sunset. Now, the sudden arrival of chattering birds reminded Alba that dark time was nigh.

Twilight was fleeting, night fell suddenly in the Australian outback. It would be upon them in just a few hours, when nocturnal predators prowled for the vulnerable and unwary.

Apart from her own mortal fear of the dark, Alba's natural hospitality made her offer the visitor a bed till morning. It was what her parents would have done, so it seemed right.

"There's a bunk in the sleep out on the back verandah It's cool out there. If you'd rather rest up until tomorrow?"

The visitor put on a appreciative face loaded with false surprise at the offer he fully expected.

"That is so good of you! I have to admit I don't relish doing more walking today. You are truly a kind hearted lady. Thank you."

Alba was pleased by the polite way the man gladly and humbly accepted. She showed him where he could use the outhouse and have a shower outside under the tank stand. A new cake of soap, shampoo and a clean bath towel where brought out for her interesting visitor.

"You won't get much lather. It's the bore water." She told him apologetically.

"No worries. It will sure be a pleasure to wash some of this road dirt off." He smiled.

Alba smiled back. He was such a very charming man. She felt drawn to him, thrilling to his macho looks and his nice manners. So much potential right here in her own home seemed like a gift.

Before going to the shower, the charmer pulled some clean clothes from his haversack, still leaving it wide open. The woman would peek inside later, when she could, of this he was certain.

As soon as he strode to the tank stand and shut the half door, Alba clambered upstairs to the attic where she could get a view of him standing naked under the overhead shower rose.

Seeing his firm manly physique, Alba felt some latent yearnings rekindle. She watched him scrub fingers through his head of thick hair and pitied that she couldn't see his fiddly bits over the half wall. Entranced, she watched as his hands worked the soap down to more intriguing lower regions.

The woman's ample proportions and sun dried complexion made her appear much older than her thirty years yet she remained young at heart. She often wondered what it would be like with a young and handsome lover. So far, she'd only known one man sexually and he was old enough to be her father.

Alba hurried back down the steep attic steps to the verandah and took a quick peek inside the man's bag. She found his wallet with a drivers licence inside a plastic cover. Alba couldn't read well but by sounding out the letters, she deciphered his name to be: Kirkwood Bonn.

The worn plastic cover over the licence made the ID photo look blurry. All the same, Alba thought the photo must have been taken when the man was much younger. A thick wad of cash bulged in his wallet as well.

So he is not just a good bum. Alba giggled at the funny double meaning in her own little joke. Pity she couldn't share that one with her usual lover, Old Bob, who she felt sure might take a dim view of her naughtiness.

Since he had so much money, Alba thought the handsome man was very lucky not to have been robbed by the bad bloke who'd left him stranded. When Alba heard the pressure pump turn off, she hurriedly put everything back into the man's knapsack, just as she'd found it.

The snooping woman went to find some fresh linen to make up the sturdy bunk in the sleep out and took a couple of steaks from the freezer to thaw for their evening meals.

2

The Bruiser

The handsome stranger enjoying Alba Jenkins' hospitality was not Kirkwood Bonn.

The real Kirkwood Bonn had been incinerated in the fireball that destroyed his Toyota Landcruiser. His killer, Bruce Luck, who'd been known as The Bruiser inside prison walls, stole Kirk's valuables and his identity.

Some children of abusive parents grow up to become law abiding, successful adults. Bruce Luck was not one of those. He felt society owed him for his poor childhood. He knew right from wrong but considered himself entitled to take out his resentment wherever possible.

Bruce Luck had come out of prison with no plans and very little in the way of assets or opportunities. With nowhere else to go, he went back to his childhood home in South Australia where his despised father still dwelt. Bruce was relieved to find his bedroom remained as he had left it. Cobwebs and all. He wouldn't have put it past his father to rent it out.

The dysfunctional relationships of the Luck family had festered, well hidden behind the benign facade of a typical suburban brick home, in a respectable neighbourhood.

As Bruce entered the house, his father, in advanced stages of dementia, had called out:

"Is that you Greta?"

"No. You stupid old bastard. Mummy dear pissed off long ago."

"Who are you?" The old man peered at his son.

"It's Bruce, your old punching bag. Don't you remember me? You idiot old fart."

"Where's Greta? I need my tea." His father whined.

Bruce's mother, Greta, had abandoned the family home many years ago, before her son reached his seventh year. The old man, Bruce Luck senior, often regressed to the past, as if the intervening years after his wife left had never happened.

Greta Luck had never taken to motherhood and grew to despise her abusive husband. She also loathed having to take their son to and from school five days a week. It seemed just too hard. Greta rarely got young Bruce to school in rainy weather and never on Mondays after her normal weekend binge drinking. This suited the boy very well. He hated school and all the rules.

The local dump was closed on Mondays so young Bruce would sneak under a gap in the chain wire fence to play there. He felt it to be his personal domain where games included throwing stones at scavenging birds and rats. He sometimes saw foxes and feral cats creeping amongst the piles of debris. Fortunately for the animals, Bruce's attempts at building traps out of rubbish did not catch anything.

Greta's efforts to get the boy to school at least three days a week made her resent the stern lectures given to her by the principal. She thought to be doing well enough. What did year one and two matter anyway? It wasn't as if they were being taught rocket science.

Greta offered her opinion to the school head. He disagreed and went off on another spiel. She'd had enough. Despite a no smoking rule, Greta lit a cigarette and blew smoke in the headmaster's face.

Despite the offence, the school principal feared confrontation with the tarty mother. To retaliate in the way he'd have liked, would be construed as improper, under lawful limitations. The man had to swallow his pride.

Rather than escalate the issue, the principal gave her a last chance to comply or he would report it to Child Welfare as child neglect, he'd said. Not expecting a win from this threat, he was surprised it had some effect on the woman. If he was not mistaken, he identified real anxiety cross her face. Although the child's school attendance did not improve, the headmaster remembered the exchange as one of his triumphs.

Indeed, Greta suffered valid concerns that Child Protection Officers could extract damning accounts from her young son. She already knew the kid wasn't smart enough or old enough to be coached out of telling a particular tale against her. If the truth came to light, she could be in deep trouble for coercing her child to commit a serious crime.

Rather than knuckle down and obey the school rules, Greta Luck packed a bag, pawned her wedding ring for a pittance and went back to the city, soliciting for work on the streets as she'd done in a happier past. Young Bruce had not yet turned seven years old when his mother left.

Bruce's father took it out on the boy with beatings until the boy was strong enough to strike back. At eleven years old, well built and bad tempered, Bruce punched his father in the mouth and told him he'd kill him if he ever hit him again. His father truly believed him.

Bruce Luck junior had a short fuse and was already no stranger to the police. He'd been in trouble for fighting at school, been caught shoplifting and looking up women's skirts from beside an escalator in the mall.

The senior Bruce Luck took to locking his bedroom door at night, having no doubts his boy

was capable of murder.

Greta Luck's joy at her escape had been short-lived when she found herself to be pregnant again and too far along for abortion. The timing meant the child had to be her husband's.

The expectant mother went back to using her maiden name, Greta Vossberg, before presenting herself to a Catholic home for unmarried mothers. She gave a convincing story of being raped and beaten, having experienced those atrocities first hand from her own spouse and others.

Greta Vossberg put her second baby up for adoption, she no more wanted it than the first one. The nuns told her the baby would be going to a very respectable and religious older couple. Greta wasn't interested in where it went as long as she got rid of it. She didn't want to meet the people and left without thanking or saying goodbye to anyone at the home.

Neither young Bruce nor his father ever saw or heard from Greta again.

Being released from prison, in his early thirties, with no job and no prospects, did not worry Bruce Luck. If anything he felt that with no strings, the world was his oyster.

His old father received help from a home care group who supplied one good meal a day and did some housework. Bruce thought the old mongrel could go on for ages and would need looking after.

The unloved son briefly considered applying for a carers pension. He thought it might be easy money. On second thoughts, taking responsibility for his dear old Dad would be even worse than finding a job. *No way.*

Bruce Luck junior looked forward to the day his old man kicked the bucket. Inheriting the family home couldn't happen soon enough for the chip off the old block.

In the meantime, the ex prisoner wanted to make up for time lost in the clink. Not keen on being shackled to some boring occupation after two years incarceration, he wanted to live a dream of taking off into the outback to look for easy pickings.

Bruce Luck's mobile phone, driving licence and various plastic cards were secured in a locked metal cash box kept on top of the wardrobe in his old bedroom. He wanted no digital trail that could track where he went.

After two years of no sex with a woman, the man looked forward to an adventurous rampage across Australia, taking advantage of as many women as he could.

The Bruiser had some cash to play with but as an accomplished thief, he planned to augment his finances along the way. He considered it would be like a gap year.

A few weeks into his escapade, Bruce Luck befriended a younger man, Kirkwood Bonn, and discovered he was travelling up to the Northern Territory coast.

Bruce had never been to the Top End. The idea appealed to him as a great destination to continue his wild spree. It had been remarkably easy to gain a lift with Kirkwood.

The ex prisoner recognised his mark had similar wavy brown hair and a ready smile like his own. A feline slant and gleam to his eyes were the clincher. Bruce knew how to use his own catlike eyes to best advantage, either to enchant or terrify, as the situation demanded.

Telling himself it was the old stroke of 'Luck' meeting a dickhead who could passably fit his own description, a devious possibility occurred to the con man.

The Bruiser introduced himself as Richie. It was the name of a cell mate he'd shared with in prison. Ever cunning, he could react to that name readily without pause to raise suspicion.

Bruce Luck, as Richie, offered to share fuel costs for a lift. Kirkwood was only too happy for the company on the long road ahead. Kirkwood's white Toyota Landcruiser had roof racks packed high with camping gear. The Bruiser assessed the younger man as being well set up and probably not short of a buck.

As a precaution, Kirkwood Bonn locked himself into a toilet cubicle and privately messaged his partner, saying he was giving a lift to a hitchhiker named Richie. He said the guy seemed genuine and would provide some company apart from sharing fuel costs.

Kirkwood's partner, Damien Cresswick, replied: "Sounds good. Take care. Miss you. Talk soon. Busy just now lots of customers. Xx" This brief and light message with its tones of dismissal would forever stalk Damien's regrets.

'Richie' paid the fuel tab and they set off on the long road north. The travel companions shared a mega packet of Minties, as the view of red dirt and grey green grassy tufts and scrub flashed by the dusty Landcruiser windows.

The long stretch of highway made for a tedious journey and since the two men had little in common, their conversation dwindled. The Bruiser had his chequered past to protect and Kirkwood did not want to disclose his personal life.

After driving for three hours non-stop, The Bruiser as Richie, offered to take the wheel for a while so Kirkwood could catch a nap. Kirkwood had found himself nodding a few times, so he gratefully accepted the chance for a doze.

While his benefactor slept, The Bruiser drove off the main travelled road when he came upon a more thickly wooded area. He parked the Toyota beside a deep but dry watercourse.

Kirkwood awoke and got out of his vehicle thinking it was just a piss stop, seeing Bruce anointing a nearby salt bush. He followed the example to relieve himself.

Turning his back on the other man was the last thing the hapless Kirkwood Bonn ever knew.

The Bruiser stripped anything useful he could carry from the Landcruiser and drove it to the very edge of the dry creek bed, chocking a front wheel with the same heavy branch that stove in Kirkwood Bonn's head.

The dead man was dragged to sit behind the steering wheel and buckled into his seat belt. Bruce placed his cheap sunglasses on the body and took Kirkwood's expensive aviator pair for himself. He undid the fuel cap before pulling the chock and pushing the Toyota to topple over the ravine. The loaded up top heavy vehicle rolled down the steep bank and overturned.

Matches and firelighters among the loot gleaned from camping equipment, got a good blaze going in tinder dry brown leaves and twigs blanketing the creek bed.

The killer hastily left the scene as bright flames crept towards the spilt petrol. Trekking back to the main road, the murderer looked behind to see thick plumes of black smoke rising to stain a cloudless sky, before a booming explosion split the silence.

Disturbed from a dead tree, a murder of crows cawed *Har Har Har* as they flew further afield. Despite himself, the murderer felt a chill run down his spine when the black birds jeered.

Bruce Luck had to remind himself to 'man up' and live up to his title. He was The Bruiser!

The man had no idea where he was but suspected he had to be miles from anywhere. It couldn't be helped. He'd just have to hoof it. Grateful for one good thing about his stint inside prison walls, it had made him wiry and physically fit.

The Bruiser shouldered his victim's backpack of stolen goods and prepared for a long trek.

After walking for an hour, the column of smoke could still be seen in the distance behind him. He hid from sporadic oncoming traffic from either direction, not willing to be seen in the vicinity of the burnt wreckage, should anyone venture off the road to check out the source of the smoke.

The thrill of danger turned into a great adventure for Bruce Luck. It reminded him of games played as a child, hiding out from an imagined enemy. He was having fun at last, out of prison, away from rules and free of responsibilities.

Apart from the victim's money, credentials and basic belongings, the killer thief was weighed down with the dead man's bottled water and snacks.

The knapsack lightened as the day wore on and The Bruiser drank and ate his way through the supplies. He discarded plastic bottles and wrappers by burying them under the red sandy soil, not out of civil duty but so not to leave any trail.

Trudging along, Bruce The Bruiser amused himself by inventing stories as to how he came to be hiking along the highway, in case he had to explain it to anyone. The best would be to claim he'd been left stranded for some reason.

The Bruiser, alias Bruce Luck, counted on the destroyed Landcruiser remaining hidden for a very long time because the wreck would only be visible from directly above. After the smoke and the smell dissipated, it would not be noticeable across the flat landscape. He imagined the body had been efficiently cremated and wild animals might scatter any

parts that weren't reduced to ashes.

He went over the details, sure it would appear as if the motorist had driven so far into the scrub to find a private place to stop or camp. Accidentally driving over the edge of the creek bank would be understandable, when overtired from the long tedious drive through the same stark countryside hour after hour.

The Bruiser had been careful to leave Bonn's phone in the vehicle, knowing if he took it, its location could be tracked. He had replaced the fuel cap before torching the leaves and congratulated himself on the perfect crime. There should be little evidence left to rake over after the explosion and inferno.

The Bruiser reminded himself he must answer to the name of Kirk as he came into view of Alba Jenkins' lonely homestead. Another stroke of the old 'Luck' was finding the place occupied by a lone woman. Forever canny and astute to signals, he found the naïve back country woman easy to read. Fooling Alba Jenkins was a piece of cake to any sly opportunist and Alba represented fair game.

Alba Jenkins had a feeling the attractive visitor would not hang about for too long. She had no work to offer him and could not afford to pay him anyway. So she had to make the best of the hitchhiker's short and timely visit. An opportunity to be with a young virile man would not be presented often, if ever again.

That night after 'Kirk' thanked Alba for the good steak and potatoes meal, she produced a bottle of rum she'd been rationing to herself in half nips since Christmas. Between them, they polished off the rest of the bottle. It was no great sacrifice as Alba had a spare bottle in the pantry behind the big flour barrel.

Later that night, Alba joined the man on the hard mattress of the sturdy bunk in the sleep out at the back of the house. The Bruiser had never seen such a wide backside. This Jenkins sheila had a booty like the back of a bus and her broad white expanse glowed like a cracked moon in the dim starlight. He would never have chosen such a lard arse but *any port in a storm* he shrugged.

As he banged into the needy woman to her lilting cries of delight, The Bruiser felt he'd paid his way with the best favour he could afford her. Though he reckoned she owed him change.

Bruce Luck's last sex with a woman had been with someone's unwilling wife. It had happened near the beginning of his journey, before he met Kirkwood Bonn. She'd bitten him hard during the rape so he mussed her up pretty badly. He made his speedy getaway in the nick of time as a gang of the woman's menfolk were hot for his blood, threatening to hang him up by his balls and slit his throat.

The Bruiser avoided the lynching by entering an empty horse float, unseen, via the left hand side door. He'd managed the escape just as the towing vehicle moved off onto the highway. He lay on a thick bed of straw, quite comfortably accommodated, as the conveyance sped him away to safety.

The rapist's pursuers had no idea how the man disappeared. They held off reporting the crime to the police, preferring to mete their own justice. Collectively, the posse considered he may not be suitably punished within the system even if he were found guilty. Adding to that likelihood, the female victim would be dragged over the coals with questions and further shamed. The Bruiser would never be forgotten and would be dead meat if the hunters caught up with him, no matter how long it took.

Landing in another small township, the felon crept out of his free ride and sauntered into the roadhouse where he spied Kirkwood Bonn for the first time. Several people occupied seats spread along the diner counter.

The Bruiser, aka Bruce Luck chose to sit on a spare stool beside the younger man. He soon began a friendly chat as they both ate roadhouse breakfasts of bacon, eggs and chips.

The Bruiser got that the younger man could fit his own description and sussed a way to get himself a new identity and perhaps some travelling money. It was to be the last breakfast ever for Kirkwood Bonn.

After masquerading as Kirk with Alba, The Bruiser had every reason to head for the Queensland coast to mingle in more populated areas and hopefully wipe his crime path.

He told Alba he had to move on as he was expected in Darwin, where he had a job to go to. That lie slid easily off his tongue as the real Kirkwood Bonn said that was his mission.

The Bruiser felt satisfied that Alba Jenkins would say her guest, Kirk, had gone to Darwin if anyone were ever to ask after him.

After giving him a substantial cooked breakfast, Alba offered to drive the man into the small townships bus depot. She didn't make a big deal of parting, not wanting any locals to notice her in the company of a handsome young buck and give rise to inevitable gossip.

The Bruiser she knew as Kirk, lifted a hand in brief farewell before Alba drove off. That was the last she ever saw of her able one night stand, except in her dreams.

Despite what happened next, memories of the wonderful sex Alba enjoyed with the handsome visitor served to enhance future encounters with her much older usual bedfellow.

A few days after seeing the exciting guest off, Alba discovered her hidden full bottle of rum had gone. Disappeared! In a panic she checked her nest egg of cash, kept in an old china teapot. The pot was empty. Empty! All the money gone. Her wonderful Kirk must have stolen it all. For the first time in her life, Alba felt violated.

Those savings were meant to cover her property rates and vehicle registration. Maybe she should have hidden the teapot in a better place than the top shelf of the pantry. She decided to put it in the back of the china cabinet in future. At least that could be locked with a little key. If she could find the key.

The startling fact remained, Alba was skint. Her social security instalment was paid fortnightly and now all of it would have to be saved for months if she were ever to catch up.

Alba Jenkins had never been able to hold down a job longer than a week. She could cook and clean but was painfully slow and unused to taking orders.

Eventually assessed as virtually unemployable, Alba Jenkins was awarded the nominal social security payment. A government case officer set up a bank account where the deposit went in automatically every fortnight.

But Alba Jenkins didn't trust banks. The bank tellers looked sneaky and Alba was aware they whispered about her behind her back. She wasn't deaf and she told herself she wasn't born yesterday either. Those bank workers had to get up pretty darn early to pull the wool over her eyes.

Alba knew numbers and the alphabet even if she had trouble reading long words and sentences. A calendar hung on the kitchen wall and first thing every morning, each new day was carefully ticked off. Government paydays were marked with big red crosses.

Every fortnight without fail, Alba waited outside the bank for the doors to open. She was usually half an hour early, with her nose pressed to the glass so those shifty bank people knew she was watching them.

Leaving only enough in the account to keep it viable, Alba withdrew the bulk in cash as soon as possible on the day the government stipend went in, before those tricky tellers could get their sticky fingers on it.

Alba paid for her purchases and bills in cash and stuffed any leftover notes in her trusty teapot. Now her carefully saved money was all gone! Stolen by that good looking man. Who could tell about anyone any more? He had been so well mannered too.

Alba Jenkins shied off reporting Kirk's theft to avoid probing questions and possible publicity. Another worry, an intimate connection Alba had with an old cattleman, Bob Bartleigh, had to be protected. Of all people, she didn't want him finding out.

Old Bob leased Alba's land after her parents passed on. People thought it charitable of Bartleigh to pay for such poor grazing, but he saw an opportunity and soon cunningly introduced the lonely and backward Alba to rum drinking and sex. It was the most excitement she had ever known, before Kirk.

Bob bobbed up every few weeks or so when he ran his cattle in to the yards for various inspections and treatments, whether they needed it or not. He'd bring a handy parcel of beef to replenish Alba's freezer and she in turn cooked a good meal for him, with his home grown meat and fresh vegetables from her own garden.

They'd sit at the table talking and drinking rum after dinner, when Alba always mentioned she was sleeping on the bunk on the back verandah, in this hot weather. Bob would accept the comment as an invitation to join her during the night, as it was intended.

Bob Bartleigh would go home to his skinny wife the next day, which suited Alba, she could only stand the old guy in small doses. Often her daydreams lingered of what it would be like to have a much younger, better looking lover. Well, now she knew and had paid the price dearly. The naïve woman's hurt and humiliation knew no bounds.

In frustrated anger over losing her savings and her last bottle of rum, Alba Jenkins stripped the bunk and bleached the sheets, working to the tune of her loud sobs and curses that rang into the empty space of her surroundings. How could she have been taken for such a mug? That knowledge wounded almost as much as the losses.

Alba's concerned dogs worried around her, puzzled. They could identify nothing in the vicinity to be the cause of their owner's unusual distress, though they sniffed and searched.

Bob was appreciated a little more after the debacle with Kirk. At least old Bartleigh was a trusted regular diversion and kept her in meat.

Alba did not want Bob or anyone else getting wind of her thieving overnight guest who called himself Kirk. She could never tell anyone.

Meanwhile, The Bruiser moved across the border into Queensland where he hitched eastward towards the coast and gradually travelled further South, enjoying his holiday and crime spree adventure.

3

Dulcy Vestige

Senior Sergeant Dulcy Vestige had transferred from the Queensland coast up to Darwin to be with her partner, Dave, who was in the army and based at Robertson Barracks.

The first important event Dulcy had to address was a missing person case. She worked with local police personnel who were more familiar with the difficulties of their vast jurisdiction.

Kirkwood Bonn, reported missing one week after his last known message contact with his partner, had been driving a white Toyota Landcruiser. The registration number, verified with The Department of Main Roads, confirmed the missing person as the vehicle owner.

Initially, Dulcy had little to go on apart from a report that the missing man had picked up a hitchhiker known only as Richie, along the way.

If Kirkwood Bonn had met with foul play, that hitchhiker was prime suspect, in which case, Dulcy reasoned 'Richie' likely to be an assumed name.

'Richie' accepted the story that his benefactor was going to a job in Darwin. In reality, Kirkwood Bonn had been on his way home to reunite with his longtime friend and partner, Damien Cresswick.

Kirkwood had been a cautious person and refrained from unnecessarily divulging his gay status to anyone, particularly not to a random acquaintance such as a hitchhiker.

Damien Cresswick had expected Kirkwood to arrive home within a window of a few days variance, given the distance he had to drive through The Red Centre of Australia and that he might camp overnight to break up the trip.

Kirkwood Bonn had visited Adelaide in South Australia and detoured to the opal mining town, Coober Pedy, along the way on his return. He hoped to catch up with some lost family down there. Drawing blanks on finding anyone, the young man headed back towards Alice Springs. He planned to rest there before going on to his home town.

The last message Damien Cresswick received had been from somewhere south of Alice Springs saying Kirkwood was giving a lift to the man named Richie. After that, there had been nothing at all and no interaction by phone or on social media. Damien knew there would be a lack of signal in the outback, nevertheless, he worried his friend could be in serious trouble and lamented not going on the trip with Kirkwood.

As hours went by with no word from Kirkwood, Damien became convinced something must be terribly wrong and reported his partner as a missing person. He supplied several photographs which were good likenesses of Kirkwood Bonn, to the police.

People perished quickly in the arid regions and it had happened too often, so any missing person claim in the desert was taken as a matter or urgency.

Dulcy Vestige ascertained Kirkwood Bonn went missing somewhere along a 1500 km stretch or over 930 miles along the Stuart Highway. Messages to truckies and motorists to look out for a white Toyota Landcruiser, possibly broken down, came up with nothing.

The equivalent of door knocking the neighbourhood, eventually brought Dulcy to the remote outback door of Alba Jenkins.

"Anything wrong?" Alba asked on being shown the police ID and badge.

"Just asking after a man gone missing somewhere along the highway, travelling towards Darwin. We're asking everyone who might have seen him."

Alba was shown the photo. She looked at it for a long time and knew it resembled the conniving handsome man she'd taken in. Alba didn't want to admit to having that hiker stay overnight. What if they found out she'd had sex with him? It was just too embarrassing.

"I'm not sure. It looks a bit like a man who hiked by here."

"The missing person was driving a white Toyota Landcruiser."

"Nope. No one like that stopped here."

Alba breathed an audible sigh of relief. It wasn't him. He didn't have a vehicle. Dulcy picked up on the other woman's vibe and noticed that her face blushed bright red.

"So, Miss Jenkins, the hiker you mentioned. Did he stop by for a while? I mean it's miles from anywhere."

Alba paused and mentally rehearsed what to say:

"Yes. He wanted water. Said he'd been hitch hiking but his last lift tried to rob him. So he'd walked a long way in the heat."

"I'm sure you'd have offered him some country hospitality." Dulcy smiled.

Alba paused again. She saw no way out of admitting more:

"I did. Yes. I offered him food and drink. Said he could kip on the verandah bunk overnight. If he needed to rest up."

"And did he?"

Alba made another lengthy pause before adding:

"Yes. He did. I let him have a shower under the outdoor tank stand as well."

Dulcy felt it was like pulling teeth to get this much out of Alba Jenkins. The woman avoided eye contact and was plainly holding back. Dulcy had an intuitive idea why that might be, watching her wring her apron and mull over every answer.

"Then he left in the morning?"

Alba was quick to answer this time:

"Yes. I drove him into town and dropped him at the bus depot."

"He must have said his name at some point."

"Um. Kirk. That was it. He said to call him Kirk. I didn't get his other name."

Alba fibbed trying for an offhand tone of voice. She would never admit to going through the traveller's belongings. Her dogs picked up on some nuance and gathered about in support, leaning on Alba's legs.

Dulcy had her lead. Kirk was not a common name. It was too much of a coincidence if the passing hiker was not connected to the missing man.

"Can you describe this visitor named Kirk, Miss Jenkins?"

"Describe?"

"What did he look like?"

"Oh. Tall. He had a hat and a bag like you wear on your back."

"Was he fat, thin, average?"

"More thin. I think. Brown like a stockman. But not a blackfella."

"A white man with a tan?"

"Yes. That's right. A whitefella been out in the sun."

"Did you notice his hair colour or eye colour?"

"Darkish hair. Eyes sort of yellowy green."

"Thank you Miss Jenkins. That is very helpful. Often people don't notice eye colour."

Alba's face showed alarm. Had she said too much?

"Well. See. His eyes looked bloodshot from the dust. So I noticed the colour."

"He would have been glad of that shower. You were very kind to that man."

Alba blushed crimson red and began to sweat. If, as Dulcy guessed, Alba Jenkins had taken the drifter to her bed, he'd probably be a pretender, not Kirkwood Bonn.

To Dulcy, Kirkwood Bonn did not fit Alba's description of a tanned stockman.

The missing man's partner, Damien Cresswick, made their gay relationship clear. According to Damien, Kirkwood was shy mannered, polite and urbane, a dapper dresser, neat and very particular about details.

"I teased him for being a fusspot." Damien said.

From what Dulcy Vestige assessed so far, she doubted if the rather dim witted, rough and hefty Alba Jenkins would have been able to entice the real Kirkwood Bonn, even if he swung both ways. These were Dulcy's private thoughts, not what she would write in any report.

Dulcy summarised: Surely the real Kirkwood would have sought a lift into town from Alba if his vehicle had broken down. He'd have wanted mechanical assistance or a tow truck. The whereabouts of Bonn's Toyota

Landcruiser remained a mystery. It seemed likely that another man calling himself Kirk had the missing person's ID but not his vehicle.

Dulcy Vestige feared she was investigating a possible homicide and the perpetrator remained on the loose. Future forays would not be undertaken alone.

Dulcy Vestige kept the details of Alba Jenkins' guest strictly confidential. She did not want the supposed impostor changing his name again at this juncture. It would be easier to track him if he still used Kirkwood Bonn's ID.

4

Crime Scene

Use of a police helicopter enabled a sighting of the burnt-out vehicle, where it lay blackened and upside down in the dry gulch.

Dulcy Vestige in the company of other officers of The Northern Territory Police Force rushed to inspect the scene. Charred human remains were discovered within the upturned Landcruiser. The diminished condition of the body was such that it would not be possible to visually identify the deceased.

The skeleton, wedged upside down in the crushed cabin appeared mostly intact. The brunt of the explosion and flames had erupted upwards and a burst water tank mounted on the roof racks had dampened the ground underneath.

The vehicle number plate, earlier obtained from Main Roads Department confirmed it to be Kirkwood Bonn's Toyota Landcruiser. The police team reconvened to discuss the incident:

"No mystery who the body is." Dulcy said to her colleagues.

"Poor bugger."

"If it is indeed the missing man and we're 99.9% certain it is, then someone else is using his identity. Our main suspect is a hiker who called himself Kirk while cadging an overnight stay at a remote property. The timing, location and the name fit our projected scenario." "Unless it's just a very freaky coincidence."

"We don't like freaky coincidences. Can we get a bead on him?"

"Trying to but he's still at large. So far."

"Our best chance to track him, is if he misuses the dead man's ID."

Further investigation revealed the Landcruiser gearstick was in neutral, just as it would be if it had been pushed over the ravine. If the vehicle had been accidentally driven over, it should have been in gear. The gear selection backed the theory that the vehicle was pushed in an act of foul play. Dulcy Vestige and the team needed no further proof that the event involved murder and robbery. Protocols were observed with removal of Kirkwood Bonn's blackened skeleton to a mortuary, where his cracked skull determined cause of death. Dulcy Vestige had the onerous duty of informing the victim's partner, Damien Cresswick, who took the hard news very badly. Damien fell to his knees and gasped in horror.

"Does it seem like.....did he suffer?" Damien cried in anguish.

"We think not Mr. Cresswick. Forensics determined Kirkwood died from a blow to the back of the head. The injury suggests death would have been instant. He would not have known or felt anything."

Dulcy did not know for certain if her last sentence was strictly true, but tried to make the news easier. She knew it would be replayed repeatedly in Damien's mind for all time.

"I hope you get the bastard who did this." Damien Cresswick sobbed.

"We will try our hardest and do our best." Dulcy's intentions were heartfelt.

Dulcy asked if Damien had anyone to stay with him. She had made him a cup of sugary tea though he'd barely touched it. He said neither he nor Kirkwood had relatives in The Territory, saying they moved to the other side of the continent to escape family condemnation for their relationship. Damien had friends he could call on but said he just wanted to be alone.

"I didn't want him to go down there but he was following a lead to find some long lost relatives. And now this! Kirkwood was a gentle soul. He didn't deserve this."

"No one does. You have our sincere condolences and I am very sorry for your loss."

The detective regretted that her common platitude must be cold comfort to Damien. Dulcy did not want the stricken young man left alone, so assigned a police grief counsellor to stay with Damien. Dulcy needed all the time available to work on finding Kirkwood Bonn's killer.

That night, Dulcy Vestige made a phone call to Queensland based Senior Detective Sergeant Dougall Grimslade. They had become good friends when working together in the past, before Dulcy transferred to the NT. She ran all the details by Dougall, to get his take on it. Grimslade liked a challenge and held Dulcy Vestige in high regard.

"So according to the last message his friend received, we've got the victim giving a lift to a man who called himself Richie. And it seems he picked him up somewhere between Coober Pedy and Alice Springs, after which Bonn disappears off the radar."

"That's right Dougall. My theory is this Richie bloke murdered Bonn and thieved what he could carry including Bonn's ID."

"Yes. That adds up. The man who mooched an overnight stay with your Alba Jenkins is definitely the prime suspect."

"And the only suspect. But furthermore Dougall, off the record, I think him staying with Alba Jenkins was a one night stand kind of thing. She's been cagey with her answers."

"He's fallen on his feet for sure. I see the time frame placing him overnight at Jenkins property suggests Bonn picked him up much closer to The Alice than to Coober Pedy."

"Yes I agree. But Bonn could have picked this bloke Richie up anywhere. Of course, Richie is not likely to be his real name. He'd be just some itinerant drifter who could be from anywhere at all."

Grimslade thought about it for a while, doodling patterns with arrows and numbers that only he could decipher. Dulcy waited. She knew and respected how Dougall worked.

"Let's narrow it down. Since the message Bonn sent to his partner mentioned the guy was contributing to fuel costs, Bonn and Richie must have had that discussion somewhere. So that's less like he picked him up totally by chance along the road."

"True. I also wondered if the meeting was random, Dougall. The victim could have been deliberately targeted for some reason. But the message the victim sent his partner sounds like Richie was a stranger to him."

They discussed possible places the pair might have met.

"We've been asking questions and checking CCTV at roadhouses, cafes, pubs and anywhere they might have been. But we also know Bonn had a lot of camping gear. He might have camped anywhere and this Richie could have been another camper."

Dougall was quick to quash that idea:

"But without wheels, Dulcy. I guess some hikers can carry enough on their backs to make a camp. But flimsy gear would not be ideal in those harsh conditions."

"That makes sense. And they'd need to carry a lot of water. Plus there's a huge area to cover when campers aren't limited to designated grounds. People can camp anywhere out there."

"It's a bloody big country." Grimslade added.

Heading out along the Stuart Highway allowed plenty of isolated places where a crime could be committed without trace. The detectives agreed the murder and robbery to be certainly opportunistic if not completely premeditated.

"I doubt the killer would have gone on towards Darwin if he knew Bonn was heading there. I mean, he might run into people who knew him." Dulcy said.

"True. Problem is, he had so many other options. He could have gone West to WA or East to Queensland. Or even backtracked South."

"As you say Dougall, it is a bloody big country."

Dougall Grimslade immersed himself in the scene, he liked using the tactic of putting himself in a criminal's shoes:

"Myself, I'd choose Queensland. Go to more populated coastal areas. Easier to get lost in the crowd where backpackers and casual travellers are common to see."

"Yes that makes sense too. The victim's partner said Kirkwood Bonn usually carried a lot of cash. So his killer would be ok for money." Dulcy added.

"So the murderer would be cashed up but it wouldn't last forever. He might try looking for casual work. If he was stupid enough he might even use Kirkwood Bonn's ID."

"Let's dote on him being stupid enough."

"He probably thinks himself smart. They often do." Dougall Grimslade stated that as fact.

The 'they' Grimslade spoke of encompassed past criminals he'd dealt with. The smallest clue could lead to their downfall yet even the cleverest made mistakes.

CCTV at a roadhouse identified Kirkwood's vehicle being refuelled by a tall man who wore sunglasses and had a wide brimmed hat, pulled well down over his brow. Whether by choice or by chance, the man's facial features were well hidden. Other images from inside the roadhouse diner showed Kirkwood eating breakfast at a long counter where a line of other diners, mostly men, sat. Zooming in on those seated either side of the victim, only gave sketchy images. The one thought to most closely resemble the tall man, kept his face averted and angled away from the security camera. The detectives decided this was a deliberate ploy and perceived their quarry to be no amateur at avoidance.

Dougall Grimslade with the help of his office staff, got onto agricultural employment agencies who routinely found casual farm work for backpackers. If the murderer attempted to misuse Kirkwood Bonn's ID, the dragnet could reel him in. In the interim, with no other clues, the wanted man might be difficult to pin down among the five million or so population of Queensland.

5

Beach Party

Blissfully unaware the police already had him on CCTV and at Alba Jenkins' house, The Bruiser hitchhiked across to the east coast of Queensland.

Dropped off beside a pretty seaside cove, Bruce Luck waved goodbye to his lift and breathed in the clean salty air. He had longed for this while in prison. The tang off the ocean smelt of freedom.

He took a lukewarm shower at the public amenities and used Kirkwood Bonn's shaving gear and toiletries to make himself more presentable. After changing into clean clothes he emerged feeling fit, fresh and hungry for hot food.

The wanted man hadn't eaten since lunchtime five hours beforehand. A small fish and chips shop on the esplanade drew him in with the aroma of fried food.

Bruce ordered a dinner of fish and battered potato scallops with salad and lemon wedges. He sat inside the shop at one of the few tables provided, placing his backpack on the floor between his feet.

He had no idea where to spend the night, but if nothing turned up, he would sleep on the beach. Weather was mild and he had a warm hoodie, another quality contribution from Kirkwood Bonn's wardrobe.

As The Bruiser ate, a pair of youthful bronze tanned girls wearing short shorts and bikini tops wandered in and placed a big order for fish and chips.

The beach girls' combined funds fell short by a couple of dollars for what they'd wanted. Before they were forced to reduce the amount of food, The Bruiser offered to put in the difference. Both girls looked him over and liked what they saw.

"Wow. That is so kind of you."

"No drama." Bruce smiled.

"Are you here for the day?"

"Passing through. But I could stay a while if there's anywhere available. I might end up sleeping on the beach of course."

Bruce angled for a possible invitation to lob down as a guest with the girls, thinking maybe they had a holiday flat.

"We're camping with a group of friends. On the beach. We've got a bonfire ready to light for a beach party, when it gets dark."

The girls exchanged glances. The Bruiser knew they considered inviting him to the beach party. He got up and inspected the ice-cream freezer.

"What's good now? I haven't had an ice-cream in yonks." he said.

The girls were quick to offer suggestions, telling him their favourite nutty chocolate covered icecream on a stick. He bought three and gave the girls one each. They enjoyed the treats while waiting for their order to be ready. The girls exchanged winks.

One girl said coyly:

"You're welcome to join our party if you like."

"That would be nice. But are you sure I wouldn't be intruding?"

"Not at all. The more the merrier."

The girls were with a group of six others, all seventeen year old school leavers, three boys and five girls. Since none were really seriously paired off and there were more girls than boys, they thought inviting the old guy might be a buzz. Plus, he seemed to be easy going and have plenty of money.

"What can I bring?" Bruce asked.

"Whatever. Drinks. Anything." They replied vaguely.

"You'll find us ok. It will be at the big bonfire on the beach."

The Bruiser detected a faint whiff of marijuana from the teenagers' hair. He hoped they had more for the beach party and decided to bring lots of snacks for the munchies later.

The girls both gave him cheeky come-hither grins as they left the shop carrying their warm newspaper wrapped parcels of food. As they sashayed away, swaying their hips, they knew the tall guy would be watching.

Bruce almost salivated. He wondered if he might have them both before the night was over. Maybe even the two together. He felt his lust rising and almost needed another shower, only colder than the last one.

A dip in the sea would be wonderful but he didn't want to leave his backpack unattended. He had the good thick wad of Kirkwood's cash to protect.

The Bruiser sat over a coffee in the cafe, waiting for sunset. Shouldering the knapsack he wandered down to the shore. The smell of wood smoke reached his nostrils before flames of the party bonfire took hold enough to glow in the dusk.

The man arrived at the teen party and offered a cardboard carton of Cokes and snacks, corn chips, potato crisps and a variety of chocolates. He produced a bottle of Bundaberg Rum from his knapsack and became the instant hero of the party.

"Wow. This is great. Thanks...um...we didn't get your name."

"Ricky." he replied with the variation on Richie just to be different from his past socials.

The eight rattled off their names but Bruce doubted he'd remember any of them. Not that it mattered since it would only be a short friendship. They soon began passing around shared spliffs and encouraging 'Ricky' to partake.

"Hey Ricky. Hope you're not an undercover cop. You're not are you?"

"Nah. I'm not The Fuzz. But I am reputed to be good at some things undercover." He bragged with obvious innuendo about his prowess in bed. No one picked up on his boast. Instead, they ridiculed his use of the passe label: 'The Fuzz' to describe law enforcement.

"The Fuzz!" One of them shouted and clapped his hands. The teenagers fell about in fits of laughter fuelled by their recent intake of cannabis.

For some reason the outdated description for police hit their combined funny bones. It made Bruce feel really old and outdated himself. He didn't let on but decided to lay off the booze and reefers and let the youngsters get wasted. It would give him an edge in taking advantage of the situation somehow.

The Bruiser waited his chance. The first two girls he'd met at the fish shop went off together to the sand dunes, supposedly to pee although they carried a blanket. He slowly got up and wandered off after them, taking his backpack.

"Have a good one." One of the boys drawled.

The others all collapsed in fits of laughter again. What he hoped to get seemed acceptable and common knowledge.

Bruce came upon the two girls who giggled when they saw him. They had removed their scant clothes and were fondling each other on the blanket placed between two sand dunes. He dropped his kit bag near some tufts of dune grass and walked the few paces down to where the girls played. They drew apart and patted the blanket in invitation.

"Anything for me?" He asked.

"Plenty. What have you got yourself?" Came the brash answer.

Bruce dropped his pants and displayed his ample and ready erection. The girls fell upon him with enthusiasm, stripping all his clothes off and pushing him down onto his back. One offered her large breasts to his mouth while the other mounted him for a ride. She finished quickly and the girls swapped positions. The Bruiser felt he had died and gone to heaven. This was a dream come true and been ridiculously easy to accomplish.

Their activities kicked up flurries of sand making the man squint but The Bruiser didn't want to miss anything. He cracked his eyes open to commit the scene to memory and spied a shadowy figure creeping towards the dune grass.

Instantly aware one of the boys was stealing towards his knapsack while the little molls kept him busy, he twigged why the sex had been so easy. He'd been sucked in by a bunch of kids. Not for the first or last time in his life, Bruce cursed himself for letting his dick rule his head.

The Bruiser tried to throw the girls aside. He was in a vulnerable position. The girls were both quite strong and far less affected by the rum and the reefers than they had made out.

"Hold him down." The boy urged, aware he had been caught in the act. Yet he still attempted to loot the knapsack, unaware he dealt against a hardened criminal.

The sneaky plan had been to grab the old guy's money and scarper while the sex tarts kept him busy. The girls believed they would not be blamed. Apparently there was no plan B.

"Hold him down will you. Can't you even do your part?"

The boy struggled with effects of alcohol and weed. The girls gasped, aware the designated robber had just implicated them in the plot.

"Trying to. You idiot."

Riding the man had been considered the best way of holding him down. The other girl, leaning over his face, attempted to kneel on his shoulders but only succeeded in holding down one arm.

The Bruiser, as Ricky, bucked his body violently to dislodge the rider, causing the girl to climax. Her cry of ecstasy was cut short as he punched her hard with his free hand. The other girl who had been trying to smother his face with her breasts had her nipple savagely bitten through. Both girls screamed and beat their conquest ineffectually with their fists.

Bruce gained his feet, kicked the girls aside and approached the thieving boy who froze in terror. The teenager distanced himself from the backpack, ready to defend himself. The Bruiser loomed over him, snarling, teeth bared.

"So you think you can play with the big boys do you?"

"I'm unarmed." The boy quavered holding his hands up in surrender.

"So am I." Bruce growled.

The Bruiser grabbed the aspiring thief by his long hair and pounded his face knocking him unconscious. Or dead. In the heat of his anger, he didn't mind which. The girls regrouped and tried beating him away from their boy friend, earning bleeding noses and broken teeth for their bravery.

The girls' screams brought the rest of their party running to help. One boy brandished a switch blade and adopted a fighting stance as he shaped up to attack.

The Bruiser had faced this exact threat in prison from far better skilled adversaries than the green juvenile. He booted the teenager in the balls and bent his slim wrist back until it cracked, easily twisting the knife from the boy's thin fingered grasp as he did so.

Bruce casually took up the weapon and faced the others, his face dark with rage and his wolfish eyes glinting eerily in the moonlight. Those still able to move, ran off, leaving the fallen to their fates.

While the knife wielder sobbed in agony and writhed in the sand nursing his bent wrist, Bruce calmly searched the boy's pockets. Car keys, a wallet and a mobile phone were confiscated.

The Bruiser aimed to put the fear of the devil into the errant teen with some sage advice:

"People like me don't like young yobs with an attitude. Best watch your back boy. Unless you're sick of living. Are you? I could kill you right now. Be easy as pie."

The man heard a splutter. "Shat your duds didn't you? Weak as piss!"

The Bruiser spat on the kid's face as a parting gesture.

Retrieving his knapsack from the dune grass, Bruce strode to the dimly lit car park area beyond the sandy beach. He clicked the key remote and a sporty Mazda blinked its lights in welcome. The Bruiser threw his backpack into the passenger seat, got in and drove away. Those of the scheming teenagers who were still upright, watched helplessly as he left.

The injured staggered back to the bonfire where the eight teens re-grouped to concoct the story they should agree upon for their police report.

Knowing the young scammers watched his exit, Bruce turned at a nearby T-junction where a main road led inland towards the West. He drove for fifteen minutes and came by a house lit up with party lights.

There was some sort of private occasion being celebrated behind high fences. Several cars were parked along each side of the roadside. Bruce paused the Mazda beside a parked ute and threw the boy's mobile phone into its open tub. He hoped that after the party, the ute owner would take it for a long drive in any direction other than down the southern coast highway.

The Bruiser drove until he found a turnoff that should eventually lead back to the main coast highway. Following the minor road through cane fields, he found a secluded spot to spend the night sheltered in the car, parked within a patch of bushland.

The dark coloured sedan couldn't easily be seen by passersby so he planned to abandon the Mazda there, before sunrise. He was pretty sure police would be looking for the car by then.

Bruce realised in mild surprise that he was still stark naked. The shorts and t-shirt he had worn had been left back in the sand dunes.

In the dark car, he searched the knapsack for his jeans that held a valued pocket knife. The scouts knife bore the initials BL, being the reason he stole it from a goody goody boy scout whose name he forgot. The penknife was the only item that might identify him as Bruce Luck but he rarely went anywhere without it. He kissed the BL knife for good luck and made sure it was secure in its leather casing, safely attached to his jeans belt.

He donned the jeans and someone's lightweight bomber jacket he found in the car. Going through the jacket pockets rewarded him another twenty dollars and a ready rolled spliff. He lit the spliff from the car cigarette lighter and relaxed, smiling to himself.

The Bruiser considered that the double action sex with those young harlots had been worth the trouble. He'd had fun getting the better of the boy wonders too and thanked his time in the clink for some of the moves he perfected there, in staying alive.

"Not The Fuzz." The man repeated to himself, amused now at the memory of the teens laughing at his choice of words. He drifted off in a cloud of cannabis smoke and slept soundly.

As dawn broke, Bruce awoke to the sounds of bird song which he didn't appreciate. The dawn chorus worsened a pounding headache, the result of sleeping in the stuffy smoke filled car.

"Damn magpies." He muttered, rubbing his bleary eyes.

In the first light of day, Bruce checked the boy's wallet contents. It held a couple of hundred in cash which he pocketed. He smirked at getting the better of the rich and entitled teens, comparing their advantage to his own poor lot, both now and at the same age.

"Stinkin' yobs got everything. Then they have to try and steal from me. Even after I bought stuff for them. I should've cut them all up. The little creeps. Making fun of me. Me!"

The Bruiser raved to himself. The injustice of it all roused his anger. What he wouldn't have given to have a new car, or any car for that matter at their age. And so much spending money. Not to mention the easy girls they hung with, willing to go all the way.

The Bruiser's resentment drove him to slash the car seats, door panels and ceiling material with the switch blade knife he took from the privileged teenager. He wedged the knife in an upright position under the drivers' seat hoping the next chump to sit there would get the point. To top off vandalising the Mazda, Bruce aimed a long stream of acrid yellow urine over the wool covered steering wheel and dashboard. He closed all the air vents and left the car locked.

Satisfied the interior would reek to high heaven by the time anyone managed to get the doors opened, Bruce hiked ahead to the main coast road, reached within fifteen minutes.

As a final celebration of retribution, The Bruiser dropped the kid's wallet, driving licence, plastic cards and car keys into a public composting toilet at a roadside rest area. He grinned seeing how the valuables sink out of sight, into the smelly sawdust.

Before long, The Bruiser gained a lift that transported him another hour further South, down the highway. Dropped off at a Maccas and feeling famished, Bruce ordered a substantial breakfast and coffee latte. He borrowed a free newspaper provided for customers and perused it for any mention of his crimes, finding none. He turned his sights to a wall mounted TV in the eatery. The Bruiser stopped chewing when a breaking news report flashed on the screen and captured his undivided attention.

The TV news hound stood on the sandy beach in front of blackened remains of the party bonfire. The reporter described an innocent group of schoolies having a quiet evening picnic and marshmallow roast, before being set upon by a deranged older man.

Older man! I'm only 31! Someone should thank me for it. Indignant over what he perceived as a slur on his prime time of life, Bruce justified his revenge. He hoped to have taught those conniving rich kids a well deserved lesson.

The Bruiser knew, with his record, he had Buckley's chance of being seen as the schoolies' victim, even if the whole episode miraculously came to light as it truly happened.

The news report went on to say: Some of the youths, including two girls, were seriously injured and hospitalised, all had broken noses and cracked teeth. One girl had been bitten in a savage sex attack and would require micro surgery to restore blood vessels to the delicate area. The perpetrator made his getaway by stealing one of the teen's cars, a late model dark green Mazda sedan.

The parents of the car owner had given the brand new Mazda as a graduation gift and it was their son's pride and joy. They appealed for help and offered a cash reward to have it returned. The Bruiser tried not to chuckle out loud at that. *Yeah wait till they see it.* He paused to wonder if insurance would write it off for 'cosmetic' damage. After all, the car would still be mechanically sound.

Tearfully, the boy's parents said their quiet and studious son had not only lost his new car but suffered a dislocated wrist with extensive nerve damage. The couple said their brave son sustained the injury while trying to protect the two injured girls from a vicious sex attack. The impaired wrist severely limited their lad's ability to pursue his dream career as a snow ski instructor. The Bruiser disguised his spontaneous hoot of laughter as a sneeze. Some diners at another booth tut tutted over the tear-jerker news report. The Bruiser exchanged glances with them and shook his head in mock sympathy with their sentiments.

"Poor kids. They were so brave. I hope they find the boy's car." One of them said.

"Lucky they weren't killed by that old maniac." Bruce said truthfully.

The Bruiser privately smirked that the kids might have trouble explaining how he'd raped two girls without the others knowing about it. He supposed the police would have kept his discarded clothes as evidence, yet they were not even his own, the shorts and t-shirt had belonged to Kirkwood Bonn.

Kirkwood Bonn had been in the habit of sending all his clothes to be washed and ironed at a laundry service. As such, everything had discreet labels printed with his name, placed under the brand tags. If the killer had noticed the laundry tags, he might have ripped them off. But Bruce Luck did neither. He carefully went over the event and saw no way it could be linked to himself.

6

Grimslade On It

Detective Dougall Grimslade picked up the trail after viewing the police incident report of the beach party attack online. Dougall knew the clothing with Kirkwood Bonn's laundry tags clearly implicated the killer thief from the Landcruiser case and felt excited over the definite link. Liaising with local police who'd been first at the scene, detective Grimslade explained the situation with the offender using stolen ID and asked them not to release the name Kirkwood Bonn to media. Interviewing the eight teenagers again, beside the local officer, the senior detective asked for a description of their attacker:

"How old was the man?"

"Um. Not sure. But he wasn't young."

"Would you say he was about my age then?" Grimslade tried.

"Oh god no. Not that old. We wouldn't have....I mean he wasn't going grey or anything." One of the girls flustered.

"Wouldn't have what?"

"Invited him to our bonfire." She said weakly.

Dougall was not a vain man, normally, but the kids made him feel ancient. He glared at the seventeen year old friends and cleared his throat:

"So you invited him? That differs from your initial statements saying he invited himself."

"He sort of did. But we let him stay."

One of the other teens jumped in with the swift excuse, an amendment delivered rather too quickly for Grimslade's liking. Earlier statements had been so similar, the detective suspected the eight kids concocted what to say beforehand, together. Now the story showed some holes. Grimslade knew the dithering teenagers had to be hiding or editing the entire truth of the matter. The senior detective let it pass because his paramount aim to find Kirkwood Bonn's killer took priority. However, a sarcastic raised eyebrow glance to the accompanying local officer suggested he should pursue the kids' collusion further, later. Grimslade continued his interview:

"Would you say he was in the ballpark of this other officer's age group?"

"No. Not that old either. He was still....I mean....um...old but more youngish."

The silly girl wavered under the severe expression of the local officer. He had only just passed his fortieth birthday. Suitably insulted, he felt primed to grill all the eight teens separately to tear their rehearsed story apart. Dougall wished he could be there for their undoing but he had bigger fish to fry.

"Have fun." Dougall winked to the younger police man.

"I will." The forty year old replied with a set to his jaw and glint in his eye.

Dougall Grimslade then contacted his Northern Territory colleague Dulcy Vestige:

"Seems our most wanted is on a one man crime spree. Now he's targeted a bunch of schoolies having a picnic. I'm not sure the kids are as innocent as they make out. But their injuries are real that's for sure. And by the way, Richie is calling himself Ricky now."

"Richie, Kirk, Ricky, he gets around if it's the one and same man. Alba Jenkins said she found the man calling himself Kirk to be well mannered and nice looking. That would often get his foot in the door." Dulcy said.

"Let's hope there is only one of him. He must be a real charmer for sure." Dougall agreed.

The laundry tags on the stolen clothes pointed to it being only one man. There was little doubt of that, but every possibility had to be considered and explored. As the detectives had that conversation, Bruce Luck tried to ignore a disquieting thought that eight young people could give a very good description of his face. Perhaps an accurate identikit image would be generated and spread across media. The man comforted himself knowing there would be many handsome men with even features like his own. It was not as if he had any distinguishing abnormalities in his face. He believed no real proof existed and he would simply deny everything if ever pulled up and questioned.

The Bruiser felt good and satisfied for the moment, having had great sex, won a fight and enjoyed a good feed within the past twenty-four hours. Those three items were high on his list of making life worth living. Trashing the kid's car had been colossal fun as well.

7

The Welshman

Bruce The Bruiser put his cares aside as he hiked along a quiet country road, humming to himself.

He waved cheerfully to a motorbike rider who sped by. The roar of the machine deafened him for a few seconds and sent a flock of pink and grey Galahs lifting off from a stand of Iron Barks.

The Bruiser envied the motorbike rider and wished he had a powerful machine to zoom about on. Speeding along would sure beat foot slogging. Though he was doing ok so far, considering his escapades since leaving his demented 'Dear Old Dad' in Adelaide.

Deep in fond memories of the most recent fun event, The Bruiser became startled and alert to a herd of about twenty cows heading his way. Some old bloke in a paddock yelled to him:

"Can yer head 'em off son?"

Bruce was obliged to head off the cattle or be run down in the stampede. He circled outstretched arms and spoke softly to calm the leaders, while the old fellow hobbled down the grassy slope on bandy legs, to open a paddock gate.

The cow man then stepped back and walked towards the rear of the mob that had begun to slow down. Between them both, Bruce and the old guy turned the small herd into the paddock.

"Thanks lad." The wrinkled old man offered his hand. "Owen Evans." he said, introducing himself in the country way.

Quick on a glib invention, Bruce recognised the old man's name as Welsh and dubbed himself with a Welsh sounding name as well, as he shook hands:

"I'm Owen as well. Owen Jones. They call me Jonesy."

It paid to be of the clan. Bruce just hoped he wouldn't be called upon to sing, knowing it to be a favoured trait of Welshmen.

"So Jonesy. I guess you're taking in the countryside on foot? It's the best way to really feel it. I say." The old Owen offered his gap-tooth smile.

"It is. Except when I'm caught out without shelter, at least. Looks like weather closing in so I'd best be making tracks."

'Jonesy' shouldered his swag and went to walk on, quite certain he already a foot in the door for somewhere to spend another night.

Dark clouds billowed on the horizon and an earthy scent of rain reached them on the breath of a zephyr. The dry leaves of a gum tree rattled in the sudden gust, preceding a telling stillness.

"Lucky for that weather coming. Might not have got all those cows in otherwise. They stick together better with rain on the way." Old Owen said.

"How did they get out?"

"I had them out to graze the footpaths. But some fool on a motorbike spooked 'em."

The Bruiser as Jonesy tutted and shook his head:

"That motorbike passed me. Going way too fast. Obviously ridden by some bloody great flaming idiot. No sense at all, some people."

Old Owen grinned broadly. He liked the lad who agreed with his own opinion.

"Come up for a cuppa tea?"

"Oh that would be very welcome. Thank you. I could murder a cuppa." Said Jonesy, the pseudo Welshman.

The Bruiser as Jonesy sat in at a scrubbed pine kitchen table as rain began to beat a rhythm on the iron roof of the farm cottage. Warmth from a hot range stove hugged the room.

Old Owen took a bowl of white dough, covered with a checked cloth, from his 'fridge. He dropped egg-sized lumps of the floury mixture into a frying pan of melting butter. Soon he had the griddle scones rising and browning. He flipped them over once with a spatula. The delicious aroma had his guest's mouth watering.

"Tea be mashed by the time these are ready." He said.

"Can I help?" Jonesy asked.

"You could get the syrup tin out of the cupboard over there, thanks son. And set out a couple of plates."

The Bruiser did as he was told. He also took two mugs from the draining board of the sink and wiped them out with a tea towel.

"Milk and sugar?" He asked.

"If you want it. I take mine black."

"So do I." Jonesy replied. He really took his tea any way it came, but strove to connect with his host.

Old Owen had rolled up his sleeves. Jonesy noticed a tattoo of an anchor inked on his forearm. It reminded him of Popeye The Sailor Man, giving the hint that the old guy might have once been a seaman.

"So Jonesy. What brings you out this way?"

"Fate. Long story. I travelled up north for job on a fishing trawler. But when I got there, found out they'd already taken on a crew and had sailed without me. Had no other reason to hang about and started back. Hitched a couple of lifts but mostly walking. To save money you see."

"You were given a red herring by the sounds of it." Old Owen sympathised.

"It hasn't been all bad. A bit of an adventure really."

Jonesy shrugged stoically, playing down how hard it had really been, wearing martyrdom like a badge. Old Owen's eyes softened in fellow feeling for the younger man.

After the good morning tea break, Jonesy cleared the table without being asked and began washing up. Owen Evans was impressed. He sat petting a sleek calico coloured cat that had made itself comfortable on his thin lap.

"What do you aim to do when you get home?" He asked.

"I'm going to apply to join the navy. If they'll have me."

Jonesy embroidered his story humbly with a spur of the moment idea meant to appeal to an old seaman. And it did.

"That's marvellous I am sure a fit young man like yourself will get in. What drew you to the navy?"

"I want to do something worthwhile. And I love the sea and ships. It's in my blood."

"Following a family tradition?"

"Yes, in a way I suppose so. It goes back to my great grandfather who was in the Welsh Merchant Navy." he lied.

Owen Evans did not mention he'd once had a son, also named Owen, in the Royal Australian Navy. He never spoke of it to anyone. The memories were too painful. His son had died young from injuries received during the Vietnam war. Owen's wife had never gotten over it and had faded before her time.

As the rain drummed down, the lonely old man lit a pipe, smoking as he mused on having this guest turn up. Himself, an honest man, Owen Evans did not question the validity of the younger man's tale.

The Bruiser respected the old man's silence and sat apart on a window seat watching the rain fall over green pastures, misting a line of distant blue hills. Steam rose off the fat cattle that now stood or crouched not far away from the window, chewing their cuds, content with the cooling shower.

"You can't be going out in this weather young Jonesy. It looks set in." Old Owen said at last.

Jonesy was shown to a small single bedroom, with a bare mattress covered in black and white striped ticking atop a narrow bed. Old Owen pointed to where sheets and blankets could be found in a hall linen cupboard.

During his prison stint Bruce had learnt how to make up a respectable tight bunk. Old Owen noticed that he ably completed this task. His approval of the young man grew. He had already formed a positive opinion or he'd never had put him in his son's former room. It was nice to have company for a change as well. Old Owen had spent years alone.

Jonesy offered to pay his way in cash but old Owen wouldn't hear of it. He did, however, suggest he'd be grateful for a hand with some chores once the rain let up.

The Bruiser felt very at home in the cosy farm cottage. He imagined what it would have been like to grow up in the care of a kindly father like Owen Evans.

For once, Bruce Luck didn't scheme on robbing the place.

The old man boiled potatoes and fried sausages for the evening meal. He asked Jonesy to cut some bread and put the Worcestershire sauce on the table. The Bruiser got that the old bloke didn't have much but was happy to share.

When the sausages had browned nicely, old Owen threw some coarsely chopped cabbage into the frying pan with them. He added the water off the boiled potatoes to the pan, steaming the sausages so they were well cooked all the way through. The Bruiser watched with interest. He'd never seen sausages done that way before.

Old Owen tasked Jonesy with mashing the spuds:

"Add a good knob of butter, lad. That's it. Now dribble in milk a little at a time until the spuds take it up. That's lovely that is. Thanks young Jonesy."

The old man did not waste anything. He added a cup of rice, a few sultanas and a teaspoon of curry powder to the potato water in the pan juices and let the rice absorb the liquid as he stirred.

"We'll have curried rice on toast for breakfast tomorrow, Jonesy." He said.

"Sounds good."

"Puts hair on yer chest." Old Owen assured him.

The old man served up the sausages and mash with steamed cabbage. He enlivened his own plate with black sauce. The Bruiser copied the old man's example and counted it as one of the best feeds he'd ever eaten.

Jonesy felt very calm and content in the little kitchen, with its smoke stained ceiling and quiet company. He listened with interest to tales old Owen related from earlier days. The man had grown up in Wales in what sounded like extremely tough conditions although he spoke of those long ago times with nostalgia.

The following few days, saw Jonesy haul hay out to the cattle, mend fences, chop wood and help old Owen do a grease and oil change on his ancient tractor. He followed the old farmer's systemic instructions obediently and both the men enjoyed the lesson.

Bruce Luck would have liked to stay on in this comfortable billet with the nice old man. But he had too many problems chasing him and worried over the outcome if the law caught up with him in the Evans place.

The Bruiser had never before cared what others thought but he now cringed to imagine disappointing old Owen Evans. He had begun to respect the man, a feeling so alien to Bruce Luck's nature, it surprised himself.

Eventually, in keeping with his lie to be off to join the navy, the fake Welshman Jonesy, had to bid old Owen farewell.

On leaving the Evans place, The Bruiser had reluctantly shouldered his backpack and taken again to the long road. Old Owen sent him off, early one morning, with a packet of fried oat cakes and half a tin of Golden Syrup.

Bruce The Bruiser wiped a tear from his eye as he trudged away. He imagined, in some parallel universe, he might have had such a good man as his own father. How different his prospects could have been.

Owen Evans did not ask Jonesy to write. He had a sense that his own time was nigh and overdue as he approached his eightieth decade.

The lad's visit had given him a well needed boost, yet at the same time, the good time had also exhausted the old man's reserves of energy. Afflicted with prostate cancer and suffering worsening symptoms impelled Owen Evans to put his affairs in order.

Subsequently, he took the bus into town where he sadly arranged sale of his remaining cattle. After facing that hard decision, an appointment with his solicitors served to record old Owen's final will and testament.

Owen Evans bequeathed his modest cottage and smallholding to a young man of recent acquaintance known as Jonesy: One Owen Jones care of the Australian Royal Navy.

His solicitor advised it was very unusual to do this and tried to talk Evans out of it. But old Owen remained adamant.

He had no one else and the lad seemed deserving. Plus, he shared the name Owen, had Welsh blood and was going into the navy, just as his own son did so long ago.

Owen Evans hoped young Jonesy would love the land and cottage as he and his family had always done. Maybe the lad would buy more cattle to restock the paddocks.

That fond thought helped the old man endure through his final months of life. The old Welshman died content thinking he'd set young Jonesy up for an easy retirement.

8

Kombi Van

After a few miles without seeing another vehicle on the quiet country road, The Bruiser came to a highway where he acquired a lift in a brightly painted Kombi van.

The Kombi roof held board racks with surf boards. As keen surfers, the two blond haired guys in the van headed for the coast, an opportune destination, the coast being just where Bruce hoped to go. He felt his old 'Luck' luck was bearing up.

He told the guys his name was Jonesy because he hadn't quite let go of his peaceful time with old Owen Evans. The Bruiser wished he really was Jonesy, the Owen Jones fabricated for the Welshman. He even regretted that he would not soon be in the navy.

The surfers asked the usual questions:

"Where are you headed?"

"South. Going to join the navy." He lied, still wrapped up in his wishful fantasy.

One replied with respect:

"Wow. Good on you. I'd do that if I could stand the discipline and being ordered about."

The Bruiser had almost caught himself up wanting the falsehood to be true. With a heavy heart he realised, with his lack of education, unqualified status and past criminal record, he could never hope to join the Royal Australian Navy. Resentment of his lot in life resurfaced.

Anyway, he told himself, taking orders and knuckling under with discipline was not one of his strengths. Funny thing was, old Owen had tasked him with all sorts of jobs and he had enjoyed being under instruction in those circumstances. Bruce missed that old man.

The strength of sentiment for an elder was new to The Bruiser. Going back to visit old Owen Evans was out of the question for the same reasons he had to leave that good place.

The abandoned child in Bruce Luck's psyche had warmed to the father figure of the kind and down to earth old man. Being under old Owen's roof had seemed magical, like another world. Bruce had felt he truly belonged there, yet he did not and never would.

In a blue funk, the whole wild adventure of running amok of the law began to pall for The Bruiser. Yet there was no going back. What was done could not be undone.

"They say that sailors have a girl in every port. So that would be alright hey Jonesy?"

"Huh. If only." he answered, despondent with facing some harsh truths about himself.

The suggestion of having a girl in every port rekindled The Bruiser's latent sexual yearnings. For some reason, he hadn't been overly bothered by excessive urges while staying in the old farm cottage with the Welshman.

The surfers pulled into a beach camping site. They had booked ahead to secure their usual berth as the place became packed out on weekends.

Bruce envied the surfing mates who had nothing to worry about except catching a wave and having a good time.

"This is as far as we go." They said. "Good luck in the navy Jonesy."

"Yeah. Thanks for the ride. Enjoy the surfing."

Bruce saluted a farewell to the carefree surfers who would never know how he envied them.

He headed for lunch to a large seaside cafe named as The Greeks. He had lost track of the days but learnt the day was Friday when he bought a daily newspaper.

Seeing nothing of the Kirkwood Bonn incident in the news, Bruce felt satisfied that the burnt out Landcruiser had yet to be discovered. Nothing had eventuated from the beach party with the eight teenagers either. So far so good.

The cafe cook turned out to be The Greek himself, a giant of a man who wore a blue and white apron depicting the flag of Greece. Bruce ordered a hamburger.

"You want the Greek Burger or the Australian one?"

"What's on the Greek Burger?"

"Lamb patty stuffed with feta and olives, cucumber, tzatziki sauce."

"Zar what? Yeah. Nah. I'll take the Aussie thanks."

Bruce shied away from a foreign sauce he'd never heard of.

"You want a fried egg on that? Cheese?"

"Sounds good."

The big man served up a luscious hamburger, Australian style with everything including a well done beef patty, fried onions, beetroot and pineapple, the generous portion pinned with a wooden spike to keep all the contents together. Salad as a side had green lettuce, cucumber and tomato. Sauces, salt and pepper were on the table as help yourself.

"Now that's what I call a hamburger." Bruce remarked, impressed.

The Greek took the compliment gracefully as his due. The big man bowed, a flash of large white teeth parted his copious jet black beard in a pleased smile.

The cook's rolled up sleeves displayed thick hairy arms as he began clearing tables and wiping the counter. The time was early for the usual lunch hour custom and only two other tables were occupied. The Greek noted his customer's substantial backpack, held between the man's feet under the table.

"You hiking through?" The Greek asked.

"Yep. Heading for home. Saving fares."

"Been up North?"

The Bruiser gave The Greek the story he'd given Owen Evans about the boat crew job that fell through, embellishing as he went along.

"It's been a total waste of time and money. But I've seen a bit of the country anyway."

"You want a weekend shift here before you move on? Cash in hand. I could use some help washing dishes, cleaning and all that. There will be plenty of customers starting tonight through to Sunday arvo. The cafe stays open 7am to 8pm. I tell no lies to you. It's a bloody long day."

"That's an idea. You lose your last worker?" He had to ask. It seemed too convenient.

"My wife. She quit. Says I smell of onions. She sick of this place. She walk out on me."

"Bummer." Bruce replied.

He gave his name as Owen Jones with the nickname of Jonesy again, supposing the surfing guys from the Kombi van might come into the diner sometime. A good liar had to be on the ball at all times.

The Bruiser's mind whirled. A cafe like this would reap in a whopping packet over a busy weekend. Maybe he could get away with more cash in hand than The Greek intended. Though he wouldn't want to get caught and fall foul of the huge hulk of a man. The big Greek could break him in two. He'd have to play it smart or at least take care to appear straight.

"Where can I stay? I didn't book in anywhere. My last lift dropped me here but I intended to move on after lunch."

"I got a caravan out back. You can stay there. My wife, Cassia, she always keep it clean."

The Greek cafe proprietor took a key from a hook on the wall. "Go have a look. The dog ok. He look mean but he don't bite. I can give you another blanket if you need it. You need the key for the shower and toilet. It's in the laundry room behind the shop."

The Bruiser had no other plans for accommodation. He thought this to be a lucky break.

"How much cash in hand?"

"Let's say $15 an hour with free food and accommodation. I pay you on Sunday night."

They shook on it. The Greek's enormous hand felt strong and very firm. No doubt it was intended as a warning.

Having the caravan and amenities for two or three nights was a godsend, so The Bruiser agreed to do the cafe grunge work for the weekend. He'd suss out how to turn the temporary fix to his advantage along the way, if he could. Receiving gratuities couldn't be counted on, since tipping is not the done thing in Australia. Nevertheless, wherever cash changed hands he might get to pocket some on the side.

The Bruiser observed that The Greek had living quarters above the cafe. So the big gorilla would be on the premises the whole time which could be tricky.

Bruce began work immediately by stacking the dishwasher and sweeping the floor. His swag, hidden in the caravan, had been shoved well back in an overhead storage cubicle with a pillow wedged in front. The resident German Shepherd guard dog looked fearsome but seemed friendly as The Greek said. Nonetheless, Bruce hoped the dog might be a deterrent to any would-be burglars.

After the Friday night clean-up, The Bruiser enjoyed a hot shower and comfortable bed in the caravan. Rising early Saturday morning, Bruce as Jonesy, helped set up for the morning rush in the cafe while the cook made a breakfast of scrambled eggs, bacon and toast.

The Greek kept a close eye on his temporary employee and was pleased to see how efficiently he worked and interacted with customers, who soon picked up on Bruce's self imposed nickname.

"Hey Jonesy!" Echoed around the room, mostly from girls giving him cheek. Jonesy gave it back in good humour and the mood in the diner was made more cheerful with his presence. The Greek lamented that Jonesy would not be staying on.

The Bruiser wore a blue and white bib apron over his shorts and t-shirt. The long apron strings wrapped around his waist with the long ends dangling behind. After the tenth time some girl pulled them undone and felt his buns in the process, he began tying them in front. Bruce enjoyed the attention but nursing an overactive boner on the job was too distracting. None of the girls dared pull the strings from the front.

The cafe closed at 8pm but the cleaning up afterwards took another hour. The Bruiser was bushed at the end of Saturday night. He had worked a fourteen hour shift on top of a nine hour afternoon and evening the day before.

He gratefully stood under the hot water jet in the shower, glad clean towels were supplied. He used Kirkwood's aromatic toiletries to wash himself and the clothes he had worn all day. He rinsed out his shorts and t-shirt in the hand basin, to be hung on the clothesline outside, then returned to the caravan with just a towel wrapped around his waist.

The days work had been relentless but fun with the boisterous crowd. Content, The Bruiser crawled onto the bedspread, falling into a deep sleep the minute his head hit the pillow.

Sometime in the night, Bruce startled awake, aware of a shady presence beside the bed. There was no latch on the inside of the door and he hadn't heard it open. The dog he trusted as a burglar alarm hadn't barked either.

"Shit!" He sat up in alarm.

"Shush. No panic. It only me Cassia. The wife."

"What? You're The Greek's wife?"

"Look. I got nowhere to go tonight. I just want to sleep. OK? I don't bite."

"Holy crap. Your husband will kill me."

"He won't know. He sleep like a log. Can hear him snoring from here." Cassia assured him.

The Greek's wife slid in under the blanket and between the sheets, her back to Bruce. He still lay on top of the covers but shivered in the damp towel he wore. The night had grown cold with a stiff breeze whistling in off the ocean.

"Mrs. Um. Cassia. I'm bloody freezing. I have to get under the covers."

"Whatever. You never heard of pyjamas?"

"I travel light." He replied.

Bruce dropped the towel on the floor and was no sooner huddling under the covers than the woman turned towards him. She ran her warm hands busily over every part of his nakedness.

"Hey!" He objected, afraid this was going to mean big black bearded trouble.

"Mmmm. You feel so smooth." She crooned.

"Listen. I'm flattered but I'm also buggered and....oh my God...that feels so good."

"You smell so good too." The woman encouraged him.

The caravan rocked on creaky springs as the inevitable happened. In the midst of her passion, Cassia clawed his back with long sharp fingernails, drawing blood with her talons.

"Ow. Ouch. Go easy woman." The Bruiser cringed.

"Huh. Big strong boy. You just a pussy." Cassia giggled.

Although the woman left the caravan sometime before dawn, Bruce barely caught an hours sleep before having to get up for the Sunday tourist influx. He dreaded working the daylong shift almost as much as facing the massive Greek man after bonking his wife all night.

Fatigued after his hard night and sorely tempted to quit, Bruce felt dangled over a barrel. Opting out meant he would lose all the money already owed him since pay was withheld until Sunday evening. In light of his night with Cassia, making waves with her husband over the pay deal seemed best avoided.

Somehow The Bruiser got through the long Sunday of drudgery helped by the cheeky banter of friendly customers.

After sweeping and mopping the floors at the end of the shift, Bruce could hardly stand up. Finally, he hung up his apron for the last time, and fronted The Greek for his pay.

To Bruce's enormous dismay, Cassia appeared, descending the stairs from the flat above. An acetone odour from a new coat of purple nail varnish wafted down with her. She blew on her long sharp nails and smiled smugly while sashaying to stand by The Greek's side. The Bruiser belatedly tumbled to a set up. He now doubted the Greeks could really be husband and wife unless their relationship was more than a tad impaired.

Hands on hips, The Greek dictated a command in his booming bass voice:

"No pay for you. You got enough. Now you go!"

The Greek owed him over five hundred dollars but it wasn't worth the argument. The Bruiser knew himself to be both defeated and physically depleted from the arduous weekend. He'd only get a hell of a beating from the burly giant if he objected. With just a sneer to Cassia, he dragged weary feet outside into the dark night.

Bruce unpegged his stiff dried clothes from the line and checked his backpack. At least it hadn't been robbed and his original money roll remained intact. The Bruiser as Jonesy the prize sucker, slunk away like a beaten dog, vowing to someday return and torch the place. Give it enough time and the act would never be linked to himself. They didn't even know his real name. Plans for revenge were his only consolation.

Bruce donned his one pair of jeans, two t-shirts and a hooded jacket to spend a cold uncomfortable night huddled against a windbreak fence above the beach, using his backpack as a pillow. He had to resist taking a blanket from the caravan, no use inviting trouble he couldn't handle.

In the morning, Bruce awoke to the sight of the Kombi van guys who trotted up from the shore carrying surfboards, dripping wet from their early session riding the waves.

"Hey Jonesy. Is that you? We thought you were heading out."

"I was. But I got offered a weekend job. Seemed like a good idea at the time. Turned out more of a train wreck."

The Bruiser managed to say that much before his raspy voice caught in a dry cough. The surfers exchanged eye rolls and did not hold back with scathing remarks:

"Don't tell us you fell for The Greek's scam with Cassia!" "Another one bites the dust!"

"I did." Bruce admitted with remorse. "And I've got the claw marks to prove it."

He bared the crisscrossed throbbing scratches decorating his back, to show them.

"Ouch. Nasty. Salt water is good for that. But it will sting like hell."

"I might brave it. Hope I'm not scarred for life."

"Ha ha. She leaves her mark that's for sure."

"We reckon it's so Cassia can cry rape if anyone dobs them in for the rort."

"I didn't even think of that. Was more worried about getting thrashed by the fond hubby."

The surfers said they could have warned him but took for granted he intended moving on to enrol with the navy.

"Wish I had moved on. Hindsight is great, hey."

"Nearly every weekend those people con some other poor bugger. Always some lone guy travelling through. Never a local."

"We've met a few of them now. Turfed out at night with nowhere to go. Full of guilt because....well you know. Helped them if we could."

"I was fast asleep. Next thing she's all over me like a rash."

"You're not the first and probably won't be the last."

"That's why we never go there to eat any more. We bring our own food supplies now."

The Bruiser gave them a thumbs up. His throat ached, so parched, he could barely continue the conversation. Fine sand crusted his hair, eyelashes and cheeks. With a mouth feeling like the floor of a cocky cage, he groaned and rolled over onto his knees to get up.

"I feel like a first class fool." He croaked.

"Nah. Live and learn hey. Come over for brekky at the Kombi. We've got baked beans and frankfurters today. Add mustard to that combination, it turns a surfboard into a jet ski."

"Huh?"

"Make sure the wind is in your face next time you fart."

"Slow on the uptake this morning." Bruce tried to emit a laugh. Failed.

"One or two cups of strong tea will set you up."

"I won't say no." He replied.

The Bruiser took a brief bracing naked dip in the briny, keeping his eye on his backpack and heap of clothing on the deserted shoreline, before meeting up for breakfast at the Kombi. Bruce Luck, as Jonesy, slurped down a big mug of hot tea, liberally laced with sweetened condensed milk. It was just what he needed along with the calorie rich breakfast.

Abashed, he didn't have the words to adequately thank the Kombi guys. Instead, he hid a fifty dollar note under his plate before bidding farewell to the helpful surfers. The Bruiser rarely gave money away. The warmth he felt from his gesture of appreciation made him fear himself to be going soft. He resolved to harden up. In his experience, the world was no place for wimps and bleeding hearts.

"I'm The Bruiser!" he whispered hoarsely, thumping his chest.

Bruce Luck reminded himself of his nickname to bolster his flagging ego. Truth be told, he felt more like the bruised than The Bruiser at that juncture.

The surfers found the fifty under the plate later that morning.

"Look at this! Jonesy left us this bloody great tip. What a great guy!"

"Wow. I'm a bit humbled for being a beach bum while he is off to join the defence force."

"Yeah, me too. Dude's a proper hero. Of all people, Jonesy didn't deserve the Greeks' con."

"It's a shame. High time someone took revenge on that moll Cassia and her big hairy ape."

The two surfer guys mulled over Jonesy sacrificing possibly his best years of life in the navy. Maybe he would have to fight in some war and get killed for his country. It was a sobering reality check.

"Fifty bucks buys a lot of fire starters. What d'you reckon?"

"Dead set. I'm in."

The surfers high fived. Thanks to several smoke alarms, the sleeping occupants in the flat above the cafe had ample warning to escape the burning building.

The arsonists hung back in shadows, long enough to witness the residents run out the back door. Unhampered by his long striped night shirt, the burly Greek man led the race well ahead of his woman. He had a surprising turn of speed for such a heavy person. Back at the Kombi, the surfers feigned being just awoken by fire brigade sirens and gathered with others gawking at the blaze.

The Greek and Cassia moved into the backyard caravan after fire gutted their business premises. Refusing to pay for better accommodation, The Greek decreed they must endure the cramped conditions until such time as insurance facilitated rebuilding.

Unfortunately, the big cook left administrative side of business to the woman. Cassia sweated knowing the policy had lapsed. Thinking a few weeks made little difference, she let it slide while shopping online for a better deal. However, far more interesting social media pop ups were such distractions that Cassia had yet to secure another policy.

At least they were far from being cold stony broke. The partners each had healthy bank accounts, for the busy cafe had been a veritable goldmine. They fleeced weekend casual workers because they could get away with it. Cassia liked the variety of sex partners, and The Greek liked saving money.

Authorities deemed the fire to be deliberately lit, going with a theory that kerosene poured at the base of wide front doors, seeped inside to soak a greasy floor mat. It was assumed fire lighters set it off. Flames spread across the internal floor, reaching the kitchen area. In swift reaction, a full fryer vat of cooking oil caught, fuelling an immense blaze, subsequently exploding several gas cylinders.

Investigators endeavoured to ascertain any motive for the attack. Yet the cafe owners could hardly admit to inciting fury from diddled casual workers. In a somewhat poetic twist, The Greek and Cassia swore to police they had no known enemies. Between themselves, the latest patsy Jonesy featured high on their private list of suspects. Then again, they could never be certain, since many more had succumbed to their shrewd trickery in the past.

Thrown together in the caravan, the big sweaty man's stale odour made Cassia gag. He really did stink of onions. She'd enjoyed a degree of separation before, with her own room.

Cassia owned an urgent need to get out before her volatile partner learnt they were uninsured. She valued her neck and long feared earning the big bully's rage. In the early days of their partnership, Cassia organised means to skip out as a precaution. Her wealth, and her passport kept in a bank deposit box, enabled a ticket out of Australia.

No culprit ever came to justice for the arson and no go-fund-me page ever eventuated for The Greek's Cafe.

9

The Bible Thumpers

After his hard weekend, The Bruiser wearily shouldered Kirkwood's knapsack of assets again and headed out to the main thoroughfare, hiking along the verge.

He would not overtly thumb a lift but had met no problems cadging lifts so far, despite the mode of travel being illegal in the Sunshine State of Queensland.

Eventually he stopped at a rest park to use the public amenities, where tap water was signed as unsuitable for drinking. He sat at a picnic table to empty grit from his boots and cool his hot feet on the soft green grass. Available water came from a creek, whereupon inspection, had edges alive with fat black tadpoles, the young of cane toads.

An old couple at a nearby table were packing up remnants of a picnic, stowing baskets and a water cooler in their car. The Bruiser heard water splashing around in the cooler. They looked promising for a lift South as their car had New South Wales number plates. He knew travellers were rarely denied water and used a ploy that had proved useful in the past.

"Excuse me." he said in a polite tone of voice.

"Yes?" the man replied, about to close the car boot.

"I wonder if I could trouble you to fill my canteen?" he asked in a shy way, "The water at this park is labelled non potable."

"Of course. Are you hiking?"

"Yes. It's a long road. I think there is a backpacker hostel in the next town South of here." He replied. "So that's where I am hoping to sleep tonight."

"Can we give you a lift at all? We're heading South."

"That would be most welcome. Are you sure I would be no intrusion?"

"None at all."

The man smiled benevolently. It had been an easy exercise for The Bruiser. The kind old couple not only filled his canteen from their own supply but gave him a welcomed lift.

Invited to sit in the comfy front passenger seat, he planted his feet either side of the knapsack on the floor, thanking his lucky stars for another good break.

The husband did the driving and his wife sat behind him where she could carry on a conversation with The Bruiser who went back to calling himself Richie.

He stuck to the story of joining the navy. It had held up so far. About five sentences into the conversation he was asked if he'd found Jesus.

The Bruiser managed to keep a bland face despite an inward cringe : *Christ bloody bible thumpers. There's always a catch.*

Ever resourceful, The Bruiser, again as Richie, launched a counter attack:

"Have I found Jesus? I have and no mistake. I have found Him in the earth and trees and in the clear blue sky above. Also in the falling rain and in the vast ocean."

He hoped that would shut them up but it only encouraged them to reel him in.

"How wonderful and eloquently said!" They exclaimed in absolute delight.

The religious zealots went on extolling their favourite topic for another hour while The Bruiser gritted his teeth behind a fake smile glued on his dial.

The woman went on and on...

"We travel the righteous path with Jesus by our sides. That's it in a nutshell."

"You can't say more than that." her husband added.

The litany wound up and the woman drew breath at long last. She seemed to expect some reply. The atheist answered, with a chant of relief that she might shut up at long last:

"Hallelujah brother and sister."

He raised his fist to pump the air, as emphasis. The religious couple squirmed in raptures and immediately ordained him into the fold:

"I say Brother Richie, I don't suppose you would consider speaking at one of our meetings? The next one is in a few days time in the next country town from here. It will be in the evening from 6pm with a tasty supper as well."

The Bruiser did a mental eye roll. That sounded like a real blast. Not. He could not imagine anything worse than making a speech to a boring bunch of bible botherers. He tried to wriggle out of it.

"Oh. I hadn't planned staying for long. Sorry. I haven't even booked at the hostel. So I might not get in either. I may have to move on."

"We have a venue booked for the meeting and you are welcome to stay there. It is a country hall with reasonable amenities. It's on our loop that we do routinely every year."

Free billet would be good but he loathed to share accommodation with these tedious people.

"Where will you be staying yourselves?"

"We booked at a motel. But it's busy at this time of year of course. You'd be lucky to find a motel or hotel vacancy I'm afraid." The man replied. "Our event takes up a lot of available accommodation with all the faithful coming into town too."

Phew

"That's ok I couldn't really afford a motel or hotel, to be honest."

"Well at least your accommodation at the hall would be free of charge. And we will stock the refrigerator with food for you. There is a microwave and kettle in the little kitchen."

"That sounds okay then. What do you do yourselves at the gathering?"

"We lead the prayers and take up the collection. Last time we had over a hundred faithful souls. So it keeps us busy." The old people smiled, rather smugly.

A big collection? No wonder you can afford to motel it. Hmmm.

Brother Richie did the sums. Over a hundred at maybe average twenty bucks apiece? He didn't like to ask how much their audience gave. He wondered how much people might pay to buy a ticket into the pearly gates of heaven. It had to be a fair wack to make it worthwhile for the hire of the hall and travel expenses. Maybe the faithful gave a lot more like double or triple his estimate. Now that would be tempting, if only he could get his hands on it.

"What would you have me speak about?" He asked, warming to the possibilities.

"Could you build on finding Jesus in your earthly surrounds? Maybe ask if anyone in the congregation had similar feelings? Largely they contribute ideas and their replies lead on into other topics. But while you're on the podium you orchestrate proceedings."

"How long would I be needed on the podium?"

"At least an hour. Longer if you can keep it up."

"Will there be other speakers?"

"One of us can take over if necessary. But we like to welcome new blood, Brother Richie."

The Bruiser weighed it up. It would give him a few nights free accommodation and food. He could probably blah on with some balderdash to keep his talk going. If he ran out of ideas he'd just make them pray for a long time. The tantalising collection sweetened the deal and he would be well placed to suss it out.

"Alright. I am not accustomed to public speaking but I would like to help you out, after your kindness to me. It is such a worthwhile cause and I could do with a rest from tramping the roads, to be honest."

The old couple clapped their hands in approval. The Bruiser felt like their golden boy.

"That's wonderful Brother Richie. What will you title your theme for the talk?"

"How about: I Found Jesus In The Ocean."

The Bruiser could hardly keep a straight face. Surely that facetious title would earn some wise cracks. It could be fun. He might get the audience laughing. His benefactors didn't catch any joke in his theme title.

"Is that what has driven you to join the navy Brother Richie?"

"You know...I think you have picked up on that before I even knew it myself."

The old couple looked pleased with themselves.

At the prayer meeting venue, 'Richie' was shown to an enclosed dorm room up on a mezzanine floor, accessed by a steep ladder-like staircase. Inside the room, two sliding windows faced out over a backyard garden, separated from a bitumen car park by a dense leafy hedge of blue Plumbago.

Inside, the upper floor landing looked over the cavernous hall space, where chairs were set out facing a low stage that held the speaker's lectern. Beneath the mezzanine floor were the kitchen and public facilities.

The dormitory held several folding canvas stretchers. Sleeping bags hung, opened out for airing over railings attached to the walls. A bathroom with WC and narrow shower cubicle completed the dormitory amenities. After The Bruiser's previous cold gritty night spent huddled on the beach, the basic comforts seemed the height of luxury.

The Bruiser opened the windows and turned on the one ceiling fan to freshen the room. He checked for locks on the doors and found none apart from a slide bolt on the inside of the bathroom.

His concern for his backpack and money came to the fore. He would have to be wary of anyone climbing up to the mezzanine. He stuffed his pack inside a folded stretcher and planned to sleep against it for safe measure.

"Are the amenities adequate for you, for a few nights?" He was asked.

"Yes. Thanks. It's as good as most hostels I've stayed in. My only concern is security. Does anyone else have access to the room?"

"Not while we have it leased. It can be all yours. We can put up a 'Staff Only' sign if you like."

"Thank you. Yes, that would be good. You see, what I have in my backpack represents my worldly possessions at this point in time. It's not much but it is all I have."

The old couple tut tutted in sympathy.

"It will be good to be issued with uniforms in the navy. I am looking forward to wearing decent clothing."

The Bruiser put on his best abashed expression. His benefactors bustled to make a Staff Only notice to put on the dorm door.

10

The Speech

On the night of Brother Richie's inaugural speech on finding Jesus, the hall filled with a throng of people, appeared to be dressed in Sunday Best attire.

Some rowdy children hurtled around shooting each other with water pistols. After squirting a few adults by accident, their weapons were taken away and the little brats chided. The Bruiser shrugged off mild surprise that guns were condoned as suitable playthings. Nothing the peace and love mob did made much sense, in his opinion.

The Bruiser noted the toy guns were placed out of reach of the kids, high on the edge of the mezzanine landing although no one climbed the ladder staircase.

Soon, the children stopped whining for their toys in favour of pigging out on cream cakes. Women of the congregation contributed plates of sandwiches and cakes to a high tea laid out on long trestle tables.

The Bruiser opened the dorm door a crack and peeped out. He had showered, shaved, and combed his hair with water. Painfully aware his duds fell short of finery, he wore the jeans and the least crumpled short sleeved button down shirt amongst Kirkwood's clothes.

After everyone became seated and opening prayers said and done, Brother Richie was introduced. He emerged from the dorm, waved self consciously from the mezzanine landing and climbed down the steep laddered stairway, backwards, as the safest method of descent.

A number of women and men in the hall secretly admired or envied Brother Richie's tanned muscular arms and tight buttocks clad in faded denim, as he negotiated his way down.

The organisers had placed an easel on the stage with a placard:

"I Found Jesus In The Ocean" by our dynamic new Guest Speaker Brother Richie.

Seeing this credit, The Bruiser felt like a minor celebrity. He gained the pulpit and surveyed the sea of faces upturned to his every movement. A sedate golf-clap welcomed him.

"Good Evening." the newly ordained Brother Richie had rehearsed his intro somewhat but hadn't advanced any further with what to say. He tried to string it out:

"Before I begin, does anyone have questions on my title theme – I Found Jesus In The Ocean?" *Please someone fill this space. Anything even a bad joke or a criticism?*

Not one person put their hand up. Not even a twitter. A pin dropped would have sounded loud in the expectant silence. The Bruiser cleared his throat. He'd just have to wing it:

"Has anyone had similar experiences?"

Apparently not. Nevertheless, the dynamic speaker soldiered on:

"Ahem. My journey began with an aim to find some meaning in life. Before I gained the righteous path, I have a confession to make." *They love public confessions don't they?*

He looked over the crowd. No response.

"I sinned along the way." *If they only knew.*

"None of us are without sin Brother." Said a whiskered man sitting in the front row.

"Let he who is without sin cast the first stone." Another one quoted.

Brother Richie gave himself a tick for making at least two of them speak up. *So they aren't all struck dumb. I was beginning to wonder.*

"Yet I beg to plead my sins which will surely surpass any committed by the good folk here."

The crowd appeared more interested by his claim. *Maybe I should shake them up:*

"Yes my good brothers and sisters, I have sinned. I have slept with the unholy, taking temptation as my bedfellow whenever it has been offered... And it has been offered to me so very many times. My body and my expertise to give sensational pleasure to others, has been my downfall."

A collective gasp hissed through the crowd.

Ha ha. That made them sit up. Nothing like a mention of hanky panky to push buttons.

He had them on the hook:

"Yes my friends. There are many who will casually partake of the carnal pleasures in life. And I have been among that number who scorn the missionary position to achieve far greater heights of physical release. A whole world of delights opened up to me at the hands of the fallen and I shamelessly fell with them, along the way."

The undivided attention of the audience came with murmurs of shock and a shuffling of feet. To tease them even more, the sinner continued:

"To my great shame I came to be acquainted with such unholy couplings as I had never imagined existed during my cloistered and innocent youth. And I have indulged with fervent lust and passion."

He intoned the words deeply while beating a fist upon the lectern for dramatic effect. The crowd, as one, agog with curiosity, appeared to lean forward, and shift to the front of their seats.

"But I will not describe those wild and erotic practices here due to the youngsters present and the delicate sensibilities of the womenfolk."

The recently ordained Brother Richie said it piously. An audible groan of disappointment from the congregation ensued. He had them in his hand.

"Any questions so far?"

A front row man stood up and asked:

"So Brother Richie. You undertook these unseemly practices before finding Jesus. How did your enlightenment curve you away from the sinful way of life?"

Shit I didn't actually want to explain it. Thanks a lot you bloody great wowser.

"Thank you. That is a very good question. It makes me explore my most inner being."

And my most inner being is trying to invent something...What if I say I got the clap? Nah. These holier-than-thou wankers want all the gory details.

The Bruiser continued making it up as he went along:

"You see, I worked on a fishing trawler where an argument took place involving a female prostitute on board."

An elderly woman put her hands over her ears.

"I thought women on fishing boats were considered bad luck." The wowser interrupted.

"Yeah right. It was bad luck. For her. And for me. You see, he was a Jezebel by name and by nature. Jezebel had been taken on board to have her favours shared among the entire crew of eleven lusty sailors."

Go on make a smart arse reply to that. Ha ha.

The elderly woman gasped and opened wide her eyes, proof she still listened.

The audience drew a collective breath of either disgust or titillation. He suspected the latter.

He lay his head in his hands as if distraught but in an effort to gain time to think up more:

"..the woman, Jezebel, was thrown overboard naked when she tried to blackmail the crew for more money. She threatened to blow the whistle to all their wives and girlfriends. I think I was the only unattached man on board."

"Naked! They threw her over naked?"

"Yes. So cruel. But I threw her a raft to save her life because we were miles out to sea."

The cynical front row member put his hand up. Brother Richie forestalled his question:

"The raft inflated automatically when it hit the water."

Thwarted, the picky interrogator put his hand down again.

"The other crewmen took unkindly to my well intended action and threw me over the side after her."

"Were you also naked?"

"Yes. They stripped me of everything. Even my precious gold watch left to me by my grandfather. May he rest in peace."

The Bruiser thought the gold watch was a nice touch and congratulated himself on quick thinking. He pretended to be heaving and trying to hold back sobs, as he looked to the rooftop, praying for inspiration and wondering how much more bull dung they could swallow. The audience grew impatient. The gabby front rower asked:

"So Brother Richie. How did that work out?"

"I swam to the raft and tried to get into it with Jezebel... but my scrambles almost upset the whole thing. She screamed at me to stop before I drowned us both. The trawler motored away and left us stranded. I was in the water."

"Was it cold?"

"No. Not too cold. But Jezebel hogged the raft I had given to save her. To be perfectly honest, I found her selfish attitude most unfair. Of course, that woman wasn't known for her integrity. Anyway, I had to cling to the side while we drifted for hours in the cruel sea."

He closed his eyes, shook his head and rocked on his feet as if reliving the ordeal. The audience allowed him a minute to get over his minor breakdown.

"What happened then?" Someone asked to kick start his story.

Give me a break. I'm trying to think.

"Then sharks began to circle us."

"Oh goodness. How frightening it must have been."

"It was. Very. I begged to be let into the raft. Finally Jezebel agreed and tried to help me ease over the side without swamping the whole thing... Oh my God. I can't bear to recall what happened next..."

The Bruiser played for time and racked his brain for some punch line.

"Stay strong Brother." People in the crowd egged him on.

"Remember Jesus is with you." Someone called from the back, which gave him a clue.

"Yes Jesus was with me. Although I know Jesus loves us all. HE seemed to choose my life over Jezebel's. Her ending was so horrible. I don't know if I should fully describe it."

"The children are asleep now Brother."

Damn them.

"Yes. Alright. So I managed to get into the raft with the wanton woman. It was very cramped and our naked bodies pressed together, moving to the rhythm of the ocean as the raft rode the swells. Up and down. Up and down. You get the picture? Jezebel suggested we might as well go out with a bang....I was stimulated by her words and even more so by her able hands. There was little else to do, as you can appreciate. Although granted, the conditions were not ideal."

"You gave in to lascivious temptation even in the face of death?"

He felt condemnation from the crowd as they emitted negative vibes and he did not want to lose their kinship.

What high ground could I occupy? Think!

"It was so hard..."

He paused waiting for a giggle that never came. It was a hard room to work but at least the sea of faces hung on his every word:

"...But you see... I endeavoured to help the fallen woman cope with her fears. I tried my hardest to take her mind off our dire predicament. So yes, I made love to Jezebel and rocked the boat very dangerously, it has to be said. Her cries of ecstasy mingled with that of the seagulls flying above.

I can never again hear seagulls without the memory resurfacing." *Phew what a save.*

All eyes remained on him. A few woman fanned their faces with prayer sheets. Having full attention of the gathering felt empowering. He raised both hands to the ceiling.

"Let us pause at this point to pray to the almighty."

No one could argue with that.

The Bruiser noticed the organisers had begun going among the aisles, passing silver trays holding little brown envelopes, like pay packets. From the vantage point of the pulpit, the speaker glimpsed the light green of hundred dollar notes being slotted into the packets. His mind whirled trying to do the maths of headcounts per dollars, knowing it had to be a substantial take. The crowd wanted more of his story:

"Amen." The wowser said aloud to mark the end of prayers.

"You said Jesus chose you over the woman?"

"That is how it seemed. You see,.after we...you know...she felt the call of nature and sat on the side of the raft to relieve herself...I counterbalanced the raft by laying against the other side. But suddenly she just went over the edge. This is horrible. Please stop me if you can't bear it." *Please please do.*

"Courage Brother. Remember Jesus is with you."

"Very well. I am sorry to burden you with this. Ahem. Sharks grabbed at Jezebel's ample nether regions that hung over the side. The vicious monsters pulled her into the ocean. There was just a blood curdling scream and then she disappeared. I hope it was quick. That poor woman. Even though she was a terrible sinner."

"Oh no! Even so. How awful."

Mutterings of sympathy rippled through the hall and the story teller could see they loved the entertaining mix of sex sin and horror. He bet they'd be bashing more than their bibles this night. He continued on a high of his new found celebrity:

"I know. It was so tragic. When I sat up and dared to look, all I witnessed was a mad frenzy of action churning up the waves. The sea turned red and gory with blood. I knew the worst but my mind would not accept it at first. I screamed as the reality sunk in. The sharks had Jezebel."

The Bruiser took a moment to dry sob and think up more:

"When her head floated up against the raft, her eyes held some sort of truth. I can't explain it any better than she looked as if she'd seen the light."

"Oh my God." the elderly woman cried. "Perhaps she had. At last."

"Yes. Perhaps so. There was nothing I could do. I lay back down in the bottom of the raft, frozen in terror, I don't know for how long. I feared any movement I made might draw the sharks to attack the raft."

"You must have been cold by then, being naked." A woman used her ripe imagination.

"Yes. Cold and numb with shock. Eventually another fishing boat sighted me adrift and took me on board."

"Did you feel the hand of God in your rescue?"

"I did. Of course I did. Yes. I felt Jesus had taken me by the hand and pulled me to safety. I was given clothes and hot food. Although the clothes were old fishy smelling cast-offs and the food basic porridge, they were the most valued gifts I had ever received."

A few women sniffed and dabbed at their their eyes. The heckler in the front row wasn't done with him:

"And what now Brother Richie, do you not feel the carnal urges any more?"

"Of course I do. But Jezebel left her mark. Her long red painted nails clawed my back in her final throes of passion. Although it has been many months since, that stigma flares up and stings painfully to remind me to mend my ways."

"What? You bear the stigmata still?"

The Bruiser slowly began to unbutton his shirt, enjoying the rapt expressions of the whole audience. He wondered if he was the first to ever do a strip tease from the pulpit. Baring his impressive muscular chest, he was rewarded with coos and sighs.

He slid the shirt from his shoulders and turned around to show his back. The claw marks Cassia gave him in the caravan still smarted. He knew the scratches remained raw and reddened. It was in no way any proof of his tale but no one denied his claim. They wanted it to be true.

"So, I take up my journey knowing I am blessed to be alive and have been granted more time to live on this wonderful earth."

A few of them chorused:

"Hallelujah praise be to God."

He wondered at the double standard of praising their god since poor Jezebel suffered her awful fate. But he wasn't going to argue with the dyed-in-the wool faithful.

"Hence," The Bruiser thought usage of the old word 'hence' gave it a classy touch, "I found Jesus not only in the ocean, but in the green fields and the blue sky up above. All around me in every living thing. In the birds and the trees. I have striven to be a better man ever after. Thanks be to my saviour. Let's hear it for Jesus."

He clapped his hands above his head like a variety show host.

As the crowd stood up applauding, Bruce made a humble bow before a speedy exit to the mezzanine floor, in case anyone nailed him with difficult questions about his fiction.

Inside the dorm, The Bruiser breathed a sigh of relief that he had gotten through the speech and it was over. He knew no one had gone up the ladder stairs but still checked that his belongings and money were all in order.

While captured on the pulpit performing his duty speech, Brother Richie observed the collection contents were transferred to a brown leather hold all. Now he surreptitiously cracked the door ajar to see where that haul of donations ended up.

The Bruiser was not the only one who coveted that bag of money. While patrons enjoyed another cup of tea, two masked bandits strode in, grabbed a young girl who happened to be standing by the door and held a knife to her throat. The girl yelped but did not struggle.

"Hand over the brown bag and don't follow us outside or she will get hurt worse."

One of the intruders shouted the demand in an odd accent that was so bad, The Bruiser knew it had to be put on.

People screamed and at least one woman fainted. The Bruiser stayed watching the event unfold from behind his cracked open door. *No way.* Whatever happened next he knew it would bring the police and he held no ambition to be a hero. The water pistols confiscated from the brats earlier, had been placed on the edge of the mezzanine landing out of their reach.

The black plastic guns appeared remarkably real and could come in handy if the crooks confronted him.

Slowly, The Bruiser opened the door wider and on hands and knees snaffled the fake weapons that were within arms reach. He managed to edge back inside the dorm room without being noticed.

Meanwhile the brown bag of donations was slid down the centre aisle to the robbers who backed out of the door, dragging the slim girl with them, as hostage. Someone in the crowd yelled out saying they had dialled 000. They might have been bluffing but The Bruiser couldn't risk it. He neither relished facing the congregation again nor the constabulary that could be there within minutes.

The only clandestine escape was through a window with a drop of five metres to the ground. Working quickly, The Bruiser shoved the toy guns into his belt, lifted a fly screen from the window track and quietly placed it against the wall. The backpack dropped out first, hit the ground with a muted thud onto soft green lawn. Climbing out of the window, The Bruiser hung onto the narrow aluminium rim by aching fingers before letting go. Landing with bent knees onto the knapsack, he rolled over and gained his feet, ready to run. He then scarpered along the Plumbago hedge thicket to a back garden gateway.

The former Brother Richie made his escape in a low crouch, knapsack slung over his shoulder. The only way out was through the car park where he hoped to dodge unseen, behind the cover of parked cars. Near the car park exit, a sporty black Ford revved at the ready. The Bruiser acknowledged it as the thieves' obvious getaway vehicle. He'd been there and done that often enough, he felt sure the escape car would only have one occupant. The designated driver would be on tenterhooks watching for his accomplices to emerge with the stolen takings.

The Bruiser crept up to the driver's side door, wrenched I open and stunned the driver senseless using a chop to the back of the neck, another useful trick he'd learnt in prison. He realised the getaway driver was a girl after he pulled her big black hoodie off. The lightweight female had been easily dragged behind the bushy hedge. She remained unconscious but Bruce jammed a dirty hanky into her mouth anyway. Without a second to spare, The Bruiser then took the place of the getaway driver, wearing her black jumper with the hood up as she had worn it. He put his knapsack on the floor in front of the passenger seat, hoping no one chose to sit there but he leaned across and locked that door to make sure.

The other two thieves emerged from the hall with their hostage. The young girl got down and lay on the ground, perhaps having been told to under threat of harm. The pair in possession of the brown hold all, sprinted to the car, dived into the back seat and slammed the doors.

"Go go go." They yelled.

The Bruiser accelerated with a screech of tyres and a smell of burning rubber. He guessed the plan would be to head for a nearby forested area where they might dump the car. It was sure to be stolen if they possessed half a brain amongst themselves.

"In here Sis. This is it." One of them directed Bruce to turn into a minor road.

Another vehicle, a common old Corolla sedan was parked by the roadside on the deserted byway. It was the only other car in sight. Taking a punt, The Bruiser pulled up behind it. The other two rolled out with the hold all. One of them keyed the sedan to open and threw the bag into the boot. They were prepared for a speedy departure and did not look back. Watching closely, The Bruiser exited the getaway car with his backpack and took the black water pistols from his belt.

"The game is up lads. Hand over the keys or I'll blow your balls off." he snarled.

The two youthful thieves spun around and exclaimed in fright.

"Where's my sister?" one gasped.

"She's dead. I shot her. If you value your hides, you better do as I say. Now lay on the ground and chuck the keys my way."

"NO. OH NO." they both cried together as they obeyed his orders.

The Bruiser picked up the Corolla keys. Keeping the water pistol on the likely lads, he put his knapsack in the boot beside the brown bag of donations. Sirens heard in the distance heralded the imminent arrival of the men in blue.

"The cops will be onto you any minute now. Best you run off into the bush, hey boys?"

The lads took his advice and took off. He could hear them crashing through the undergrowth. The Bruiser slid behind the wheel and sedately drove off in the Corolla, reaching the highway within a few minutes. He passed three squad cars with lights flashing and sirens blaring going in the opposite direction, back to the hall.

The Bruiser sang as he drove away.

"Hallelujah. Hallelujah. Hallelujah."

11

Cousins

The Corolla fuel gauge showed full so The Bruiser planned to make tracks as far as it would take him before having to dump the car. It could be reported as stolen as well.

Back at the crime scene, the girl getaway driver came to, spat the disgusting handkerchief from her mouth and staggered into the car park. The hostage girl was just getting up from the ground. The two girls were cousins and had planned the heist with their brothers.

"Jesus girl! You're supposed to be driving the getaway! What are you doing here?"

"Some big yob jumped me and knocked me out. God my neck hurts. I just woke up under the hedge. I guess he hijacked the car. So where are the guys?"

"They got the money bag and took off as planned. And keep your voice down Cuz."

"What? They've been kidnapped!?"

"That's what it looks like. And here come the police. Play dumb."

The four cousins had long resented the religious sect and despised the prayer meetings they were obliged to attend. Convinced their devout parents were being fleeced, they planned to purloin the donations as retribution. The plot was to split the loot among themselves and each secretly buy mobile phones they'd long been denied by their frugal god fearing parents.

The police arrived to an uproar in the hall. Some children were howling because their toy water pistols could not be found. In the confusion, the two girl cousins easily intermingled with the familiar crowd, and just as easily played dumb.

The old couple who organised the cult meeting were bereft. They didn't even think of checking on Brother Richie until much later.

Meanwhile, the two boy cousins heard the Corolla take off and doubled back out of the bush. They regained the stolen getaway vehicle and drove it to within walking distance of the hall. The stolen Ford was abandoned again and the would-be thieves intermingled with the crowd of people who knew them well.

Seeing the two girls had the boy cousins cry out with relief. No one noticed their little drama in the uproar going on with everyone in a tizz, talking at once.

"We thought you were dead!" the boys whispered to their getaway driver cousin.

"As you can see I am alive, just have a splitting headache and a sore neck."

"So you guys got kidnapped with the money. How did you get back?"

"Some big guy held us up at gunpoint and told us to run into the bush. So we had to do it or he was going to shoot us as well. He said he had shot you dead."

"But he didn't. Obviously."

"We had to believe he did. Anyway, he left the Ford but took Mum's Corolla and the bag."

"After he left in Mum's car, we drove the Ford almost all the way back and walked in."

"You'll have to report Mum's car as stolen. Won't you?"

"No. Mum didn't know we were borrowing it."

"She'll report it stolen though when she finds it missing."

"Yes of course. But it won't be connected to any of us."

The four cousins failed to gain the money but at least thought themselves to be free and clear of any suspicion.

By then, the old couple who'd cajoled Brother Richie into doing the talk, discovered he had absconded out of an upstairs window. The removal of the fly screen supported this finding.

It disappointed that the eloquent speaker had run away in the face of danger. General opinion of the audience was he'd given the best talk they'd ever attended and most said they gave more generously as a result.

Speculation surfaced that Brother Richie might have been a party to the robbery. The rumours kept the guilty cousins well out of it.

Detective Dougall Grimslade caught the evening news story on TV. Footage showed the

congregation being questioned by local police and took in the billing for Guest Speaker Brother Richie. Richie! Could it be?

The case was out of his area but Dougall strove to find out more and made a speedy trip to the country hall. After clearing it with the officer in charge, he interviewed the event managers.

Adding to the name Richie, the description given of a handsome, well built and charming person fit the picture of the man he pursued.

"You say it was a memorable talk given by this Brother Richie, yet no one took any photos or video?"

"No. It is not allowed. We frown on that type of interference during our gatherings. It is, after all, primarily a prayer meeting."

"May I ask what Brother Richie's talk was about?"

"He described a life of debauchery that was turned around after a life threatening experience, when he came to find Jesus as his Savior."

"Did that ring true. I mean, how was it accepted?"

"Oh yes. We could all see Brother Richie had seen the error of his ways. He even showed his stigmata."

"His what?"

"He bore some permanent physical scars."

"Uh huh hmm. And that was accepted as some kind of proof?"

"It backed up his story."

Dougall paused while he assessed the people as extremely gullible, they assessed him in turn and tried to offer him salvation and everlasting life:

"May I ask: Have you found Jesus Detective Grimslade?"

Dougall replied curtly:

"HE has not been on my search list so far. That will be all for now. Thank you for your time."

The busy detective made a hasty retreat, returned home and phoned his colleague Dulcy Vestige. Dougall wanted her opinion on whether the story teller, Brother Richie, could be the man they chased.

"I don't know. They say a girl was taken hostage and it involved at least two others. Our suspect acted alone in the past, so far anyway." Dulcy mused.

"I agree. Though much of what they said sounds like him. The fact he asked to have his canteen filled to cadge a lift, isn't that how he got a foot in the door with Alba Jenkins?"

"It is. That's right. So it could feasibly have been him doing the speech. Maybe not the heist though. He is more likely to act on his own."

"Yes. The theft could be completely separate." Dougall concurred.

"He'd want to get out of there before any police arrived."

"That's it. He would. And it seems he did. I'm betting he did it."

"Found Jesus?"

"Get real Dulcy."

The Bruiser did indeed want to get away before any police arrived. He drove the Corolla away from the main highway and headed ever southbound on lesser used country roads.

Finding a secluded spot, he spent an hour pulling cash from the many brown pay packets, estimating the haul to be a whopping five thousand dollars plus change.

The Bruiser had no remorse over keeping the prayer meeting treasure. He felt to have earned it with his entertaining speech.

The brown leather hold all with the empty pay packets was left in the boot of the Corolla. He locked the car and left the keys under a wiper blade.

Finding the garage vacant, the Corolla owner reported it as stolen but could not find any sign of a break in. She insisted adamantly that her

Corolla had been locked in the garage and the keys kept inside the house. Indignant denial met a police suggestion of an inside job.

"We are a family of staunch Christians." they had huffed.

The lady's car containing the incriminating evidence was found within three days.

People in the Christian group gossiped over the staunch church member's vehicle being implicated in the robbery. The robbers had specifically asked for the brown bag. Only the sect followers would know donations went into that brown bag. The huge scandal surpassed even Brother Richie's stimulating talk for entertainment.

The cousins' parents got together to discuss the obvious culprits, since their children were in and out of each others homes often. All had access to the house, the car, its keys and the garage keys. The guilty teens stubbornly refused to confirm or deny anything. The adults saw the light, but each blamed the others offspring. A family feud was born. In order to avoid their relatives and the sniping innuendos from the church congregation, the cousins' parents dropped out of the religious sect. The four cousins were reasonably pleased with the outcome but went without mobile phones until they went to work and earned their own.

After dumping the Corolla, The Bruiser once again took to hiking the roads but now perceived himself to be very vulnerable with so much money in his possession. Weariness threatened to overtake the fugitive who yearned for somewhere safe to lay up for a few days.

The catch-22 in finding himself rich in cash: He couldn't buy a secure place to sleep. ID needed to be shown to book into motels or hotels. Using

Kirkwood Bonn's ID was an option but he dared not use it in case the name was flagged on national databases. He would never rest easy with the threat of being raided a possibility.

With no immediate options, the man sought out places where homeless people spent their nights, bedding down on flattened cardboard cartons and newspapers, always with his backpack as pillow and one hand on his knife. While weather remained mild, he could bear the conditions yet could not relax enough to gain deep sleep. The riches had to be guarded. The money came to own him.

The Bruiser saw that real freedom meant having nothing to lose.

12

Bouncer

Bruce Luck hiked from town to town and made an effort to keep himself looking clean, shaven and reasonably respectable. He did not want to attract police attention for looking like a grubby vagrant.

The man sometimes paid to enter public swimming pool facilities just to use the change rooms and hot showers. Showgrounds, whenever events were on, also gave access to hot shower amenities, provided for paying exhibitors. It seemed no one policed showground bathrooms when horse or dog shows were held and his usage was never challenged.

During a regional agricultural show, he underwent a ten dollar haircut at a show tent barber shop. While there, he heard talk of a horse drawn camper trailer being offered for sale, on the grounds.

The Bruiser did not imagine the old fashioned mode of transport would suit himself. Nonetheless, he wandered over to have a look at it, out of boredom and curiosity.

The offering comprised a canvas covered framework fitted onto a box trailer. It was adapted to be horse drawn, except for having no drivers seat. The sturdy grey pony gelding that represented its one horse power, needed to be led at a walk by a head halter and lead, while towing the wagon.

Inside, the trailer was equipped with a bed roll, blanket, small butane stove, pan, kettle and a couple of big metal buckets. The foam rubber mattress lay over a sack of pony pellets and two bales of lucerne hay. Some spare pieces of harness and horse brushes hung from S-hooks fixed into the frame walls.

There was not much headroom but the space seemed cosy to crawl into, to someone who had been sleeping rough.

The Bruiser imagined the small gas stove could only be used outdoors but he saw the potential in having a little mobile home and being able to walk along unencumbered by the weight of his backpack.

Several interested onlookers listened as the seller demonstrated how to feed, water and harness the pony and tether him out on grass if necessary. The asking price of six thousand dollars was poo pooed by most of the spectators, who sneered or laughed and walked away.

Among comments bandied about were: "You'd be lucky. Ha ha. What a rip off."

A handful of children and The Bruiser were the last left contemplating the deal.

"Why are you selling it?" He asked the vendor.

"I have to go into hospital for a big operation and I need the money."

"Fair enough. Will you take four?"

"I'm asking six."

"Nah. I don't see six in it. The trailer and camping gear is maybe worth fifteen hundred tops. So you've got four and a half on the pony?"

"That's a very reasonable asking price for him. He's Welsh bred. Only ten. Quiet and a good worker. In his prime he is. Hard footed. Never needs shoeing. And he don't eat much. For a horse. He just wants his ration, about five good big buckets of water a day and curry comb his coat once a day. He likes that. I'll even throw in the curry comb."

"What's his name?"

"Bouncer."

The name might have given a clue but the pony looked in good health with shiny coat and bright eyes.

The Bruiser knew nothing about the equine species but the idea of a camp trailer grew on him. After the ordeal of having nowhere pleasant to sleep for the past several nights, the spongy rubber mattress under private cover held enormous appeal. He knew he could buy it outright and be sleeping comfortably that night. The stolen money burnt a hole in his pocket.

"Five is my top offer."

The Bruiser said it in an offhand indifferent tone of voice.

The owner seemed reluctant but five thousand might be the best he'd get. He had already touted for two days and paid a fee to the show society for the spot. As his buyer prepared to walk away, the seller compromised: "Suppose I could take five if it's in cash."

Greatly surprised that the bloke actually had five thousand dollars in cash on him, the vendor supposed he might have collected a big win somewhere. He didn't dare question it. There was something about the tall guy that boded ill of falling foul of his temper. The seller had a soft spot for the pony but it was supposed anyone paying five thousand would look after their investment.

The money was carefully counted out, they shook on it and the haul from the 'I Found Jesus In The Ocean' talk was exchanged for Bouncer the pony, and the mobile camper trailer.

The Bruiser walked his one horse mobile home to the next town, yarded the pony over night at another showgrounds and camped beside him. As he lay in comfort wrapped in a blanket on the mattress, listening to Bouncer munching his feed, he felt content and slept well at long last. Woken not long after sunrise to the sound of girly voices cooing over Bouncer, the man felt revived from his eight good hours of sleep.

"Good morning." The Bruiser unzipped the canvas flaps and poked his head out.

"Oh hello. Sorry if we woke you."

"That's ok." he yawned.

The girls appeared to be perhaps eleven or twelve years old. Both wore jeans and pony club t-shirts. He asked if they would mind his camp while he went to the bathroom. They said they were glad to do it. On return, he asked if the girls might be able to guard his lot for a bit longer. He needed to shop for supplies for himself and promised to pay the kids for their trouble. At the same time, he realised the flaw in having the pony and camper, which was no more secure than a tent.

The possessions tied him down and he had to be responsible for Bouncer's welfare and for replacing the fodder. Bouncer ate like a horse and would be through the current supply within the week.

The Bruiser returned with a few food supplies, teabags, coffee, powdered milk, cereal, fruit and tinned beans. The girls had been busy curry combing Bouncer and he noticed they had also refilled the pony's water bucket. He gave them ten dollars each for their efforts.

"Oh tar very much. We loved looking after the old fellow. He is good for his age isn't he."

"Forgive my ignorance. I don't know much about ponies and I haven't had him long. Is ten old for a pony?"

"No. Ten is not old. But Bouncer is over twenty you know." The girls seemed sure of that.

"What!"

"Don't worry. He is fit and could go on into this thirties. If you look after him. He's got a little splint on his nearside fore though."

"He's got a what on his what?"

The pony clubbers pointed to a lump on the inside of Bouncer's cannon bone. The Bruiser got that nearside fore meant left front leg. Why they didn't just say left front leg was a mystery to him.

"I think I was diddled out of paying too much." he realised aloud.

"These quiet old ponies are worth their weight in gold." the girls assured him.

The pony clubbers then gave The Bruiser a lesson in ageing horses by their teeth. Not that he envisaged ever needing that skill. He was used to taking each day as it came and didn't look too far into the future.

The Bruiser spent some quiet and relaxing days trudging from town to town, accompanied by the tap and patter of Bouncer's unshod hooves. At times, he unhitched the pony and held him to graze, taking note of the pony's liking for green milk thistles and particular grasses.

He grew fond of the old pony whose white lashed, liquid black eyes studied him patiently. The ex-prisoner who had never known or shown any tenderness to another living being, now doted on Bouncer with extra strokes of the horse brush. He found the pony enjoyed a scratch behind the ears and gave him this affection without any ulterior expectations.

The flawed individual, proud of his nickname The Bruiser, learnt giving could be its own reward. Bouncer's whicker to greet his feed times endeared him to the man who felt he had formed a trusty bond with the solid little pony.

There were downsides to travelling gypsy style. The Bruiser weighed up the downsides against having a comfortable bed and shelter every night. Boiling the kettle for a hot drink and a snack along the way was a definite boon.

Main thoroughfares had to be avoided but that was no hardship. Most people who passed the man and pony along country roads, smiled and waved. Some form of wholesome goodness seemed imbued to the man just by being in the company of the pretty pony and old fashioned way of travel.

The enduring problem was finding somewhere suitable to stay overnight. Choices were limited to towns with showgrounds, vacant sale yards or rural free camping areas.

The Bruiser came upon a small town with not much going for it except a pub in a decrepit old timber building that had a jaunty lean to one side. He craved a tot of rum and had the money to buy a whole bottle. It was too good a chance to pass by.

There was nowhere good to leave the pony and wagon, but a snot nosed raggedy boy had begun walking alongside. The kid wore baggy pants, a ball cap turned backwards and a shirt two sizes too big. The shirt sleeves bore evidence of being used to swipe his runny nose more than a few times.

"How'd you like to earn a quid?" The man asked the boy.

"What's a quid?"

"A couple of dollars. Easy money."

"Are you a sex pervert?" the boy asked with a wet sniff.

"Yes. But rest assured you don't appeal to me in that way." the man admitted truthfully.

"So what's your name?" the boy asked, in no way offended.

"Aloysius Cackleberry." The Bruiser lied.

"Wow. Same as mine." the smart-mouthed kid made the claim without batting an eye.

"Okay Aloysius. Can I call you Al?" The Bruiser asked.

"Pretty sure you could. It isn't that difficult." the kid wisecracked back.

Uppity little prick. If Bruce Luck hadn't craved the rum so much, he'd have walked on.

"Do you want to earn some money or not?"

"What would I have to do?"

"Just mind the pony and my stuff while I nip into the pub over there."

"Five bucks for ten minutes then another dollar for every minute you're late back."

The boy looked at his own bony wrist to emphasise the point although he wore no wristwatch.

"Okay. Deal."

The man readily agreed, he could almost taste that rum and was eager to get it. The Bruiser felt sure he could get to the pub, purchase the rum and get back easily within the five dollar time slot. He shouldered his backpack and hurried to the tavern.

Emerging from the pub the man strode across the street peeling off a couple of fives. Elated by obtaining the rum, he had decided to be generous because the youth seemed needy and he reminded him of himself. But the boy had scarpered. The Bruiser made a quick check of what was missing from the trailer. He'd gotten away with the camp stove, kettle and a big bag of food supplies. The theft was worth far more than the promised five dollars. The Bruiser knew it was exactly what he would have done at the same age. He raved his anger to the unconcerned pony:

"Bouncer, that puny little bastard played me like a fiddle. The time limit he set, the exacting payment deal, all part of his distraction. And like a prize fecking mug, I fell for it. Hook, line and sinker. Shit oh dear. Taken in by a bloody little kid!. He couldn't be more than ten years old. I should kick myself. Could I be losing my touch? No, please don't bother to answer me, Bouncer, because then I'll know I'm losing it for sure."

The Bruiser now had no stove to boil up for a cuppa or heat some beans. In fact he had no food supplies at all. He cursed the day that stinky boy drew breath. He wished bad luck to shadow the brat's footsteps throughout his entire life, which would not be a long one if he every caught up with the thieving little sneak. Catching up would never happen if the snotty boy was half as wily as Bruce had been at the same age. At least the kid had tied Bouncer's lead rope to a fence before nicking off. Bruce acknowledged, that in his shoes, at the same age, he would not have bothered tying the pony up, just to be ornery.

The sale yards where The Bruiser planned to spend his next night were on the far side of a deserted country show grounds, a long way from the shower block. He left the pony hitched to the trailer with a big pile of teased out hay under his nose to keep him occupied. The man longed to freshen up and took his backpack into the vacant facility.

The Bruiser didn't trust kids anymore and no youngsters were about to ask for help anyway. He was in the amenities block for quite a while, using the toilet then deciding to shower, shave and rinse out the whiffy underpants he'd worn for at least a week.

The man couldn't believe it when he came out to find the pony and wagon gone. All the hay had been eaten yet he did not consider the possibility of Bouncer going AWOL.

The Bruiser believed his pony and camper trailer had surely been stolen. The country was full of thieves. He should know. Bruce could not gamble on reporting the theft to police in his circumstance of being on the run from that very same law force.

The man strode about the grounds and up and down the roads, looking for any clues like hoof-tracks or even horse dung, but found nothing. It was as if Bouncer and his cosy mobile home had evaporated into thin air. He cursed his bad luck and the bastard who stole from him.

Bruce wondered if the thief had been Aloysius Cackleberry, for want of a better name. Had the snotty boy followed him to clean out the rest of his stuff? But he doubted the kid would have tracked him so far or risked getting collared.

In fact, the town The Bruiser lobbed into that day was not far from the pony stud where Bouncer had been born and raised. The old pony had simply taken himself home at the first opportunity of finding himself free to do so. Once on the homeward path, Bouncer raised a brisk trot with the trailer rattling along behind him.

The spritely grey pony duly turned up at the stud farm gate. His owner, who had lied about needing an expensive operation, shook his head and laughed in triumph.

"So you've bounced back again old lad. It didn't take you long this time."

The pony and wagon had so far been sold three times over as many years and Bouncer had found his way home, towing the trailer, each time. No road registrations were required by law for the pony cart and the vendor made sure no traceable paperwork went with the sales.

Some paddock mates neighed welcomes to their old travelling friend. Bouncer snorted, whickered in greeting and licked his lips in anticipation of expected home comforts.

His owner mixed up a warm bran mash with molasses for his cash cow pony and gave him a good rub down. Old Bouncer kicked up his heels on being turned out to graze with the rest of the herd while his crafty master began to plan the next time he sold the outfit.

Losing his investment was not the only sorrow for The Bruiser. He had never in his life owned a pet and had enjoyed having that beautiful pony. He felt the weight of sad loss as he shouldered his backpack and trudged onwards, again with nowhere to sleep in comfort.

Wandering with the horse drawn trailer seeking suitable camp sites had led The Bruiser further inland. At least, losing the pony and camper meant he could again roam at will and stopover almost anywhere.

Once more, the wanted criminal turned eastward towards the coast. He preferred to mingle in more populated areas where hiking backpackers were commonplace, and he wouldn't stick out like a sore thumb.

Win some. Lose some. The Bruiser thought glumly.

13

Three Sisters

The Bruiser was savvy enough to new technology to assume there could be a chance of Kirkwood Bonn's ID being red-flagged on national databases, if it were reported missing.

If his original crime had been uncovered, there had been no news of it, but he knew it could only be a matter of time before it hit the fan.

When the burnt out wreck were found, The Bruiser hoped Kirkwood Bonn's credentials would be assumed incinerated with the rest. Yet, he cautiously avoided using the stolen ID, deciding it must remain hidden unless good reason or dire necessity forced him resort to it.

The Bruiser still had the bulk of Kirkwood Bonn's cash roll but knew how easily money got whittled away. Apart from buying rum, he tried to be thrifty.

Bored with being on the run, depressed and road weary, he yearned for somewhere comfortable to hole up for a while.

With that in mind, and at a loose end after losing Bouncer, the wandering felon applied for casual rural work to tide him over and provide temporary accommodation.

The Bruiser risked showing Kirkwood Bonn's ID to a small rural recruitment agency that placed backpackers in temporary seasonal jobs. The one person agency seemed like a hick affair that might not be well connected to the mainstream.

Authenticity of the ID was not questioned at the small rural recruitment agency, as Bruce Luck's face resembled the one in the photo. Being fit, strong and capable looking, the applicant easily gained a farm pickers position under the name of Kirkwood Bonn.

The agency manager assured him the job came with comfortable shared accommodation and very good home cooked meals. The employers were long time clients of the agency and well respected. It was just what the jaded fugitive wanted.

He set forth to the address given, to take up the post, where he would call himself Kirk to distance the name from the more distinctive longer version of Kirkwood.

Armed with the registration form from the recruitment agency, The Bruiser's next port of call landed him at The Calenda Market Gardens.

The fruit and vegetable farm, owned and run by three blond and blue-eyed sisters, had been passed to them after their father died.

The three pretty Calenda sisters, Marcha, July and November were so named for the months of their births. The youngest, November, went by the nickname Nova.

The young sisters were the third generation of their family to run the market gardens. Since their father had never hidden the fact he would have preferred sons for the sake of the farm work, the girls determined to keep up the rate of production, or even improve on it.

Using the extensive library in their home, they studied horticulture and argued pertinent points of various growing methods, back and forth, around the kitchen table.

Sometimes their father had gruffly explained reasons things were done as they were. The girls listened and learned. He was proud of his girls but rarely showed it.

At one stage, the sisters' father had been interviewed on a rural television program. Asked if the family tradition would endure, he infamously said that wasn't a given since he *only* had daughters.

The comment earned some viewer backlash. The farmer's wife had joined in the condemnation of her husband's words: *Only daughters* indeed struck a nerve since she had been denigrated for being *only a daughter* herself.

The old man had set his jaw and said no matter what the girls wanted to do, they had to face facts: They were heavy tasks they just could not manage as females.

Arguments flew back and forth and the old man set the girls difficult jobs to prove his point. When a big bloated roo carcass washed down the creek, he tasked them with pulling it out and making a funeral pyre.

The girls doggedly attended to the fire and its gruesome occupant. When they noticed their Dad striding down to check, they deliberately began happy chats and warming their hands on the malodorous blaze.

Their father had to hide a smile. They were good girls. Chips off the old block.

As the old man grew frail, he came to rely on his robust daughters to get the work done. For all intents and purposes, the three young daughters became the family breadwinners.

After the man of the family passed away, the womenfolk had to admit to their physical limitations and come up with permanent coping strategies.

Selling the farm was absolutely out of the question.

Steps were taken that made up for any weaknesses, so despite their gender and frail builds,

the farm prospered.

Marcha, the eldest at twenty, initiated the use of seasonal backpacker labour. She tendered a winning bid on a disused one room school house for removal. Marcha assessed it could accommodate several workers if necessary.

Rainwater tanks held run off from the roof as the water supply. Bore water could augment the tank supply if necessary. Most temporary workers complimented the generous and varied meals and did not complain about the facilities, which were kept scrupulously clean.

The workers' old school house had been set beside an existing under cover barbecue area that already included a sink, septic WC and shower.

The farming family had always used the barbecue area at lunchtimes to save walking up to the house and having to change boots. Now it became the communal dining space for their itinerant work force. The cupboard was kept well stocked with biscuits and the 'fridge with milk and fruit drinks for in between meals.

The plumbing and bunks were basic but no one ever went hungry at The Calenda Market Gardens and the three sisters earned a good reputation as employers.

The single bathroom had to be shared but only male backpackers were recruited.

Marcha and July blatantly found fun with some of those guys. It suited them that the conquests were ships that passed in the night, with never a lasting regret.

An independent delivery service, consisting of one man and his van, had been employed instead of trucking their own supplies to market. The van driver was expected to help with heavy loading as part of his contract.

Marcha was smart enough to have a rider clause built into the terms. The section named any faults or behaviours on the van driver's part, that would void the contract.

After their father passed away, the girls' mother went to live with her older ailing sister in a seaside cottage. So the three girls maintained the family market garden business together with occasional male hired help when necessary for muscle power.

As eldest, Marcha adopted the role of matriarch and did most of the cooking and office work. Being fussy, she liked to do these tasks herself and the younger girls were glad to get out of it. July and Nova did the laundry and cleaning of the workers quarters.

Other housework was shared but skimmed over if it impinged on more interesting pursuits.

Marcha loved the extensive in-house library in the family home and was never happier than finding time to curl into an armchair and immerse herself into something studious. Her particular interest lay in Latin terms and English grammar, subjects the others considered to be too high brow.

July and Nova preferred reading romantic novels. A favourite *Lemon Tango* had been read twice by them both.

The sisters attracted their fair share of male interest though choice was limited in the small rural community. July usually had a fling with any itinerant worker who wasn't dead ugly and didn't stink. Marcha would have a go at a reasonable one as well. Sometimes the elder two sisters tossed a coin for a good one. Their angelic appearances were quite deceptive.

Nova knew her older sisters indulged in casual sex but, so far, had not seen any young man who took her fancy. At fifteen years old, Nova told herself she could afford to be choosy.

"Nova, bring up some ripe tomatoes next time you come in. Please." Marcha asked

"Sure. What are you making?"

"Shepherds pie. Needs tomato under the mashed potato like Mum used to make."

"Yum." July and Nova both approved.

The girls appreciated Marcha's cooking and they all loved good food.

"Speaking of yum. Did you see the latest fella the farm agency sent?" July said.

"Bags him if he's any good." Marcha said.

"Mine I think, Marcha. I saw him first and you got the last one." July replied.

Nova rolled her eyes.

"He looks kinda dumb to me." Nova said. "But I guess that's not an issue. Hey girls?"

"Nope. Not planning on keeping him. Ha Ha."

"What if he isn't interested?" Nova asked unnecessarily.

"He will be. They always are." Marcha replied.

"True." July confirmed.

July and Marcha laughed wickedly. Nova told them they were both unspeakable trollops.

"Thank you. We try." July grinned.

"We succeed." Marcha amended.

All three sisters laughed together, sharing a ribald moment.

"True again." July added.

"This place has become almost bearable since Mum moved out." Marcha said.

"Bless her." July answered.

"I'm glad Mum likes living at the beach and helping dear old Aunty Florrie out," Nova added, "No one nagging me to do this and that all the time. Still. I miss Mum a little bit."

"However, you really should tidy your room, little sister." July said primly.

"Don't you start on me July. You're no saint."

"Never claimed to be either." July retorted.

Marcha intervened in the mild spat:

"Enough arguing. Are you getting the tomatoes or not Nova? I need them now."

"Okay, I'm going. Hey, that big dumb guy is the last of them now. Will we invite him to eat with us?" Nova asked.

"NO." Her older sisters chorused emphatically.

The sisters realised having workers in their private home space could become problematic.

The house, set on higher ground, overlooked the rest of the farm. Any shenanigans happened in the workers quarters or in the barn. At times, even the green houses had been used for the purpose of a quick encounter with the hired help.

The farm labourer calling himself Kirk was considered to be a good looking brawny backpacker with an exceptionally good body. Although he wasn't in the ideal age group, neither was he way too old. July had her eye on him from the start.

The man, as Kirk, knew July had summed him up but he lusted for Nova when he saw her picking tomatoes. He liked girls fresh, firm and a bit green just the way he liked his tomatoes. The Bruiser began making plans to nail Nova before his time ended at this farm. It teased at his vivid imagination but gave him an extra interest in staying on.

It was helpful to The Bruiser's intentions that the other few back-packer pickers had headed out for the city before their time was up. The girls didn't blame their hired help for quitting, since a massive tropical cyclone brewed just off the coast, and moved towards to the mainland. With the cyclone threatening, Kirk had the workers accommodation to himself.

The weather event had potential to be catastrophic for the area, unless it petered out after making landfall. The girls hastened to secure what they could in preparation.

July volunteered to take Kirk a plate of shepherds pie on a tray, with a bowl of jellied rhubarb tart and custard for dessert. She eyed him off but he barely met her gaze, just thanked her politely. July imagined he was very shy.

The Bruiser had never been shy but avoided eye contact with the girls after he noticed the real Kirk's eyes were described as green on his driving licence. His own were more a yellowy hazel shade. They might never twig to the difference but it paid to be careful.

"Just leave everything on the tray when you've finished. I'll come back for it later. Let me know if I can do anything else for you." July offered suggestively.

The Bruiser knew if she came back after dark, his eye colour would not matter. He might let her know what she could do for him then.

If the man was capable of analysing his off-hand attitude towards females, he might see it stemmed from being used and abandoned by his mother:

Bruce Luck's mother, Greta, had been his idol, his Wonder Woman, a superhero and best friend. Secretly, the grown man still thought of her as Mummy, though he could now hardly picture her face. His Mummy had shared his loathing of the school and facilitated his absent days. He loved spending time with her, she taught him fun things like how to shoplift and break into cars.

The little boy suffered heartbreak when she left. Worse, he blamed himself for her desertion. He had miserably failed in a trick his Mummy wanted to play on his Dad. Ever after, the reality haunted his nightmares.

By chance, Greta invented the 'trick' when she noticed her drunken husband had fallen asleep in his bath. Her hairdryer was kept plugged in on a shelf above the vanity basin. The woman quickly assessed the situation and asked her six year old son to sneak in, turn the hairdryer on and throw it into the tub.

"You must run outside straight away. You hear me? Can you do that for me?"

"Yes Mummy. It will be so funny." Little Bruce shared a naughty giggle with his mother.

When the boy entered the bathroom he felt afraid. He didn't want to look at his father naked in the tub, and he could not reach the high shelf unless he stood on the slippery rim of the bath. What if he fell in the water and woke his father? It was too awful to think of that happening. Plus, Bruce knew his mother really liked that hairdryer a lot. He worried he might ruin it by throwing it into the water.

So the boy decided a better joke would be to pour a whole bottle bubble bath into the bathtub, instead. He could do that without waking his father and the froth would cover the yucky private parts in their nest of hair.

As the suds frothed over onto the bathroom floor, Bruce ran outside, sure his Mummy would be highly amused and glad he had not damaged her good hairdryer.

But the boys' mother was nowhere to be found in the house. Running outside, he was puzzled to find his Mummy had gone next door and missed the whole trick. The let down disappointed the six year old.

"Mummy. Mummy." He had called urgently.

Greta emerged from next door.

"What's the matter Brucey darling. Is anything wrong?"

"You missed the whole trick Mummy."

"What's he talking about?" The neighbour wanted to know.

"We better go see what he's done now."

Greta indicated that the neighbour should follow her inside. The boy took his mother's hand and led her to the bathroom. His father still snored in the tub, obviously still alive.

Little Bruce got into trouble for making such a mess on the floor. His dejection multiplied knowing he had failed to do the proper trick. The neighbour only laughed and Greta had to hide her disgust.

"You silly useless boy." His mother had seethed after the neighbour left.

"I'll do it proper next time." Bruce had cried.

"There won't be a next time." She said, smacking him hard.

Young Bruce grew up quickly after Greta abandoned him. Within a few more years, the boy realised he had been set up to electrocute his father. His mother had gone next door as her alibi. If Bruce had slipped on the bathtub rim trying to do her bidding, he might have been boiled alive in the tub as well.

That final betrayal fed The Bruiser's low opinion of all females.

Despite being run by three lowly females, the Calenda Market Farm job provided good food and accommodation. The Bruiser decided he shouldn't crap in this good nest for a while. He bided his time and lusted over the slender youngest sister, Nova.

14

Cyclone Larry

Severe Tropical Cyclone Larry formed out of a low-pressure system over the eastern Coral Sea 710 miles (1150 kms) off the Queensland coast in 2006 when The Bruiser stayed at The Calenda Market Gardens.

The farm was impacted by floods as run off from heavy rainfall gathered in the hills and combined to inundate the land and cut roads. The occupants became blocked in for days.

The three young sisters who ran the market gardens were not afraid nor without necessities or comforts. They were well prepared with food stocks and had spare fuel for the generators, should power fail. They had survived cyclones before and this would not be the last.

Farm losses were the major concern. Everyone laboured to harvest what they could before crops were lost. The sisters were thankful that at least one farm worker remained to help out, and he did not complain.

The man called Kirk toiled beside them in the rain, rushing to reap and store melons and pumpkins high in the hayloft of the barn.

In past great flood events, the barn had a foot of water run through it but the loft always remained high and dry under the gabled corrugated iron roof.

Kirk The Bruiser kept abreast of news on the radio in the workers quarters. He'd heard nothing of the missing Kirkwood Bonn. If the sisters got wind of it, he would somehow have to make tracks out of there in a hurry.

Getting away could be difficult with the flood rising. By the same token, he must try to control his lecherous urges for the youngest girl, with no quick way of escape. In the meantime, he made use of the middle sister, July, who came to join him one dark wet night, wearing a raincoat and little else.

July afforded him a quick welcomed release and did not hang around, for which he thanked his good fortune. The Bruiser had no use for clingy women and believed gratitude was best shown by letting him get back to sleep. He could not envisage having failed to fully please a woman and been confident he'd given the girl a robust servicing.

As a pearly daylight outlined the eastern hills, July ran back to the farmhouse through the grey and rainy predawn.

Disappointed with the sexual encounter, she found the handsome labourer to be completely lacking in emotional warmth. July assessed the man as being nowhere near as good as his looks promised.

Although she hadn't wanted much from him except a bit of fun, his cold indifference and air of entitlement made her feel cheap and used, even though it happened at her own instigation. Only having herself to blame gave no comfort. At least she could give him a bad report to her sisters.

On return to the house, July went straight into a hot shower to wash away the man smell and shampoo her hair. Wrapping herself into a towelling robe with a dry towel around her head, she crept into Marcha's bed.

"So. Was he worth it?" Marcha moaned awake.

"Nope. Not nearly as good as he looks. Mechanical. Robotic. Vacant." July replied.

"So the old saying is true; Never judge a book by its cover: Cucullus non facit monachum." March quoted one of her Latin favourites.

"I thought he was shy at first but now I think he is just totally self absorbed."

"They so often are." Marcha agreed sleepily.

"I might as well have been a blow up dummy, only a vessel for the pestle."

"So no cuddle. No back rub?"

"Not even a peck. I vote we work the arse off him today."

"Planned to anyway." Marcha replied.

Nova nudged the door open with her hip, bringing in a tray with three cups of tea to the bedside. She got into Marcha's big bed with the other two.

"You're an angel Nova. A nice hot cup of tea. Just what I need." July smiled.

"So what's the verdict on Kirk?" Nova asked.

"Love as in tennis. No points. No score." July replied.

"Good. I never saw you riding off into the sunset with him. Does anyone else find him a bit strange?"

"We both think he is self absorbed."

"Too far up himself?" Nova asked.

"Succinctly put." Marcha laughed.

"Is there a Latin term for that?" uly wanted to know.

"I think it is 'ego refundatur' I'll look it up later. But we better get a move on. Work to do."

"The porridge is on anyway." Nova said.

"Wonderful. Porridge with honey and cream. Who wants to take Kirk his?" Marcha asked.

"Not me. Thanks." July shivered.

"I did the porridge and the tea." Nova reminded them.

"Okay. I'll do it this once." Marcha offered, with no argument from the younger pair.

July had been an interesting diversion but The Bruiser's desire remained focused on Nova, her slender young sister. So near and yet so far, Nova became an obsession for the man. He had no idea whether girls shared personal experiences but hoped July told her how well he performed. Perhaps Nova would have her appetite whetted. Not that he cared for her feelings, but taking her would be easier, if she was primed.

Another new day dawned to a guttural croaking of frogs and a sea of brown flood water lapped the edges of the barn and other outbuildings. The staff amenities and dorm block remained clear but would be awash in a matter of hours.

Torrential rain teemed down non stop, meaning the sisters were faced with accommodating Kirk in their own home. None of them wanted this but they could hardly expect him to sleep in the loft after he'd worked so hard. Hefting melons and pumpkins was heavy work and the three agreed he deserved their respect. They decided to ask him up to the farmhouse later in the day, but only after all the produce was safely stored in the loft.

A heavy metal mesh crate, bolted to a wooden sled, had been filled to the brim with the last of the vegetable harvest. The crate had a hinged lid and one side opened as a gate. Marcha used their small tractor to tow the sled into the barn out of the pouring rain.

Water had already begun seeping over the hard earthen floor of the barn so they'd sheltered the produce under cover with no time to spare.

The crate gate opened out to access the remaining pumpkins, which were a mix of types, Butternuts, Kents and Queensland Blues. The Blues being heaviest of all, were the most difficult to heave up to the loft.

"I'll go get dinner started. If the rest of you can stow this lot in the loft?" Marcha said.

"Yes. You go on. We can finish up here." Nova said.

Nova looked to July and Kirk to include them in the last of the heavy work. She'd be glad of a hot dinner warming in the range when all was done.

They were all soaking wet and the girls fought against exhaustion. The man seemed less tired and they appreciated his strength, harking back to their late father's words for the need of man-power.

July had turned her ankle in the heavy mud, and try as she might, proved to be not much use. Nova lost patience with July's stoic efforts to endure, so sent her up to the house:

"You go on up July, get into a hot bath. Put some liniment on that ankle. You're actually slowing us down now and this should be done in an hour or so anyway."

July was in more pain than she let on. Needing no further persuasion, she limped away leaving Kirk and Nova alone in the barn, to finish the work.

The Bruiser, as Kirk, hefted each pumpkin up to Nova who caught and stowed them in dry straw beside the stack previously put up. Each hard skinned vegetable would have to be turned daily in an attempt to stave off mildew in the warm, wet, humid weather.

Nova prided herself on never dropping a pumpkin but this time, so weary, she fumbled a catch. A heavy Queensland Blue splashed down to the flooded floor, and split open to reveal its seed filled golden core.

"Pumpkin soup for that one." Nova said wiping her brow.

"That's the last one anyway."

"Thank goodness for that Kirk. You better get your gear and take it up to the house. I think the workers quarters will flood tonight."

"Okay. Will do." he replied.

"I'll be along soon. Just having a rest." Nova told him. "I'll bring the smashed pumpkin up to the kitchen. It won't go to waste. Marcha makes great soup."

Nova fell backwards onto the straw and heaved a sigh of relief. She'd held a hooked hand tool ready to shift and open another straw bale but found she did not have the energy to complete the task.

The Bruiser was about to leave when he noticed the soles of Nova's boots up high on the edge of the loft. She obviously lay with her legs apart. He climbed the ladder with stealth and saw the girl was stretched flat on her back, eyes closed. Nova's damp clothes clung to her shape, leaving little to his imagination.

As the man watched, his blood rose. The beat of his burning desire thrummed throughout his whole body.

The Bruiser knew Nova was unaware of his presence. He watched her for a full minute, knowing they were alone and the other two would not be back. With the ideal opportunity presented, the versed rapist could no longer control his carnal urges.

High in the darkening barn loft, rain drumming on the iron roof drowned out Nova's startled cries as the man tore at her clothes and beset upon her in a frenzy of lust.

Nova's hand tightened over the wooden handle of the double pronged hay hook. Raking the tool down the man's face, gouged deep red furrows across his brow, cheek and down to his chin. Enraged, The Bruiser punched his victim in the head, opening a cut above her eye.

Powered by panic, Nova attempted to squirm away on her back. She tried to dig her heels into the slithery loose straw on the floorboards of the loft. Unable to gain much purchase, the girl did not retreat far.

Nova took advantage of a slight reprieve when the man knelt upright to feel the stinging bloodied wounds she inflicted.

Raising both legs together, Nova pushed him as hard as she could with her booted feet. The man overbalanced and fell backwards over the rim of the loft.

Taken by surprise, The Bruiser hurtled down to the hard packed earthen barn floor, fifteen feet below. A hands depth of flood water oozing into the building, somewhat broke his fall.

Panting and shocked, Nova peered over the edge of the loft. All was silent apart from the driving din of incessant rainfall.

The man lay spreadeagled on the flooding barn floor, his yellowish eyes staring up at her. She thought he must surely be dead...until he blinked and groaned.

In terrified panic, lest he come after her again, Nova clumsily struggled down the ladder, half sliding over the final eight rungs, scraping her shins, in haste to get away.

Rain rinsed Nova's bleeding eyebrow cut, to drip onto her ripped shirt and cold bare chest as she fled up to the safety of her sisters, who were both in the warm kitchen.

Marcha basted a tray of roast vegetables and July rested before the warm range stove, her swollen ankle raised on an old milking stool, a tabby cat in her lap.

Marcha and July gasped as Nova burst into the room and fell to her knees on the floor. The tattered wet shirt exposed her small white breasts, reddened by bite marks. Seeing her like that, the older sisters screamed causing the house cats to scatter.

"Oh my god. What happened? You're bleeding."

"Kirk attacked me." Nova cried.

"He what? No!"

"Where is he?"

"On the barn floor. I kicked him over the hayloft. But he's alive." Nova gasped.

Marcha went straight for the rifle, her face grim. Vermin was expected to invade with the rising flood so the gun and ammunition were kept handy. The sisters had lost three pet dogs to brown snake bites in the past, so lethal reptiles would have their heads shot off.

Marcha gritted her teeth, fully prepared and equipped to shoot the head off the male vermin who attacked her little sister.

"Take care of Nova." Marcha said in a deceptively calm voice.

"I will. You take care yourself Marcha."

July was already limping to help Nova up onto a chair.

"Be careful Marcha. He might be on his way up here." Nova warned.

Marcha wished they still had a couple of farm dogs but she loaded the gun and strode out bravely alone, into the rainy gloom.

The Bruiser had been stunned from the fall. He cursed himself for letting his dick take control of his common sense, as usual. If only he'd waited before trying the girl, he'd be up in the house having a hot meal and be offered a comfy bed, maybe even with July.

The Bruiser admitted to himself, his timing was way off. He also thought he could have seduced Nova to take him on willingly, if he'd been smarter and patient. In any case, as soon as the flood receded he could have scarpered more easily.

Now, water rose a few more inches around The Bruiser's prone body and he knew he must soon get up or drown. Gingerly he tested his stiff limbs. His arms and legs seemed to be in working order, though it felt as if an axe cleaved his spine.

He had landed beside the farm sled, its platform a good foot off the ground and the crate gate still wide open. Painfully, The Bruiser hauled himself into the empty crate up on the sled, out of the water. Sitting awkwardly, wet and suffering, he needed time to recover. All he could do was wait for the angry onslaught he knew to expect from the other sisters.

Despite the inches of floodwater, Marcha kicked the barn doors ajar, the rifle aimed ahead and her finger on the trigger. As her eyes accustomed to the darker interior, the enraged eldest sister was able to make out Kirk propped up in the sled crate.

Saying nothing, Marcha waded to a locker where she found a heavy padlock by feel, in a tin box where she knew it to be. All the while she kept the gun on Kirk. Wisely, the young woman did not trust that Kirk was as incapacitated as he made out.

The Bruiser watched Marcha through slitted eyes.

Marcha put the rifle down momentarily to padlock the crate door. That done, she spoke gruffly to the man who she had caged like an animal:

"Tell me why I shouldn't blast your fucking head off." Marcha snarled.

"She came on to me. I've been so lonely. I haven't been with a woman for so long."

"Liar." She raised the rifle and aimed it between his legs.

The Bruiser shrunk against the crate wall, holding his hands up in surrender.

"Don't shoot. Look. Let me go. I'll leave straight away. Tonight." he said.

"You can't you feeble-minded bloody idiot. The place is completely flooded in."

"I'll take my chances."

"Sure. And we will rest safe in our beds knowing you've gone." Marcha sneered.

July limped down with the use of their father's old walking cane. She set the torch she'd brought onto the work bench.

"Nova's in a hot bath. Says she'll get her pyjamas on and feed the cats." July whispered.

"What d'ya reckon July? I shoot his balls off?" Marcha asked loudly.

"That'd be a great start." July answered.

The Bruiser felt his bowels loosen but managed back chat in a show of false bravado:

"Yeah. Like you didn't enjoy a bit of rough yourself." he smirked at July.

"You weren't that good Kirk. Notice I didn't come back for seconds?" July replied.

"So do I shoot his balls off?" Marcha repeated as she levelled the rifle.

"Sure. Why not. He deserves it."

July folded her arms and pretended to await the gory entertainment with avid anticipation. July felt ninety percent certain it was a bluff to torment Nova's assailant but was in no doubt that Marcha itched to do it.

Marcha's cool and calm demeanour seemed calculated. As the minutes ticked by, uly felt savagely inclined towards wanting to see the man de-sexed. *Do it. Do it.* Her mind urged the punishment. Yet maiming him might get her sister in trouble, and she didn't want that.

The Bruiser resisted the urge to cover his genital area with his hands. Instead, he set his jaw and stared them down, his yellow wolfish eyes unblinking. He judged the girls would never do it. But you never could tell with women. He suffered agonies during the long impasse, only keeping his composure with great difficulty.

"The water is rising. I reckon he'll be drowned before dawn." July mentioned casually.

"You're right. Why waste a bullet." Marcha replied.

Spitting at the man, Marcha lowered the rifle.

The Bruiser tried not to show his tremendous relief but he slumped down, exhausted by his ordeal so far. He began to shiver.

"I'm unwell. I need help." He pleaded.

"Tough."

The joint one word reply held no option for negotiation. The sisters walked to the front of the tractor, peaking quietly. They discussed whether Kirk might escape via the top hinged section of the crate, and decided he might.

July found a coil of nylon rope amongst the paraphernalia under the work bench. Between them, the sisters passed the rope in several wraps over the top of the steel mesh crate, securing it tightly to metal lugs embedded along the side of the sled. The Bruiser watched and smiled slyly to himself, thinking: *Stupid bitches.*

Having secured Kirk as best they could, Marcha and July returned to the house, both soaked to the skin. Before changing into dry clothes, they locked all the doors and windows, something none of them could recall ever being done before.

"Do we have to worry about him getting in the house?" Nova asked in a shaky voice.

"No. Not at all. Just locking up for our own peace of mind." Marcha replied.

"He's well and truly locked in the crate." July placated her little sister.

"Did he say anything?" Nova asked.

"Begged to be let go. Said he'd leave right away." Marcha replied.

"As if." July shook her head.

Cosy in pyjamas, Nova huddled in front of the warm stove, and stroked a cat on her lap to calm her own jangling nerves. The bite marks Kirk inflicted had been dabbed with iodine and gauze applied over her split brow with a band-aid.

Marcha took the roasted meal from the oven and set it out, restoring a sense of well being.

15

The Stinker

Comforting each other, the sisters collaborated on what to do next: "Will we tell Mum?" Nova asked.

"If you really want to. Do you want to tell her Nova?" July asked gently.

"I'd rather not. What do you think Marcha?"

"No. Why worry her? She'll only panic and want to move back in here."

"And she'll have to bring Aunty Florrie because Mum is her official carer now."

"Cripes. Not dear old bloody Aunty Florrie."

They all imagined how the older women would step on their toes in many ways.

"We have to report it to the police though." July supposed.

"Not tonight. Let him suffer. Even if the police can get in by boat, they'll keep us up talking all night and I'm stuffed." Marcha said.

The sisters retired for the night. Well fed and exhausted, they slept deeply in their warm beds after the horrific day. The house cats crept in to snuggle at the end of various beds, content to be indoors out of the wet weather.

Up first to put the kettle on, Marcha peered groggily out into the dim morning at a view curtained with more relentless rain. The man Kirk was on her mind. He'd have spent a cold wet shivering night trapped in the cage. She hardened her heart. *Serves the bastard right.* Marcha's tough stance changed in a split second. An unbelievable sight through a gap in the downpour came to light. Floodwater had risen to halfway up the sides of the barn. That would put the pumpkin crate entirely under water.

"SHIT" Marcha shrieked.

A china cup she had held, dropped into the hard porcelain sink shattered. July and Nova rushed to the kitchen, pulling dressing gowns around themselves in the chill of the new day although the temperature would climb to a hot steamy day later. Marcha pointed to the barn.

"SHIT." July yelled, echoing Marcha's alarm.

"Double shit." Nova cried.

"Actually, that's triple shit."

Marcha corrected automatically; she could be pedantic in any situation. The sisters stared in horror. Their captive had to be dead, drowned in stinking floodwater. All three had a hand in killing Kirk. Nova kicked him over the loft albeit justifiably in self defence. July and Marcha had not been serious when telling Kirk he'd drown, knowing floods had never come up as high before. It seemed impossible. Yet they'd left him caged and were to blame for the man's death. The three sisters imagined Kirk screaming and crying out for help but nothing could be heard over torrential rain pounding on the iron roof of the farmhouse.

"What will we do?"

"We can't get him out until the flood goes down."

"He's going to stink the barn out by then."

"Could we tow the sled further away somewhere?"

"Get real. The tractor is never going to start. The engine will be completely underwater."

They got onto the latest weather predictions and ascertained the flood level would be maintained or even worsened over the coming few days.

"We might get charged with murder." July supposed glumly.

"I don't think so. Not after his attack on Nova. What else could we do?" Marcha reasoned.

"They'll say it was three against one." July worried.

"It wasn't though. You were lame with a turned ankle and Nova was injured and in shock from his vicious attack. We had good reason to fear him."

"Yeah. I guess. When you put it like that."

They digested possible outcomes for the dilemma.

"Fear is beside the point. He is still going to pong to high heaven." Nova said.

"We'll have to give it some serious thought. No point in dropping our bundles over it. What's done is done. So let's soldier on and think about it as we go." Marcha replied muttering "factum est" in Latin, for it is done.

"Yep. We factum good." July agreed.

Marcha remained stoic in any crisis and her practical approach had a soothing effect. The sisters set about attending to their normal ritual of combing and braiding each others' long hair. Then, they needed to eat breakfast. All agreed, it was no use facing the unsavoury problem on empty stomachs. Marcha threw some bacon and tomatoes into the pan while July made a pot of black tea and Nova sliced thick chunks of wholemeal bread.

"One egg or two? I'm having two today." Marcha said.

"Two for me." July chirped.

"Two for me as well and some fried bread would be good." Nova added.

The three sisters munched their way through hearty breakfasts and all had second cups of tea as they pondered on what to do about Kirk's spoiling body.

"We could always clear out the big chest freezer and stow him in there."

"But we can't even do that until the flood goes down. He'll already be ripe by then."

"True. And be ruining a good freezer. Forget that idea."

"Guess we'll just have to leave it up to the police to get rid of him."

"That could take days. And Mum is going to find out for sure."

"That will be an even bigger stink."

"Maybe we could fumigate the barn with some kind of smoke. Like incense."

The sisters washed and dried the breakfast things and went and got dressed, all thinking up various ideas. They met around the kitchen table again:

"What if we drag him down to the river with his knapsack on. It'll look like he got drowned trying to move out."

"How are we going to drag him to the river? Everything is so muddy and boggy."

"I don't know. But I guess he'll be really heavy, being so waterlogged and all."

"What if we tie his ankles together with rope and have three lengths leading off so we can all drag him together? At least he might slide along easily in the mud."

They all considered this option as feasible. Only Nova voiced one downside.

"What if he starts to...you know...come apart." Nova pulled a face.

"He won't by then. Remember that time we had to move the dead 'roo? It was older than that." July said matter-of-factly.

"That sounds like a plan. We wouldn't even have to inform the police. And Mum will never need to know." Marcha mused. "Good thinking July."

They shared high fives and considered the problem solved. It just remained to be achieved.

Marcha's phone, on the table, rang its jangling tune, making them all jump in fright. The three were rather more on edge than their nonchalant attitudes suggested. Their Mum called to check how they were faring. Marcha put the phone on speaker to save them each separately going over the same ground with discussions. Their mother was assured they were all well, safe, yes the flood was higher than ever before but nowhere near the house. Yes they had plenty of supplies.

"We're glad to hear you and Aunty Florrie are high and dry and enjoying the weather too. And yes we will look after each other. We always do." At least that was the truth.

They rang off sharing guilty looks of complicity.

"Ok. We're all liars." Nova said.

"But pretty good ones." July shrugged.

"Now we just sit and wait it out." Marcha added. "I might as well make a cake."

Marcha began creaming butter and sugar together with the edge of a wooden spoon, and at that very same time, Detective Dougall Grimslade's office staff discovered a Kirkwood Bonn had been recorded with a small rural employment agency, not long before Cyclone Larry hit the region.

Immediately informed that the wanted man had been sent to work at Calenda Market Gardens, Dougall got straight onto Dulcy Vestige in the Northern Territory:

"Eureka Dulcy. We found Kirkwood Bonn's ID is in use."

"So, the killer is stupid enough to use it. Well done Dougall. What now?"

"As soon as the roads open, I'll pay a visit to the Calenda farm and see if the owners can shed any light on the subject."

"Here's hoping you catch up with Kirkwood Bonn's impostor, Dougall. But of course, if you can get in, he can get out."

"I doubt if he is still at the farm, he won't want to stay in one place for too long."

"But you've tracked him down and are on his tail. You're a bloody legend Dougall."

"Shucks. Thanks for the accolade but I'd rather you just threw money."

"Noted. But don't hold your breath." Dulcy laughed.

16

Sisters United

Rainfall eased off within a few days but Marcha had made two more cakes before water receded enough to reconnoitre the situation in their flooded barn.

Sunshine steamed and sweltered the land in the hot tropical Queensland climate. The water inside the barn would be cooler than that outside but not cold enough to preserve a corpse.

Reluctantly, the girls deemed Kirk's remains should be accessible and dreaded the task of dragging his fetid body out.

"This is it girls. Be strong." Marcha told her younger siblings.

The three sisters began making their way to the barn, judging the water to be low enough to disclose the drowned man locked in the crate. There could still be about a foot of water over him or he might be floating. They weren't sure what would be worse.

The whole area reeked in the aftermath of the flood, with rotting vegetation, drowned wild life and farm animals washed down the creek to putrefy in steamy conditions.

The girls had disposable rubber gloves in their pockets and wore scarves tied over their faces, expecting a fouler stench than already pervaded the atmosphere outside the barn.

Before reaching their destination and dreaded assignation, an imposing 4x4 vehicle drove up the farm driveway and stopped in front of the farmhouse. The girls had pause for alarm. They had not realised roads had been opened.

"Who can this be? What god awful timing."

"Cripes. Lucky we weren't doing the...you know...thing to get rid of Kirk."

A grumpy looking man exited the vehicle. He introduced himself as Inspector Sergeant Dougall Grimslade and flashed his badge.

"Oh great." Nova exclaimed.

July elbowed her little sister which was not missed by Grimslade. He pretended not to notice the nudge.

"Pardon?" He asked.

"Just saying. Oh great. The roads must be passable now." Nova said lamely.

Marcha intervened before the other two stuffed it up.

"Good morning Inspector." Marcha said. "What can we do for you?"

"I'm enquiring after a man who was working here. A Kirkwood Bonn."

"He was working here. But I'm afraid he is no longer with us." Marcha said in all honesty.

She sincerely hoped the snort heard coming from July was not a snicker.

"When did he leave here?" Grimslade asked.

"All the workers left because of the cyclone." Marcha hedged.

"But when did Kirkwood Bonn leave? How long ago?"

"Um. He was the last to go. Must be about a week ago now. I think."

"Don't you keep pay records? I mean to pinpoint his departure more accurately?"

"No. The backpackers work only for food and lodging. I don't count every bean."

If the detective considered it a lax way to run a business, he kept a poker face.

"Marcha does the cooking. And they are really well fed. A lot of them say this is the best place they've worked at." July added, in case he thought they were only fed beans.

"So no money changes hands?"

"Sometimes we offer cash incentives to keep them working competitively. Like who gathers the most for the day." Marcha told him.

"But only if they seem slack. We expect a fair return out of them." July added.

Grimslade observed the lookalike fair haired sisters. The three gazed back out of identical wide blue eyes, pictures of pure innocence. Only the youngest one blinked and she had a sticking plaster over one eye.

"Did you have any problems with Kirkwood Bonn?"

"He was a good worker. Fit and strong." Marcha replied without a lie.

"Did you have any problems with him? At all?" Grimslade repeated not to be put off.

"We were glad he was gone before having to invite him to sleep in our house." July said.

"Because the workers' place took on some floodwater." Marcha explained.

"We like to keep our house private." Nova added.

"Uh huh. Hmm. I see. Of course you would." Dougall replied.

The detective had a hunch he was being railroaded by the young women for some reason. He observed the outbuildings. Noting what looked like the workers' cottage situated between the house, and a barn that still sat in a couple of feet of water.

"So. The man left before the flood rose? Do you know where he was going?"

The three simultaneously thought *straight to hell.*

"Couldn't say." Marcha replied.

"Is that the workers accommodation?" Grimslade pointed to the schoolhouse.

"Yes. We were just going down to clean it up. The floor will be covered in mud."

"Could I take a look at where Kirkwood Bonn slept?" Grimslade asked.

"Sure. If you like." Marcha replied.

They hadn't been down there since the floodwater receded. The sisters wondered why he wanted to look but they could hardly deny the request. They all vehemently hoped he wouldn't want to inspect the barn as well. Marcha carried a torch and saw the detective take note of it. She justified it before he asked:

"Could be snakes under the beds and lockers."

"Have to be tough handling all this." Grimslade commented, biting his tongue on adding *for girls.* It was what he thought but knew from his own womenfolk the assumption would not be well received.

"You can take the torch if you like. We've got other outside stuff to do." Marcha offered.

Grimslade entered the workers' facilities alone, through the barbecue dining section. A large blackboard where Marcha chalked up the daily menu, had a note scrawled in big chunky print: JULY U ONLY PITY FUCK HA HA.

"Hmm. I wonder what this means?" Grimslade asked himself.

The girls belatedly realised Kirk's back pack would still be in the school-house, giving lie to the story that he had left the farm.

"Cripes. That buggers it." July said.

"What will we do?" Nova asked.

"Don't panic. Wait and see. Worse case scenario: We admit to it all and throw ourselves on the mercy of the law." Marcha told them.

"*Goonies numquam mori* – never say die." she added a favourite Latin adage.

"Goonies gunna get us." July moaned.

They followed the detective into the BBQ kitchen ready to explain the presence of Kirk's backpack. Dougall stood transfixed, contemplating the rude message on the blackboard.

The girls saw it at once and shared a frisson of dismay.

"It's about me." July admitted, red faced.

"She turned him down." Marcha added in the first outright lie she'd told the detective.

"So you did have problems with him." Grimslade said.

"Yes. Well it is too embarrassing. That's why we didn't say." July genuinely blushed.

"I'm not here to judge you. I just want to determine where Kirkwood Bonn went."

"Can't say." Marcha repeated her earlier short answer.

They showed Grimslade into the schoolhouse. He inspected the sleeping area but found no clues. The schoolroom and its lockers were bare. He found nothing under the mattresses except the wire frames of the single beds.

Marcha surmised Kirk probably hid his backpack in the crawl space of the ceiling. She frowned seeing July glance at the manhole cover. Fortunately the inspector missed that hint.

An obnoxious stale odour of dampness pervaded timber floor of the school building. Grimslade went back out to the kitchen area to look in the cupboards. Relieved he had not noticed the manhole in the ceiling, Marcha herded her sisters away before one of them gave the game away.

"This place stinks. Come on girls, let's get out of here."

"When did he write that?" July whispered, as they hurried outside.

"Had to be after lunch the day we finished putting the pumpkins up."

They had all lunched together in the BBQ kitchen that day. Marcha remembered cleaning off the last menu she'd written on the black-board, before they went back to work.

"So that means Kirk planned to attack Nova and leave during that night doesn't it?"

"But he couldn't have known she'd be left alone with him."

"That was sheer luck on his part. Maybe he planned to do it some other way. Like, he knew we'd have to invite him into the farmhouse."

"Cripes. We were. I even told him to take his stuff up to the house." Nova remembered.

Despite their claims and in view of the blackboard message, Dougall surmised the girl named July may have had a fling with the man misusing

Bonn's ID. Perhaps the worker had overstepped his welcome and been run off the place.

Dougall phrased his questions carefully:

"How do your workers leave here? I understand they are always backpackers. So do you drive them into town?"

"Not usually. Most of them just hike out."

"Did Kirkwood Bonn hike out?"

"I can't say he did. We just woke up one morning and he had apparently gone." Marcha replied, loosely sticking to the truth.

Three sets of wide blue eyes regarded the detective with feigned artlessness. The detective strongly suspected they had their guard up and were stone-walling for some reason.

"Thanks for your help. I may want to speak to you again. Please take my card and let me know if anything else comes to mind. Anything at all. Anytime."

"Will do." Marcha nodded, absolutely certain they would do no such thing.

Dougall Grimslade felt there was more to the story but the sisters had united in not telling. The detective returned to his vehicle and surveyed the surrounding area. He put himself in the shoes of the man he hunted.

If the roads were flood bound and he had been run off the place by three tough irate women, there would be no other option in the prevailing weather conditions than to hike over the surrounding hills.

Checking GPS, Dougall Grimslade ascertained there to be a small village on the other side of the low range, he aimed to head to that township next.

Grimslade tried for a friendly departure as he waved goodbye, but his lop sided smile didn't cut the mustard with the cool blonds.

The three Calenda sisters were relieved to see the policeman leave at last.

"Holy hell. I thought he'd never go!"

"We'd better get rid of Kirk's body before he comes back."

"What if he does come back and catches us at it."

"We'll cross that bridge if or when we come to it." Marcha set her jaw.

Two and a half feet of floodwater still pooled stagnantly around the barn. It proved too much, even for the three wiry sisters together, to force the large double doors open.

They could enter via the overhead loft door under the eaves, and decided this was preferable in any case. A ladder that had not been used in years, hung on the outer wall of the barn, for the express purpose of gaining the high entrance.

Together they wrestled the heavy ladder into place. The ladder legs sunk inches into the softened ground which they hoped might stabilise it. Marcha took charge:

"I'll go first. Then you July. Then you Nova."

Marcha secured her powerful torch by its handle to her belt and began a shaky ascent. She waited for the other two to arrive before taking the dreaded look.

They all pulled their scarves tighter around their faces. Eyes wide, they nodded to each other and crept to the edge of the loft to peer down on the crate with its ghastly contents.

To their triple amazement, Kirk's dead body was not in the crate and nowhere to be seen in the barn. The hinged lid of the crate gaped ajar. They could scarcely believe it.

They wheeled about, with the idea the man might have regained the loft. If not dead or unconscious, he could be hiding amongst the bales and produce, perhaps watching them.

Marcha hefted a machete from where it was wedged in the barn framework. Used for cutting baling twine, it made a formidable weapon. She cautiously checked behind the stacks of straw.

Nova picked up the same clawed tool she had used on Kirk's face. Unafraid with her sisters there as back up, she felt prepared to do more damage if necessary.

July grasped a pitch fork and prodded any mounds of loose straw, finding only a black snake that tangled into the prongs. The red-belly was duly flung out via the loft door. An owl, perched high in the rafters, watched with interest before launching on silent wings to follow its path. As the reptile hit the ground, an opportunist Kookaburra swooped down on it.

Gobsmacked that Kirk had disappeared, the girls took little interest in the fate of the snake.

"What the hell? Where could he be?"

"Crikey. He's gone by the looks."

"Thank the lord for that. Now he really is our dearly departed."

The girls pulled their face scarves down.

"He's bloody well got out and scarpered."

"Looks like the ropes have been cut."

"He must have had a knife! Why didn't we think of that?"

"Where would he have gone?"

"Thank God he didn't come up to the house." Nova shivered.

"No he wouldn't dare. He'd have thought the police were on the way. He must have gone over the hills." Marcha finally realised.

"So that's when he wrote on the blackboard. The bastard!" July added.

The reality sunk in. They'd been dreadfully worried over killing Kirk and been wrong in withholding information from the police investigator.

"I bet Kirk is wanted for other crimes." Nova said.

"Very likely. That detective was keen on finding him. We know he tried to commit rape and he is probably a thief as well."

"He is for sure. I wondered where all the biscuits went. I noticed the cupboard looked empty when the nosy cop poked his sticky beak in there."

"So he cleaned out all the biscuits. And he ruined that good length of rope too. We were going to use that to drag him." July exclaimed in anger.

"July, honey, we don't need to drag him now." Nova said with an eye roll.

"I know. Just saying." July replied, "But it was a damn good roll of rope, was that."

"Logically, one way or another it was going to be wasted on him." Marcha rationalised.

They all flopped down to sit on bales of hay, regardless of possible snakes.

"I have to tell you, I've been dreading this. And then that bloody cop showing up!"

"I know. Then you had to say *he is no longer with us.* I nearly peed myself." July chuckled.

"Well. At least I tried not to lie." Marcha said.

The sisters fell about laughing with relief.

"We could turn the pumpkins while we're up here." Marcha sobered.

"Or we could go back for a nice cup of tea and chocolate cake." July suggested hopefully.

"Vote we turn a few and earn the cake." Nova said.

"Good girl." Marcha replied.

They set about turning melons and pumpkins and opening dry bales of straw to air out.

The owl returned to the rafters and surveyed its shadowy domain with unblinking round eyes. Perhaps it had done for other resident snakes as no more were found that day.

"Hey. Do you think we should phone the cop and say Kirk probably went over the hills?"

"Nah. If he's any good at his job, he will find that out all by himself."

"What if Kirk gets caught and we are called on to testify in court?" July asked.

"We let sleeping dogs lie." Marcha said.

"Yes. That would be easiest." Nova agreed.

They hoped it was the last they saw of the detective despite that they hadn't murdered Kirk.

"Suppose we really have to clean out the workers' house now." Nova sighed.

"We were always going to have to do that. By the way, I hope there aren't any snakes in under the furniture."

"Would have been funny if the police bloke found a couple."

"I'll bring the torch," Marcha said, "but we'll have tea and cake first."

"First thing I want to do, is clean the blackboard." July declared.

"So, just wondering, what does pity fuck mean anyway?" Nova wanted to know.

"Charity." Marcha explained shortly.

"Wow. He really was right up himself, hey."

"Yep. Almost inside out." July agreed.

17

Evacuating

The Bruiser kept his folding knife in a pouch on a leather thong attached to his belt. Secreted in a jeans pocket, he'd made sure the girls had never seen it, since it bore the initials BL.

The pocket knife was part of confiscated items handed back to Bruce Luck on his release from prison. He'd only done a scant two years for abetting a robbery. Bruce drove the getaway car but alleged he hadn't known his mate was going to rob the bottle shop. He claimed to only have sped away because he didn't want to miss the start of a football match.

Bruce acted out a plea of innocence, saying it took him by complete surprise to learn his companion had not paid for the alcohol. A dour magistrate perused the lengthy list of the serial offender's prior violations. The implausible excuses had not been swallowed. Bruce scowled as his punishment was imposed, laced with a parting shot from the judge:

"Thank you Mr. Luck. Your testimony has been very entertaining. I regret the system does not allow for a harsher penalty."

Bruce Luck resented the sentence. Yet he didn't mind prison life too much, given the regular three meals a day. He also took great pride in his nickname, The Bruiser, gained in prison for being one to be feared.

Some good friendships were formed in prison too. A sex offender, Richie, reciprocated with wonderful blow jobs. The Bruiser regretted having to leave Richie but that inmate still had another five years out of seven to serve for rape and aggravated assault.

Richie had kept Bruce entertained with lurid stories of his exploits that fuelled the younger man's lust for violating women. The Bruiser couldn't wait be freed so he could act out his own vivid fantasies.

Despite going down for two years, Luck felt he had beaten the establishment, since his worse crimes had gone unpunished. He had no record for committing sexual assaults and causing grievous bodily harm, since he'd evaded capture every time.

Lately, he added another feather to his cap and congratulated himself on getting away with murder and identity theft. The fact that the Calenda Farm females thought they had him beaten, was laughable and every success bolstered The Bruiser's ego.

As soon as Marcha and July left him alone in the dark barn, The Bruiser began sawing at the nylon ropes with his razor-sharp pocketknife. Within an hour he managed to get free of the crate although it proved a difficult exercise after falling from the hayloft. Urgency drove him to persist through his pain and hunger.

Once free and out of the barn, The Bruiser waded through rain and rising water, towards the darkened bunk house. He found packets of biscuits in the communal cupboard to add to his supplies. His knapsack, stowed in the ceiling cavity, held a bottle of rum and a few chocolate bars along with what he'd stolen from Kirkwood Bonn.

Grunting with the effort, the man stood on a dressing table to access the manhole, and dragged his knapsack out from the ceiling cavity, to be dropped onto the bed. In his habitual practice of leaving no clues, he carefully replaced the manhole cover.

Bruce Luck knew his only option of escape was to trek up through the wet wooded hills, with no time to lose. He was sure the girls would report his crime to the police and hoped dogs would not be deployed, certain they could track him even in the enduring heavy rain.

The desperado strove to keep going all through the long dreary night, only pausing to swig sips of rum. To stave off hunger and boost his energy, he nibbled on chocolate and biscuits while on the run.

Eventually he came to the end of a high ridge, and dimly made out through the rainy gloom, lights of a settlement far below.

An island of buildings surrounded by a brown sea, stood proud of the flood. All about, rooftops of houses and cars pierced the swirling floodwater surface, in varying degrees of submersion.

Rain bucketed down without let up, seeping through every layer of clothing and into The Bruiser's boots. Miserably wet through to the skin, he could no longer remember ever feeling warm and dry.

The fugitive had to rest for a while or pass out from fatigue. After perhaps half an hour, head in his hands and with his eyes closed, his vision cleared enough to make out activity around the largest of the lit buildings. The place looked to be part of a town centre, a town hall or a church.

The Bruiser knew if he didn't make a supreme effort, he'd fall asleep and die where he lay. He forced himself up and began a long downward trudge towards the small township, with no clear path to follow but drawn by signs of civilisation and hopes of comfort.

Startling a mob of kangaroos that sheltered under dripping Banksia and Lantana, the runaway tripped, faltered and slid down a steep embankment.

The Bruiser rode atop a sudden landslip caused by the weight of his fall on the sodden ground. Emerging covered in muck, the misstep at least delivered him a lot closer to his destination. Stumbling on, unrelenting rainfall rinsed the worst of the sludge from his backpack and clothing.

Finally arriving at what was an evacuation centre, the bedraggled man staggered in out of driving rain for the first time in twelve hours. He dropped his sodden knapsack, holding it between his feet and collapsed on a nearby pew. Some concerned Country Womens Association ladies hurried to fuss over him.

Gasping, he told them his name was Richie. If they had asked for ID, which they did not, he'd have said he lost it in the flood.

"You poor dear. You look like part of the mud army. Doris, show this poor fellow where he can get a hot shower and find some dry clothes for him."

A dry t-shirt, jersey and shorts were soon found for The Bruiser amongst donations from an Op Shop bin.

"I am so grateful. Thank you all." The Bruiser smiled wanly.

"Never you mind young man, we'll soon get you sorted with a big bowl of Irish Stew and a nice hot cup of tea."

"Goodness, how did your poor face get so scratched up?"

"I fell out of a tree," it was the first thing he thought of, "I almost drowned trying to save a little cat."

"Oh dear. What happened to the poor cat?"

"She climbed higher. I guess she'll come down when the water recedes. I hope she'll be ok."

The kind woman patted his back and told him he was a brave fellow.

"Have a good hot wash and we can treat those scratches with iodine. Might sting a bit but better than an infection."

The Bruiser allowed himself to be organised by the good women of the CWA who allocated a bunk to him, after he'd eaten the nourishing meal. He was given newspaper to scrunch up into his sodden boots to help dry them out. Firstly, he scanned the newsprint to find any mention of his past crimes and was pleased to find nothing.

That night, The Bruiser slept well wrapped in warm blankets, his belly full and his knapsack stowed safely under the camp stretcher.

Early the next morning, while the Calenda sisters worried over Kirk's drowned body in their barn, the refugee enjoyed a cup of hot sweet tea and listened to news radio broadcasted through the church hall. He heard no mention of the missing Kirkwood Bonn, nor of any search for himself.

Bruce thought his good old 'Luck' luck was holding. He endeared himself to the volunteer helpers by assisting with ladling out oatmeal porridge to other stranded people who lined up for breakfast. It gave him an opportunity to consume plenty of extra carbohydrates to restore his energy. He knew he must move on as soon as roads were opened.

In the meantime, the wanted man sussed out the other thirty or more temporary guests in the evacuation building. Most of them looked worse off than himself. An attractive young mother with a few little kids looked a tempting possibility. Bruce amused himself with what he might do with that one. But the time and place were wrong. He did not even speak to the woman as he couldn't stand being around her brats. Too much trouble.

All the while he bunked in the evacuation centre, The Bruiser craved more swigs from his rum bottle. But, he didn't want to fall from grace with the CWA brigade. More so, he didn't want to share his rum, so the treasured square shaped bottle remained well hidden in his knapsack.

After another day and night in the centre, The Bruiser sorted out his belongings preparing to leave. A fungal odour emanated from some clothes that had mouldered in the damp bag, so the articles were discarded in a bathroom bin. Bruce helped himself to dry replacements from the Op Shop donations, stowing the dry clothing in plastic bags from the hall kitchen, and tightly repacking the knapsack.

The Bruiser still had a good wad of Kirkwood Bonn's cash and the dead man's shower bag with shaving gear. His own BL branded pocket knife and about half a bottle of rum completed his possessions. He felt well set up.

After 'Richie' vacated the mission centre, overworked volunteers remembered they had not obtained his details. It seemed an excusable oversight in the circumstances with the way he'd arrived and since they had so many other mouths to feed and people in need of help.

Displaced people began straggling back to their own homes to begin mopping up and assessing damage. No one gave another thought to the tall man who had been and gone in such a short time. 'Richie' was soon forgotten as the task of cleaning up the facility became the next mammoth project.

A couple of cleaning ladies pulled some mildewed clothing from a bin in the shower room. They could tell clothes were very good quality and worth restoring.

The cleaning women noticed a name printed on iron-on laundry tags. No matter, they said, the tags could be removed or the name bleached out.

"Pity these would be too small for my bloke. We'll fix them up for the op shop though."

"Unusual name, never heard of a Kirkwood before. Have you?"

"Nope. But you get some weird names these days. One of Doris's grand kids is a Phelony."

"That's tragic."

The senior ladies enjoyed a laugh together, it was the best part of volunteering.

18

A Fart with Fred

The Bruiser shouldered the knapsack and considered his options while tramping up the damaged highway.

Fallen trees and other debris had been removed but some sections had half road closures with temporary traffic lights or manned stop-go signs to control traffic flow.

Coming up beside a line of delayed traffic, The Bruiser cadged a lift with a truck driver, again calling himself Richie. He told the driver his own vehicle copped a fallen tree during the cyclone and was a write off. Now he just wanted to get home to his wife and family further South.

As the truck sped along the highway, The Bruiser felt he was absolutely free and clear of the troubles he'd created. He'd chewed over and over his every move and been certain nothing could be linked to himself, Bruce Luck.

The truck driver, Fred, liked country music and they sang along cheerfully as they travelled. Fred said he intended driving throughout the night before stopping over at a motel. The Bruiser, as Richie, said he wouldn't mind a sleep over at a motel, he could do with a little luxury. Privately, he wondered if Fred's ID could procure a twin room that he might be able to share. He would raise the suggestion later when he thought up a tactful way to phrase it, maybe claiming his own wallet with ID had been lost in the flood. Just lucky, he'd say, he kept some cash aside.

Towards evening, Fred stopped at a Truck Stop for diesel and a feed. The Bruiser insisted on paying for the food. He needed to bolster the friendship with hopes of a night in a motel on Fred's ID. The free ride and the singalong had lifted his spirits as well as looking forward to a comfortable nights sleep.

Fred glimpsed the thick wad of cash when his hitchhiker peeled off a note to pay the meal tab. The van driver noted the money roll was stowed back into a zippered side pocket of the man's knapsack.

Back on the highway with two more hours behind them, The Bruiser let go of a gigantic and sonorous fart. *Braaack Pitpit Splutter.* the sound of which reverberated around the truck cabin and fouled the atmosphere.

"Oops. Sorry Fred. Must have been all that coleslaw. I think I need a bog break."

"Better out than in." Fred said, winding his window down to let in a blast of fresh air.

Fred pulled over into a lonely truck stop, in a layby beside the highway. No other vehicle occupied the spot that was dimly lit by a single solar light over the entry to the public toilet block. Fred was glad his passenger requested the stop over, he'd been going to suggest it himself.

Feeling an impending need for urgent relief, The Bruiser hurried into the roadside convenience before they had fully stopped and even while the vehicle motor still idled.

As soon as Fred heard the bog door slam, he extracted the wad of notes from the knapsack and crept his truck back out onto the highway. Fortuitously, a line of traffic roared by and muffled the engine sounds of his sneaky exit. In a fit of generosity, Fred chucked the hitchhiker's knapsack out on the verge, as he left.

"So long sucker. That's the most expensive shit you'll ever do, son." Fred laughed.

The Bruiser had barely wiped his bum before realising his folly. He knew before looking that he could wave goodbye to Fred and his handy stash of Kirkwood Bonn's money.

"Damn and fuck it all. The bloody arse hole frigging cunt. I'll throttle that bastard if I ever come across him again."

The Bruiser ranted and punched a few holes into the plywood bog door. He had no idea how to trace Fred and couldn't report the theft, since it was second hand and backtracked a definite link to his own worst crime.

In the high beam of oncoming vehicles, he saw his knapsack outlined on the roadside and exclaimed: "Thank hell for small mercies."

He ran to pick it up. A jangling of glass told him the rum bottle had broken. He carefully fished out the shards and chucked them against the trunk of a big white gum tree, cursing eloquently as spatters of rain fell, preceding a heavier downpour.

The Bruiser sheltered inside the smelly toilet block where he spent an uncomfortable night nursing his bruised knuckles. He hoped in vain that another truck might pull in and give him a lift. At least the rain stopped during the night though all traffic had zoomed by.

The Bruiser perched on a guard rail, in the cold grey light before sunrise, trying to thumb another lift. He felt famished, having only one soggy chocolate bar remaining which he'd eaten during the interminable night.

The knapsack smelt of rum and he mourned the loss. He loved the rummy odour but rinsed the bag at an outside tap for only one reason: Smelling like rum might not be conducive to acquiring a lift. At least his spare clothes were in plastic, courtesy of the small town missionary centre.

As dawn broke, a small sedan limped into the layby. A fat woman got out and leashed an incredibly large and ugly tan coloured dog, leading him out from the back seat. She began to walk her pet along the grassy edge of the roadside. The enormous mutt sniffed around the white gum tree and lifted his leg on it.

To begin his pitch to acquire a lift, The Bruiser said:

"Do be careful Ma'am, there's broken glass around that tree."

"Oh. Thanks for telling me." She replied, seeing the sharp remnants of a smashed rum bottle, just in time before the dog stood on it.

The chubby woman hauled her big dog away by its thick studded collar and heavy leash. If he had objected, the woman would surely lose control of such a powerful animal. Yet the dog complied readily casting adoring eyes to his mistress.

The woman, who looked remarkably like her hideous dog, except for having her dark hair pulled up into a knobbly bun atop her head, was perhaps in her mid forties. The Bruiser slyly checked her out with a rating of: *Dead tragic. Legs like tree trunks.*

"What a beautiful dog." The Bruiser continued his insincere spiel.

"Oh thank you so much for saying!"

The woman reacted with a broad grin. She loved her heavy piggy eyed unlovely dog and had never before received any compliment for him.

"What's his name?"

"Mortimer."

"A handsome name for a handsome dog." The Bruiser smarmed.

"Yes. And he is a good boy too." She replied, overly flattered for her dog's sake.

The woman returned Mortimer to the back seat of her car where he stretched his bulk out on a quilted tartan rug. His length took up the entire width of the vehicle. The Bruiser noted with revulsion the wet end on the tartan from where the dog had been drooling or possibly leaking from somewhere else.

The Bruiser stayed sitting on the guard rail, deliberately looking the other way. He intuitively knew the woman considered offering him a lift. He desperately needed the ride but did not want to appear keen or begging. The woman saw that the man ignored her now and got the impression he seemed harmless and unobtrusive.

The Bruiser waited for the woman to make an overture and soon received his bingo moment:

"I say," the woman ventured, "do you know anything about cars?"

Bugger all. The Bruiser admitted truthfully to himself, but he'd already noticed one of her front tyres was very low.

"I know a bit." He said, attempting to make it sound like an understatement.

"It's just that, mine has been behaving erratically. I hope it's not a steering problem."

"I can have a look if you like." He offered.

"Oh would you? That is so kind."

"I'll just release the bonnet catch."

Opening the driver side door, The Bruiser pulled the latch with the objective of seeing if she had a handbag in sight. He noted her bag shoved under the passenger side bucket seat. At the same time, he glimpsed some horse gear in the rear floor well.

Mortimer eyed the man and emitted a low menacing growl. *Fuck you Mortimer you god awful ugly mongrel.* The instant mechanic sent the unspoken message to the repulsive dog in one quick withering glance. The Bruiser closed the car door, lifted the hood and tapped a few things, humming and harring all the while.

"I see. It's just the overhead mid circular tap bolt sprocket needed tightening. All good. Should go ok now. By the way, do you have a spare tyre? I see your nearside fore needs changing as well."

At least he did know how to change a tyre and employed the extent of his horsey knowledge to cosy up to the woman's interests. Even to The Bruiser, the woman, Amelia Boole, seemed extraordinarily grateful. He felt no surprise that she fell into his plan for a lift. Little did he know, it was also the wicked woman's own plan as soon as she encountered the handsome young man, down on his luck, ripe for picking.

Destiny had them play into each other's hands. The Bruiser settled into the passenger front seat. As they drove out, he told Amelia Boole his name was Richie.

"I guess your trip has been delayed then. Were you expected somewhere soon?"

"Not really. But I didn't need that delay. You see, yesterday, I hitched a ride with a fellow who had made an improper pass at me. I was terribly shocked at being propositioned with such blatant sexual intentions."

"My God! What is the world coming to?" Amelia exclaimed.

He choked out more of his story in a halting distressed tone of voice:

"I could do nothing but lock himself in the toilet until the guy gave up and drove off."

He told the woman that with nowhere else to go, he had been forced to spend the entire night in the horrible place, just to keep out of the rain. That part held some truth. He saw the story hit home, Amelia Boole appeared dismayed and sympathetic. The main fiction, straight off the top of his head, had Bruce chortle at how stupid women were so easily fooled. His mirth was hidden by pathetic little coughs.

"Oh no. You poor thing! Do you want to report it to the police? Did you get his number?"

"No I didn't think of getting his number plate, unfortunately. But yes. I think I jolly well should report it in any case, after I get to civilisation and have something to eat."

He adopted a righteous face.

"Oh. Are you hungry? Sorry that's a silly question. You must be. I think I noticed a shopping mall up further along the way on my way up. So, I'll stop for a morning tea break." Amelia promised.

They came to the outskirts of a large town where an off ramp to a huge shopping centre loomed up ahead.

"Ah. I thought so. This looks promising." Amelia said.

"There must be a bakery. I could really go a hot meat pie." He replied.

"Now that would be nice. I'd like one as well. Let me get it. I really owe you for all your help." She smiled.

"But it was nothing really. And I appreciate the ride."

"Thanks but I need a little trip to the ladies room anyway." She admitted.

The car park was crowded but Amelia found a space eventually, down towards the back, facing the highway. She thought she could give Mortimer another little walk on a nearby nature strip after she returned with the food.

The Bruiser's mind whirled with ideas. Perhaps he could steal her car? No, they'd be onto him in a flash. Okay. Maybe just steal her handbag somehow and scarper. Could work. He'd have to play it by ear. He noted a culvert ran underneath the highway. It looked to be a good escape route and the railway line ran parallel with the road along the other side. There must be a train station not far away. He might be lucky enough to catch a train.

The Bruiser scrabbled around the bottom of his knapsack where he knew several gold dollar coins rattled. It was the last of his worldly wealth. He offered his loose change hoping she would leave her handbag. He had to risk it.

"Look I have all this shrapnel to get rid of. You take these coins Amelia. I'll be glad to lighten my load. The pies can be my shout. I insist. I'll stay and mind Mortimer."

"Alright thanks. Do you want peas with yours?"

"Yes please. I hope they have those mushy mint peas."

"I love those as well. I'll be back soon. Be a good boy Morty."

"Do you want me to walk Mortimer while you're gone?"

"No that's ok. Morty is sort of a one-woman dog. He can wait until I get back."

Bruce had no intentions of handling the horrible animal but thought the offer sounded good. Not wishing to share the car with Mortimer, The Bruiser stretched his own legs by walking around the car and leaning on the bonnet. The dog slobbered on the car window and cast malevolent designs on the man.

The Bruiser briefly rejoiced as Amelia walked off ..until she paused with a sudden thought and came back for her handbag.

"I might as well grab a few groceries while I'm here. I'll be as quick as possible."

"No worries." The Bruiser replied mildly. *Damn it.*

She'd left the car keys in the ignition. Once again, he considered taking the car and dumping the dog. He eyed the dog, and the beast snarled. He did not relish getting back into the car with Mortimer, without Amelia being present to control the monster.

The Bruiser's position now meant he had no money at all and felt starved. He really wanted that hot meat pie with peas. He'd just have to go along with conning Amelia for a while longer and might get another chance to rob her later.

19

Cold Trail

After departing Calenda Market Gardens, Dougall Grimslade drove around the ranges and sussed out the erstwhile evacuation centre.

He looked through the open door. The interior smelt of pine disinfectant. It had been scrubbed clean and the folding bunks, trestles and other furniture stacked in a corner.

Dougall walked around the building and came across an elderly gardener pruning roses in the church cemetery.

"Good morning sir. I am looking for someone who might have stayed in the evacuation centre during the flood. Can you tell me who might know anything about it?"

The old man liked being addressed as 'sir' and was happy to help, directing the detective to the CWA lunch room, where most of the ladies would be busy making sandwiches and cups of tea for customers.

When Dougall entered the dining room, several heads turned towards him as he was very obviously not a local. He had removed his tie but in his business shirt and suit pants he stood out like monkey's balls.

"Copper." someone whispered. A few heads nodded in sage agreement.

Although the majority had nothing to hide, everyone felt guilty for something with the unexpected visit by plain clothed constabulary. Dougall went to the counter, ordered a cup of tea and a ham sandwich in his deep well spoken voice. Two senior ladies who served him, one making a fresh sandwich and the other fetching the tea, were instantly smitten. He wasn't a bad looking chap when he remembered not to scowl.

"You're new around here?" one asked although she knew the answer.

"I am. Just on a job actually."

"Are you with the police?"

"How did you know? I say, you country ladies are very smart."

His comment, accompanied by the smile his mother always counted as precious, was well accepted by the senior ladies.

"How can we help?"

"I'm chasing a missing person who might have stayed in the evacuation place recently."

"Oh. We were there. Who are you after?"

"Chap going by the name of Kirk. Or Kirkwood. Surname Bonn."

The ladies looked at each other. They could not recall anyone by that name. One of them with a voice like a town crier, yelled over the chatter in the room: "Anyone remember a man named Kirk or Kirkwood being in the evacuation centre?"

A loud exclamation came from the back of the kitchen area. Two women who had cleaned the bathrooms in the temporary retreat, were excited to assist the handsome detective.

"You know what? We found some good clothes binned that had that name on the laundry tags. We remember Kirkwood something. It's such an unusual name. Sounds a bit posh."

"Really? That is amazing. You actually remember that."

Grimslade enthused sincerely. It gave him a thrill knowing he had picked up the trail of the murderer. The cleaning ladies beamed. Dougall felt he was a winner at this charming the older ladies stuff. Pity his talents hadn't worked on the Calenda girls.

"Yes. And those duds were really good quality. Just had a bit of mildew. We got it sorted and put it all in with the church charity clothing. A shame none of it would fit my old man."

"Well done. But, you remember no man going by that name? No one that seemed new to the area?"

"There was one we didn't know. Named Richie. He was really helpful too. Helped us serve out breakfast."

Richie! Another eureka moment. Grimslade tried to keep a bland face.

"Does anyone know where this fellow Richie went after here?"

"He was hitching. Poor thing. He said his car was a write off. Tree fell on it. And his face was all scratched up too. We dabbed iodine on it for him. Must have stung like hell."

"Yes. That's right Doris. I remember now. He fell out of a tree trying to save a poor cat."

"Not many blokes would risk their necks trying to save a cat up a tree in a flood. Richie was one of the good guys for sure," Doris said smiling, "he was a real good looker too."

"Keep yer knickers on Doris" her friend advised.

"Shut up. I still have eyes in me head."

"If you caught it you wouldn't know what to do with it. Ha ha."

"Says you."

Dougall left the senior citizens bickering amongst themselves. He surmised 'Richie' would have looked for another lift. It helped that only one main road ran through the area.

The deal with the blue eyed girls began to make sense in light of the outlaw's scratched up face. Dougall Grimslade considered going back for another talk with those feisty young women. But the stubborn sisters, obviously in cahoots, were never likely to break ranks without thumb screws. Maybe not even then. He doubted the Calenda girls would know or care where the man had gone anyway. With no time to lose in the pursuit, he decided to push ahead.

Down the highway, Dougall was held up with roadworks. Being first in the queue, he got out of his car and spoke with the stop-go lollipop man. That proved to be a long shot that partially paid off.

The traffic controller did recall a hiker taking a lift with a van driver. It was the only hiker he'd come across during that time, on that pot holed stretch of road. The road worker was vaguely familiar with the delivery bloke who frequented that route while making his weekly round of deliveries.

"So you know the driver who gave the hiker a lift?"

"No. I just know him to look at. Old bloke. Big sort of delivery van. Probably refrigerated. Has a symbol on the side like a map of Australia with something else. I forget exactly."

"If you see him again, it would be really helpful to let me know. Or ask him to call me."

Dougall gave the man his card.

"You're with the police?"

"I am. And I want you to know, that van driver is not under any suspicion but his hitchhiker might be."

"Always glad to help the men in blue." The lollipop holder said, whether it was true or not.

He turned the sign to GO and Dougall went.

Back at his office, Dougall phoned the NT detective Dulcy Vestige to bring her up to speed.

"Dougall. Hello. Find anything?"

"Yes a thin trail. The impostor worked as Kirk on a farm that exchanges food and lodging for casual backpackers in return for market garden work. Our elusive friend probably tried it on with a girl there and bit off more than he could chew. Got his face scratched up. Then he lands at an evacuation centre calling himself Richie again and endearing himself to the doting old CWA ladies."

"Goodness Dougall. You've done well!"

Dougall Grimslade always amazed Dulcy. Sometimes he seemed to possess a sixth sense.

"But that's where it ran cold. A slim chance a traffic controller might put me onto a truckie who gave a man a lift. Could be him. Or not. Don't hold your breath on that one."

"We can be certain our murderer likes calling himself Richie, Ricky or Kirk."

"Yes, and using Bonn's ID is his first major mistake. We have to keep the case under wraps, so he isn't warned against using it again."

"We must. It's really our only chance of nabbing him. Do you think we can probably assume he resembles Kirkwood Bonn's ID photo?" Dulcy asked.

"Maybe. Or, you know, perhaps it wasn't scrutinised all that well by the recruitment mob."

"True. There can be a sameness with even featured faces. Crooked, scarred or disfigured ones are far more memorable."

"Sure. No one forgets my ugly dial as far as I know." Dougall laughed.

"Now you're fishing for compliments."

"That is my only nod to sport Dulcy. Don't knock it."

20

Mad Dog

The Bruiser really enjoyed that hot pie with mushy peas and supped on a can of cola as Amelia walked Mortimer again before continuing the journey.

The woman did not ask her passenger where or when he wanted to be let off but continued driving southbound. Although the man wanted to head in that direction, he also began to feel discomforted enclosed in the car with the heavy woman and her despicable dog. The situation began to creep The Bruiser out.

They travelled on until late afternoon when Amelia turned off the highway into a rural residential area where homes were spread well apart on wide acreage plots.

"Where are we?" The Bruiser asked.

"Almost home." Amelia said cheerfully.

"I've taken enough of your time. I should really get on now." he said.

Amelia took his consent to visit her home for granted and he felt out of control.

"Oh dear. You don't think I'd dump you the roadside at this time of day? You could find yourself lost in the dark. There are no streetlights out here you know."

"That's ok. I always get by." The Bruiser replied.

"No way. I'm not that mean Richie. I have a spare room and glad to have your company. So don't you go feeling beholding now."

"Gee thanks." he said not meaning it at all.

Amelia had begun to irritate him. He liked autonomy and she took liberties with his independence. He felt at her mercy, trapped in her car. Short of jumping out at a red light, he had to wear it, telling himself he was becoming paranoid.

Yet, the man gripped the handle of his knapsack and prayed for a red light. But there were no traffic lights in the rural area Amelia drove through.

Before long, they arrived at a two storey home set back from a lonely road and partially hidden amongst shrubs and trees. The property, surrounded by a high fence, had ornate double iron gates at the entrance of its long driveway.

At Amelia's bidding, The Bruiser, acting as Richie, got out and opened the heavy front gates. It seemed too late to get out of the home visit at this point. He could have turned back down the road on foot but his knapsack was still in the car with Amelia and Mortimer.

The woman drove in and parked under a carport attached to the house while her reluctant guest shut the front gates.

Amelia opened a side door leading into a kitchen and waited for Richie to enter her home before setting Mortimer free in the spacious house yard.

The dog uttered a few deep rumbling barks and ran around to the back of the house.

The woman closed the kitchen door and smiled so broadly, her piggy eyes almost disappeared in the folds of her orange tinged fake tanned complexion. The Bruiser thought she so resembled her dog, they could be kin.

He decided he'd be out of there early the next day but for now, a free feed and a bed would see him through another night.

For want of something to say, the uneasy visitor commented: "Nice place."

In truth, although The Bruiser had dossed in some miserable digs, he felt repulsed by a stale and musty smell in Amelia's house.

"Thank you. I've done a lot of redecorating since I bought it."

"Been here long?" Not that he cared but had to attempt further conversation.

"Several years now." Amelia smiled.

The Bruiser began to sweat in the close stuffy atmosphere. He longed to open a window. But even he knew that would probably be rude. He looked to the closest window and saw it had security bars.

"What's it like living here? Are there many break-ins in this area?" he asked.

"There have been some. But I have Mortimer patrolling the yard of course and I turn on the electric fences at night. So no one could easily get in."

Or out Bruce realised with a growing foreboding.

"Now. You must want to freshen up. Let me show you to your room. Do you need ointment for those facial scratches? They look nasty. How did you get them?"

The Bruiser gave her the cat in the tree story, being easier than thinking up something else. Liars had to have good memories. Constantly checking his own every word, he knew it could not be disproved.

"Oh I knew straight up you were an animal lover. Just by the way you admired my Morty."

Amelia gushed.

The Bruiser adopted a saintly expression while a newsreel tape in his brain scrolled: *Fuck me dead. Now I know she ain't piss-chick. That's for sure.*

The woman bustled ahead going up a staircase to the second storey. The Bruiser followed his hostess into an enormous bedroom decorated in shades of pink, red and black. A large four poster bed topped with a black satin quilt dominated the room. Heart shaped cushions echoed the wallpaper pattern which depicted crimson hearts.

A pink and black tiled ensuite, visible through an adjoining door, reminded the man of the type of lollies known as licorice all sorts. But not in a good way. He supposed the decor wouldn't matter in the dark and only for one night. The accommodation was nonetheless luxurious compared to his last night in the roadside dunny.

The Bruiser at first worried he'd been shown to Amelia's own bedroom.

"My room is just down the hall."

Phew. He almost uttered that gaffe aloud.

"Yell out if you need anything. And come downstairs when you're ready. I have to feed Mortimer then I'll put something nice on for our tea."

"Don't go to a lot of trouble. I'm easy." He replied, hoping for a thick t-bone with spuds and something like sticky date pudding with ice-cream for afters.

The Bruiser explored the guest bedroom. A balcony could be accessed by double doors. Gratefully he threw the doors wide open to let in some fresh air.

Mortimer sat just below the balcony, his black lips lifted over lethal looking pointy white fangs in a silent snarl as he met the man's gaze. The place seemed more secure than the House of Correction where Bruce Luck spent a recent two years as an inmate.

Mortimer turned and pricked his small ears, hearing Amelia whistle him to be fed. The Bruiser observed Amelia open a roll up door to a large garden shed, where she appeared to take the dog's food from a refrigerator within.

Mortimer wolfed his meal down in a few seconds and looked to his mistress for more. *Choke on it you hell dog* was The Bruiser's wishful thought. He and that animal disliked each other with equal intensity.

After the dog trotted out with an extremely large bone in his slobbering jaws, Amelia reappeared carrying a couple of biscuits of hay. The Bruiser heard the rattle of chains and click of a padlock as she re-locked the shed.

Mortimer settled under a tree further away to gnaw contentedly. The sounds of gnashing teeth and cracking bone, eerily audible in the still of evening, grated on The Bruiser's nerves.

Amelia threw the hay over a paddock fence and a couple of small ponies trotted over. It was a no brainer that she didn't ride them. He imagined their short legs splaying under her weight.

The Bruiser bathed under a hot shower and hastily dried himself on one of the thick and fluffy pink towels hanging on the bathroom rails. There were no privacy locks on the doors and he dreaded having the woman burst in unannounced. The overbearing Amelia made him fear she might be capable of such an intrusion.

He pushed his backpack well under the bed where the obese Amelia should have trouble getting to it. He didn't want her going through his things and seeing Kirkwood Bonn's credentials. His BL pocket knife had been kept hidden in his jeans pocket as usual. After his shower, he dressed in clean shorts and t-shirt, and as a precaution, slipped the knife under the mattress, next to the side where he planned to sleep. At the same time, it seemed ridiculous to hide a weapon there, yet having it handy felt reassuring.

The smell of grilled lamb chops wafted up making The Bruiser's mouth water and his belly growl with hunger pangs. He couldn't avoid Amelia for much longer anyway, so returned downstairs to the kitchen.

"Can I help with anything? He asked, aware she would expect him to ask that question.

"No. You're my guest Richie. You just sit and relax. Flick the box on if you like. News should be starting soon." Amelia replied pleasantly.

He was glad of the opportunity and went into the living room area in the open plan space.

No mention of the missing Kirkwood Bonn came on the news. The Bruiser was surprised but thankful the burnt out Landcruiser had apparently not been discovered. Maybe a flood came down and covered it over. Cyclones did effect some of the Northern Territory but he had no idea if that particular dry ravine might have filled up.

In any case, the murder scene would be growing colder by the day. He still thought of it as the perfect crime and regretted he couldn't brag about it to anyone. His mate Richie in prison would be the only one he could ever tell. Maybe they might catch up again sometime in the future and share a laugh. That was something to look forward to.

"Penny for your thoughts." Amelia chimed, annoyingly interrupting his musings.

"Just chilling. You know." He replied.

"This is ready now. I bet you'd like a beer with dinner."

"I sure would. Wow this looks great."

Amelia served grilled lamb chops with browned pumpkin slices, mashed potatoes and peas.

She offered apple pie and ice-cream for dessert, followed by coffee. Her guest tucked in and decided she wasn't all that bad. Nevertheless, he still wanted to leave early the next morning.

That night the man slept well, his belly full, the bed comfortable. The sound of the chain rattling woke him before sunrise. Amelia was again doing something in the shed and Mortimer hung close by on her heels.

The Bruiser hurried downstairs with the idea of going out to tell her he'd soon be on his way. But he could not get out. He tried the front, back and side doors. All locked. Again he noticed all the windows had security bars. Whether on purpose or otherwise, he was imprisoned. He went back upstairs, not wanting Amelia to twig to his discomfort. At the sound of the back door shutting, he wandered down, faking a yawn as if he'd just risen.

"Good morning. Sleep well? I'll put the kettle on." Amelia said cheerfully.

"I'll just have a quick cuppa and be on my way." he replied.

"Oh. You're not leaving so soon? I planned a special treat for later."

"That's kind of you. But I really must be off."

"As you wish. I can't tie a good man down."

Amelia laughed. Stopped. And laughed again as if she had a private joke.

The Bruiser drank a glass of fruit juice and accepted a large mug of tea and piece of toast. The hot brew burnt his tongue in his haste to get it down and be gone.

All the while Amelia waffled on. *Blah blah blah for Christ's sake shut up* he thought trying to nod and smile at the right times in her dead boring litany about who knew what.

He returned upstairs to retrieve his backpack. Feeling woozy of a sudden, he lay down for a minute. By the time The Bruiser woke up again, the sun had set on another day. He couldn't believe he'd slept the whole day away. He stumbled to the bathroom and stood under a cold shower to revive his muddled brain.

Amelia had another tasty meal set out ready when he came downstairs.

"Oh you're awake at last. I guess your ordeal caught up with you. Nothing restores the body like sleep. Hey? I know you planned to leave but I didn't want to disturb you."

"That's okay." He said. Although it didn't feel okay.

However, the meal smelt good and he felt famished having not eaten since breakfast. Again Amelia's house guest sat at her table and cleaned his plate.

"Why don't you go into the lounge room and see what's on the news? I'll pack the dishwasher and join you in a tick." She said.

He did as suggested but chose a single lounge chair. No way would he sit next to Amelia on the long couch. The news still did not mention anything about Kirkwood Bonn. As it wound up with the weather report, Amelia came in carrying two tumblers.

The Bruiser smelt the delicious scent of rum and the sound of ice clinking in the glasses made sweet music to his ears.

Amelia set the glasses down on the long, heavy coffee table, pushing his towards the end where he sat and placing her own in front of the couch.

"I thought we'd have a little night cap. Though as you've slept all day, you might not be ready for bed again so soon. Hmmm?"

"Maybe not. I do love a rum and Coke though. Thanks."

The woman thought so. She detected a faint smell of rum when she went through his backpack. After ascertaining his real name was Kirkwood Bonn, she carefully stowed the bag back under the bed just as she'd found it.

Knowing 'Richie' would be out like a light with the cocktail of drugs drunk in his morning fruit juice, Amelia went shopping. She stocked up on more groceries, Coca-Cola and a couple of bottles of rum.

The rum went down well. The Bruiser had been craving his favourite spirit and sat back relaxed as it permeated his bloodstream. Amelia suggested they have another. He didn't say no. She made a good strong drink without stinting on the rum.

Night darkened the room. Amelia handled the TV remote and flicked it onto a porn movie she had set up ready to view, beginning with an erotic scene of a naked couple copulating.

The Bruiser could see where this was headed but the strong rum drinks blunted his inhibitions with Amelia.

"I love it doggy style best." She crooned.

That didn't surprise him in the least.

Amelia placed a cushion on the coffee table and knelt on the thick carpet. Leaning across the cushion, she flipped her skirt up. The Bruiser knew she was offering her bare essentials although the sight was mercifully in shadow. His thoughts of a bird in the hand being worth two in the bush, was later to have another connotation.

For now, he took the woman's invitation and screwed her lustily in the position she liked best. He collapsed back into his armchair feeling that he'd more than paid his way.

"Oh I knew you'd be good." she said.

He shrunk away from her advance. There was no way he could come at kissing or cuddling.

His words sounded formal even to his own ears:

"Thanks Amelia. You've shown me great hospitality. But I really must leave, come morning."

He thanked the devil she backed off from an impending embrace, although her toothy smile and glittering eyes were weird. For the first time in his life, The Bruiser knew some self disgust. His knees hurt after the effort as well, despite the thick carpet.

What a spook. Can't wait to tell Richie about this one. Privately, the man made light of the sexual encounter with Amelia to get over his lapse of self worth. Propping up his ego came easily, confident his jailbird mate would laugh and call him a bit of a rogue.

The Bruiser slept well, he'd had a good feed, plenty of rum and some sexual relief, however repugnant.

Morning sunlight lit the room, he knew Amelia had been up early, having heard the shed chain rattling. Vaguely he wondered why she bothered locking the shed, surely with Mortimer on guard the place would be safe from burglars.

Amelia had scrambled eggs and bacon ready for his breakfast. He drank the fruit juice she offered and hoed into the hearty breakfast. She'd been good for a free feed.

"I can't thank you enough." He told her, though in his opinion he had thanked her plenty.

"Just don't go outside until I chain Mortimer up." She said, with a quirk of her mouth and an eye roll that suggested good reason for this warning.

"No. I won't. Would he attack me do you think?"

"Oh yes. He would I'm afraid." she nodded, pursed her lips and widened her piggy eyes.

The Bruiser went back upstairs thinking perhaps he had only been kept locked in as protection from Mortimer. He shouldn't have doubted the fat cow who was obviously just lonely.

Elated at being able to leave at last, he straightened the bed and sat down to pull his backpack out from under. That was the last thing he remembered before waking again to another sunset.

Despite his benumbed brain, Bruce finally twigged that he was being drugged to keep him from leaving. It angered him, but he would bide his time to get back at the mad bitch. He figured it would be no use trying to reason with a crazy woman. Best he keep up the charade.

Amelia had another nice meal ready. In a repeat of the previous night, she brought out rum and Cokes again which he couldn't resist. She set them on the coffee table in front of where they sat separately, as before.

Before taking a sip, The Bruiser asked:

"Have you got any other movies? Anything spicier than last nights?"

"Sure. Let me see." Amelia seemed elated by his response and eager for his attention.

While she rose to look through her stack of DVDs, he quickly swapped glasses. Amelia knew he would swap the glasses, but the drug wasn't in either of them.

He gulped half his drink in one, knowing he needed some motivator to perform for her again. This time he tried his best to hurt her but the harder he pounded into her and pinched her pudgy flesh with his fingers, the more she liked it.

His athletic efforts pushed the heavy coffee table halfway across the room. It didn't do his knees much good but Amelia knew herself to be falling in love.

Finally, The Bruiser went up to bed, thankful that the woman did not suggest sleeping in it with him. He'd have to kill her if she wanted to do that. Come to think of it, that wasn't such a bad idea.

Maybe he could kill her. Or knock her out at least. But then, he still had to get past the locked doors and Mortimer. He went to the balcony and sussed how difficult it might be to climb down, assuming he could somehow incapacitate the horror dog. The dog was definitely the main problem.

As soon as Amelia went outside the next morning, The Bruiser crept downstairs and selected a carving knife from the back of a kitchen drawer. He thought being so far back, she probably didn't use that knife much so wouldn't immediately miss it. His own BL pocket knife was considered too good to sully on the detested woman and he really wanted something a lot longer.

The Bruiser went back to his ensuite bathroom, removed the cover from the toilet cistern and hid the knife in the water tank. Tilting the lid to seat it back into place, he glimpsed some writing on the under side. Scrawled in black marker pen the message read: *Run for your life. Don't drink the juice.* He almost dropped the ceramic lid in shock.

Going out to the balcony, he observed Amelia working in the shed again. He immediately bobbed down so she wouldn't see him. Peering between the slats, he saw Mortimer run out with another huge bone in his jaws. That big ugly dog could really get through them.

This time the dog chose to gnaw his treasure closer to the balcony. The Bruiser watched in disgust. It looked like...*Oh shit NO! It can't be!* The bone looked like a man's forearm, from the elbow to the wrist. It was inked with a whole sleeve of tattoos. It had to be what it looked like. Now he knew why Amelia kept the shed locked.

Amelia came out of the garden shed with more hay for her ponies. Seeing where Mortimer had gone, she urgently called him back and pointed to the tree where he usually went to chew his bones.

The dog obeyed and went further away. But the man had seen what the dog had. At once both sickened and terrified, The Bruiser realised just how barking mad was Amelia.

He didn't drink the juice that morning, saying truthfully, he was feeling a bit off. He couldn't stand to be near the woman so said he would go back to bed for a while.

"Oh you poor boy. I will check on you later." she crooned.

Her captive didn't mention leaving again, knowing, belatedly, she would never willingly let him go. His best chance of survival was to play along.

As soon as Amelia went out again to feed her animals, he went to the fridge and helped himself to several swallows of Coke straight from the bottle, hoping to boost his sugar levels and settle his churning stomach.

Amelia foresaw he might do that and had drugged the Coke as an added measure of control. It would have gone into his rum and Coke later in any case. Once more The Bruiser fell into a coma like sleep. He wasn't sure how long he'd been out to it when he next opened his eyes.

"Wakey wakey."

Amelia stood over him, the embodiment of his worst nightmare, her rolls of flesh suggestively garbed in a flimsy semi transparent black negligee. She had undone her usual topknot bun, and a straggle of long hair hung down past her shoulders.

Dazed by the sight, the captive man felt he must be hallucinating.

Amelia handed him a glass of rum and Coke. Befuddled and parched, in dire need of a drink, he gulped the strong brew and breathed heavily trying to keep it from coming up again. In a while, the strong alcohol served to calm his nerves.

The corpulent woman smiled and wiped beads of sweat from his brow, with the hem of her sexy ensemble.

"You're doing well." she said fondly.

Amelia dropped her gown to reveal the vast continent of her ample body. The Bruiser stared in repugnance at the mountainous terrain of breasts and dumpy stomach above a matted thicket of pubic hair, the bushy abundance of which he had never imagined possible. Before this chunderous unveiling, he had been spared seeing all her naked parts clearly, in the light.

The Bruiser knew himself to be entrapped. The past drug filled days had left him weakened and vulnerable. In terror of what she was feeding to the dog sapped his strength with waves of nausea.

If he didn't please her sexually, he was sure to end up the same way as the tattooed bloke. He wondered if that man had written the warning inside the cistern....or it could have been another. He had no way of knowing how many unfortunates had gone before him.

Bruce realised the only way out of this mess was to humour the mad cow. His revolt as she straddled his body on the bed made him doubt he'd rise to the occasion. To his own great amazement, he did so very well.

Amelia had met the erectile dysfunction problem many times before. Viagra added to the cocktail of drugs made victims sustain rock hard ability. Through trial and error, she perfected her personal seduction recipe. After a couple of oops episodes, she found the magic concoction that no longer caused premature deaths, but enhanced her playtime.

Amelia rode The Bruiser relentlessly for what seemed an eternity to her involuntary subject. He twisted her bulbous purplish nipples in an attempt to cause her enough pain to slow down but that only egged her on, bringing her to shrieking multiple climaxes.

Amelia's mania for rough sex proved insatiable. The Bruiser identified with her lascivious excesses but did not like being on the receiving end of such unbridled lust.

A thin stream of vomit drooled from Bruce Luck's mouth as his head pounded against the backboard of the bed. His penis had never felt so raw and sore.

The man's discomfort and biliousness went unheeded by the rabid woman, who was in seventh heaven, lost in passionate pleasure.

What did I ever do to deserve this? The Bruiser thought tearfully, gritting his teeth. Although he knew he'd done plenty.

To keep his mental libido up and suffering down to a minimum, he resorted to recalling lurid tales told to him in prison, by his cell mate. That seemed so long ago now. He hoped he would get a chance to relate this nightmare to good old Richie sometime in the future. But The Bruiser's future was not guaranteed and well he knew it.

"I need to pee." He pleaded at last, almost choking on his own bile.

"Don't pee long. Ha ha. My darling."

Head over heels in love, Amelia coquettishly batted her eyelashes. She'd never before had such a cute and uncomplaining young man as playmate and forgave the naughty boy for giving her a false name.

The Bruiser extracted himself from the bed of torture, went to the bathroom and shut the door. Quickly and quietly, he extracted the carving knife from inside the water cistern. He waited behind the door, ready, fully expecting Amelia to breach his privacy. And she did.

"Are you okay?"

Amelia cracked the bathroom door open after waiting ten minutes and not hearing any flush.

She glimpsed her toy boy's reflection in the glass shower screen, dismayed to see he hid behind the door and had a knife poised ready to strike.

Caught totally unaware, Amelia tried to pull the door shut but The Bruiser wedged himself into the gap and pushed her down to the floor. The heavy woman fell backwards onto her well padded backside.

Frantic that her worm had turned, Amelia scrambled over onto her knees in a vain attempt to get up. Her broad dimpled buttocks parted as she did so. Disgusted by the display presented, her prisoner hefted the knife.

Enraged for what she'd done to him, The Bruiser delved the knife repeatedly into Amelia's thickly forested nether regions as he snarled ten disjointed words in time with the multiple thrusts: "How's - this – for – doggy – style – you – sick – demented – fucking - bitch."

The irony of that accusation was lost on him in his blood lust and killing frenzy.

Amelia's screams combined with Mortimer's frantic barking, filled the room in tune with the murderer's words. In her dying throes, Amelia grasped at the carpet, breaking her fingernails, while her dog's voice changed to a strangled yodel.

Somehow the animal knew the moment his mistress drew her final breath. The massive dog bayed his grief and leapt up towards the balcony. Being too heavy to gain purchase, he had no hope of reaching the bedroom where Amelia lay.

When at last, Amelia expired, her killer withdrew the blade. He would have left the knife in the twitching corpse but reasoned, practically, the weapon might come in useful later.

Panting, sweating and covered with red spatters, The Bruiser got under the shower and turned the hot water on full blast. He washed himself down, paying tender attention to his painfully engorged penis which had grown fully erect during the crazed slaying.

He became aware, as his mood cooled, that his cock stung like one big blister. He peed into the drain as the shower jet blasted over his head. Urination scalded like acid.

The Bruiser cursed, having experienced similar results from unprotected intercourse in the past. Weakness and rage almost overcame him before he managed to exit the shower.

He collapsed heavily onto the toilet seat and bawled:

"That dirty slag. The filthy bitch has given me the clap."

Obtaining a prescription for antibiotics would be highly problematic, unless he could get back to his father's house and use his true identity.

Amelia's loathsome body filled the space outside the bathroom door. The Bruiser thought about burning the house down. But that would bring the authorities and he still had no way around the dreaded guard dog that kept up a constant keening. Mortimer's prolonged mournful howling impeded the man's ability to think straight and come up with a viable plan.

In shock at his own wild butchering of the defenceless woman, Amelia's killer stepped over the mound of her bloodied naked body. He resorted to reclining on the end of the bed with a pillow over his throbbing head to block out the dogs noise.

As The Bruiser pondered on ways to cover up his second murder, and escape the house of horrors, the funeral for his first victim was being organised by Damien Cresswick.

21

The Ghost

The police insisted that no criminal connection to Kirkwood Bonn's demise be made public, due to the ongoing nature of the investigation.

People were given the impression Kirkwood had died in an off road vehicle accident. It was not an easy exercise for Damien Cresswick to organise the funeral for his partner, while keeping homicidal details of his death strictly confidential.

The pair had made many friends and acquaintances through their wellness centre and health clinic, established and managed together.

Close friends had to be fobbed off as they hinted to learn clearer details of Kirkwood's accident. Many felt there had to be more to the tragedy but were obliged to respect Damien's privacy and bereavement. Nevertheless, speculation circulated amongst those trying to come to terms with the loss.

Damien wanted the funeral notice to appear in the newspaper so there would be a good turnout in honour of his lover. Dulcy Vestige had no problem with the funeral being made public in the local press, knowing the suspect had left The Territory and would be unlikely to ever see it.

Since deaths occurred every day, standard notices did not attract national interest.

Alba Jenkins found out about the funeral when she greeted Bob Bartleigh on another of his regular visits. He'd brought her a good pack of beef, a bottle of rum and a couple of recent newspapers.

"Thank goodness you brought more rum. I was all out." Alba smiled.

"You went through the last lot in a hurry then." Bob laughed.

"No Bob. I did not. I was being a good Samaritan for a needy traveller and he robbed me."

"Jesus girl. Now I wondered about that good looking young guy you dropped off at the bus depot, without a word to anyone. That was him, right?"

"What? How did you know that?"

"Someone noticed. You know what the place is like for gossip."

"Yes I do. You can't sneeze without everyone wanting to know if you were up or downwind."

"So Alba, did you report the theft?"

"No. Same reason. No one's business but mine and I don't want them making things up. That goes for you too Bob."

Alba rarely spoke harshly to the old cattleman. He observed her blushing face and sussed a fair idea why she wouldn't have reported it.

Bob had to swallow his jealousy. After all, he couldn't talk. *Pot. Kettle.* So the ageing philanderer had to remind himself not to spoil the convenient arrangement he had going with the voluptuous Jenkins woman. To be fair, it was not as if she owed him either.

Keeping some cattle on the Jenkins place gave Bob Bartleigh the perfectly innocent excuse to spend time there without his skinny wife ever suspecting his main agenda.

He revelled in having such a young lover at his disposal and thought of the arrangement with the backward Alba, thirty years his junior, as a godsend.

Bob Bartleigh had no qualms about the age difference and reasoned he looked after Alba Jenkins well, with the agistment money, the meat and the rum.

"So what's new?" Alba asked to get past the tricky question.

"You know that queer couple at the wellness centre? One of them died."

"What of? Aids or something?"

Bob liked educating Alba and loved shocking her. In the past he'd told her all about aids and homos, as he put it. She was so unsophisticated and naïve, like a blank page to be scribbled on, Bob took every opportunity to have fun with Alba.

"No. Not by Aids. By car accident. They reckon the funeral will be a bloody big one."

Bob turned to the public notices page in a local newspaper. He knew Alba to be quite illiterate so he began to read it out aloud:

"A celebration of the life of Kirkwood Bonn..."

"What!?" Alba gasped.

In dismay, Alba almost upset their drinks as she jumped up from her chair.

"Did you know him?" Bob asked, surprised at her abrupt reaction.

"He's the hitchhiker who robbed me!" Alba blurted out.

"No. Couldn't be." Bob said.

"Has to be. That is not a common name is it." She said, grabbing the paper to peer at it.

"No Alba. They say he died in a car accident a while ago somewhere South of here."

"But...he said..." Alba faltered in confusion.

"Couldn't be the same bloke Alba. Unless he's the walking dead."

Bob quavered the latter sentence in a spooky voice. Alba Jenkins' eyes bugged out fearfully. She'd always been deathly afraid of the supernatural. Now the idea of having slept with the walking dead was going to haunt her nightmares for a long time.

Bob knew he'd put the wind up Alba and got a big kick out of it. He laughed to himself while giving her a stricken face as if he truly believed she'd entertained a ghost. Bob enjoyed his amusement and didn't mind causing Alba some worry over her dalliance with the handsome young stranger.

"Do you think..?" Alba had paled.

"Well who knows? Stranger things have happened. But it is certainly eerie if you ask me." Bob said, winding her up ever more tightly.

Bob topped up their glasses with more rum and they got stuck in to it. That night Alba clung to him like never before and he liked that. *It's an ill wind* he told himself.

Without a word to Bob Bartleigh, Alba decided she'd just have to attend that funeral to make some sense of it. She was certain Kirkwood Bonn was the same name she had sneakily checked out in the handsome hitchhiker's bag. But maybe she was mistaken, knowing her reading skills were not her greatest talent.

Alba couldn't do the trip and go to the funeral all in one day. Her dogs were her main concern but she'd give them a good big feed of meat just before she left early on the day of the funeral. If returning before sunrise from Darwin City the following day, she hoped to get back before sunset to feed the dogs again. She decided, as a precaution, to also leave a bucket of dry kibble in a basin of water to keep ants out.

The dogs would miss her but they shouldn't go hungry. It's only for one night, she told her family of pets. Her dogs did not look convinced, they read her unsettled mood.

With the dogs meals sorted, Alba found a mid length black skirt and ironed it well under a damp cloth. Next she went through the wardrobes. She had never parted with her mother's things and remembered a few nice silk blouses. The largest one, a grey spotted print with pearl buttons, fitted her well. She gave it a good rinse out with perfumed shampoo to dispel the fusty wardrobe smell, and hung it in the shade to drip dry.

Packing a few items for her short stay away, Alba felt excited to be going somewhere overnight, tempered by the fact she would miss her dogs. All four had begun shadowing her steps, tails down, with the notion something different was afoot and they didn't like it.

Last of all, Alba filled an esky with several bottles of water and some snacks. She stowed everything into her fifteen year old Nissan Patrol, checked the oil and kicked the tyres.

The funeral was planned for early afternoon, to give people time to travel from outer lying areas. Alba sat at the back of the church not wanting to intrude as she did not know the family or close friends of the dead man.

A memorial booklet was handed to Alba as she entered the vestibule. The cover had a portrait photo with the name of the deceased in fancy script. She sounded out the letters in her head as she had done when first viewing his driving licence. Once again, she deciphered the name as Kirkwood Bonn. She was sure it was the same name she'd seen when peeking into the hitchhiker's bag.

A much larger framed photo of Kirkwood Bonn rested on a stand in front of the closed coffin, which was on a bier and covered with leafy wreaths and white roses.

Alba tried to recall the face of her handsome hitchhiker to compare with the portrait on display. It could be him but she remembered her guest as being more rugged looking. The man in the images presented, looked younger. Alba reasoned perhaps they used the best photos they had of him. It was confusing but she couldn't ask anyone at the funeral.

Alba regretted coming as she felt to have learnt nothing more and could not lay the ghost of her hitchhiker. She kicked herself for leaving her dogs overnight and for wasting money on a wild goose chase.

During the solemn ceremony, people gave tearful testaments to Kirkwood Bonn. The crying made Alba's own tears brim over in the sad atmosphere. She searched her handbag in vain looking for a hanky and felt thankful when someone kindly handed her a tissue.

Looking up to thank the kind person, she met the enquiring eyes of the police lady who'd come to the front gate and asked after a missing man. That first meeting had made Alba uneasy.

Now, Alba's scalp prickled being in the holy church and having this police woman appear by her side, almost by magic. Alba took it as some kind of omen.

Dulcy Vestige, in turn, felt surprised seeing Alba Jenkins at Kirkwood Bonn's funeral. Not only for her presence there, but that she looked so suitably and finely dressed. Clearly Alba had made every effort to respect the occasion.

The police inspector had only attended Bonn's funeral as a matter of course, to see what might arise that might be helpful, although she did not expect to find anything.

Neither Dulcy nor Alba planned to attend the burial or the wake. The requiem mass was a lengthy ritual to be sat through, so, as various members of the congregation rose and made their way slowly down the aisle to receive holy communion, Alba and Dulcy took the chance to quietly exit the church.

Dulcy knew Alba must have good reason to be present in the church that day. It was a long drive into Darwin City from where she lived, and not an easy one. As they walked together to the car park, Dulcy asked if Alba might like to get a cup of tea at a cafe. She did. After some general chat, Dulcy tried to guess Alba Jenkins' motives in attending the service.

"Alba. I have to say you look lovely in that smart outfit."

"Thank you." Alba reddened. "This blouse belonged to my mother. I am glad I kept it."

"Indeed. Though, I did feel curious to see you at the funeral. I am wondering why you made the long journey to attend. Then only sit up the back and leave early."

Dulcy phrased the enquiry with a smile to soften her words.

"You likely know already. I thought he must be the hitchhiker who stayed at mine."

"That's right. You said his name was Kirk. But how did you connect him to the deceased?"

"It's an unusual name...but look...a friend was telling me my hitch-hiker couldn't be the same man as the one who died. Unless he was the walking dead."

Alba appeared upset and visibly shaken. She carefully placed her cup back in its saucer to avoid spilling the hot tea.

"The walking dead?" Dulcy echoed. *What next?*

"Exactly. But who else could it be? So that got to me. The walking dead idea has given me the heeby-jeebies. It's not like you can lock the doors on that. Or sic the dogs onto it. I'm glad of my dogs but they can only do so much. It can be eerie out there alone sometimes."

Alba tried to explain as best she could but the expression that crossed Dulcy's face was not encouraging. Dulcy hadn't imagined an explanation that bordered on the occult with a possible zombie involved. Momentarily stymied, the detective tried to sort it out:

"So you needed to...what...make sure he had died?" Dulcy asked.

"Sort of...I don't know. The photos look like the hitchhiker who came to my place. But younger. Though of course the man had walked a long way and was pretty worn out when he got to my house. That's why I offered him lodgings overnight. It's just a mystery. But no, I am none the wiser for having come here. I'm sorry to say I just don't know."

Alba sighed and sipped more tea. Dulcy tried to make sense of what the other woman said. Apparently Alba thought she may have entertained a ghost.

"Do you believe in ghosts Alba?" Dulcy asked gently.

"It depends. I might. It's easier to believe in ghosts when the wind blows and rattles the windows and whistles in the trees. Day or night, but more so in the dark of course. Or when a man appears out of a dust storm, like from out of nowhere at all."

"You mean your hitchhiker of course."

"Yes. I do mean Kirk.   Then my friend, old Bob, who has lived a long time and knows more than I do, told me that man in the funeral notice was supposed to be dead before he got to my place. Unless he was the walking dead. Do you see?"

Dulcy did see how it would be spooky and disturbing for Alba, living all alone in the creaky old homestead, miles from anyone. Whoever this old mate Bob was, he had to be getting a lend of poor Alba, pulling her leg to scare the wits out of her. Not that the simple woman had many wits to spare.

Dulcy wondered what would become of the childish woman, in the long run.

22

Fingerprints

Alba sipped her tea, worried this nice police lady must think her a nutter. Never having had a female friend, that notion caused disappointment. She couldn't wait to get back to the motel room now, kick off the tight shoes and get out of her tortuous foundation garments.

Alba would have started back home without delay if it wasn't such an arduous trip, but knew it made more sense to get some sleep and return early next morning. Despite the comfort of her dogs, Alba did not relish getting home in the dark with the ghost of Kirk looming eerily over her shoulder. The spooky thought made her shudder.

Dulcy observed the woman and understood more than she could voice. The policewoman usually worked with black and white facts and this spiritual aspect was a grey area. She strove to put the frightened woman at ease:

"Alba. Can you keep a secret?"

"Yes I surely can. I promise."

Alba loved a secret and was glad to be taken into confidence. Maybe Dulcy didn't think she was nuts after all.

"Well. That Kirkwood Bonn we just said goodbye to? He is not the same man you took in."

"Oh! How do you know that?" Alba was intrigued and relieved. "Then he wasn't a ghost?"

"No. Not a ghost. But this is the secret you must keep. Cross your heart Alba."

Alba solemnly crossed her heart, describing a big X over her ample bosom.

"I promise." she vowed in a stage whisper.

"Police believe your hitchhiker stole the real Kirkwood's things and was just pretending to be him." Dulcy said. "But we don't want the thief to know we are on to him. It will be a lot easier to catch him if he doesn't know."

"Oh goodness me! No wonder he robbed me." Alba said it without thinking. *Oops.*

"He robbed you?" Dulcy picked up on it immediately.

Alba looked guilty:

"Yes. I am afraid so. I only found out a few days later. He took my savings that I keep in a pretty willow pattern teapot. Oh, and a bottle of rum." Alba admitted.

"Why didn't you say so when I first came to your house?" Dulcy tried to tread softly but it had to be asked.

"I know I should have. But people talk. Make up things. I didn't want it made public."

"Oh dear. I'm afraid your mercy might have helped him get away."

Alba looked stricken. Dulcy hastened to add:

"But it isn't your fault. No one blames you Alba. Not at all."

Dulcy said the last quickly to keep Alba on side.

"I feel awful now. I helped a thief." Alba said, downcast.

"Lucky he only robbed you." Dulcy said.

Alba made no reply, not sure what else Dulcy might mean. She hoped it wasn't about having sex. It seemed best not to ask. Let sleeping dogs lie her parents always said.

The Jenkins woman would find out she assisted a murderer eventually when the whole story came out. But Dulcy felt she'd divulged enough at this stage. Alba kept thinking on it.

"He seemed like such a nice bloke. Well mannered. You can't trust anyone these days."

"The most successful crooks are good at what they can get away with." Dulcy replied.

They ordered a second pot of tea and a plate of pikelets with plum jam and whipped cream. Alba had trouble coming to terms with it all.

"Do you think this Kirk I took in robbed the poor man while he lay dead in his crashed car?"

"Something like that." Dulcy hedged.

An awful possibility occurred to Alba: "He didn't...I mean...did he hurt him on purpose?"

"We are treating Kirkwood Bonn's death as homicide." Dulcy replied quietly.

She had to admit it looked like Alba's guest committed murder. Alba would find out soon enough and Dulcy didn't want to lose her trust in case more to the story might be uncovered.

Alba thought about that unusual word: Homicide. She remembered it was to do with murder. Maybe it had been in one of the Agatha Christie stories her parents used to read to her. She needed more of an explanation.

"Does homicide mean that the man I looked after, killed the one in the coffin?"

"It could mean he did. But we don't know who your traveller was or if he has a previous police record. We do both know he committed thefts. I guess you'd have washed up everything he used by now so there would be no chance of lifting his fingerprints."

Alba thought of how she had scrubbed everything and even bleached the sheets. Only one item had been stored away in its original condition, apart from it being empty.

"All except the rum bottle." Alba told her.

"The rum bottle? Didn't you say he stole it?"

"Not the first one. That is my Christmas bottle. He stole a new full one out of my pantry. He must have had a good look because I had it well hidden behind my big flour bin."

Dulcy's mouth fell open:

"Wait! You're saying you have a rum bottle that might have his finger-prints?"

"Yes. I kept that bottle because it has a special Christmas label."

"And you're sure the bloke touched it?"

"Yes he did. He liked rum and he topped up our glasses more than once."

Dulcy stared at Alba Jenkins. If viable fingerprints could be lifted off the glass bottle, they could be checked through the The Australian Criminal Intelligence System database.

"This could be really helpful Alba. Are you sure you didn't wipe the bottle?"

"I can't remember wiping it, like, it didn't look dirty or anything. I put it up in the attic beside the Christmas tree so I wouldn't throw it out by mistake. My friend Bob gave it to me as a gift and it has my own name on it with a greeting. It says Merry Christmas Alba."

Dulcy felt a frisson of excitement and dared to hope:

"Alba this is so important. You could help us solve the crime and catch a dangerous criminal. When are you going home?"

"Early tomorrow morning. Very early that is. I have to feed my dogs again and they aren't used to me being away all night. They will be worried."

"Please let me follow you home. Where are you staying? I will meet you as early as you like."

Alba Jenkins was thrilled to please Dulcy and be in on catching the bad guy. He owed her so much. She wondered if she'd be able to get her money back.

Dulcy phoned Dougall to give him the news. He had given up on the idea of finding useful fingerprints from the Calenda farm or the flood evacuation centre.

"This could be the big breakthrough. Fingers crossed." he said.

"And toes." Dulcy agreed.

They eagerly awaited results to see if the prints from Alba's Christmas rum bottle would meet with any match in the database records.

Meanwhile, Damien Cresswick tried to come to terms with his devastating loss, while keeping the business running.

23

Family Tree

Kirkwood and Damien had made each other sole beneficiaries of their wills.

They had separate suites with office spaces in their home, and now Damien ran his hands over Kirkwood's desk trying to feel some latent vibe of his loved one. He'd been sleeping with Kirkwood's favourite silk pyjamas imagining the fibres held a faint essence of his cherished partner's being.

Mail had arrived for Kirkwood in his absence. Damien had placed the lone letter on his friend's computer keyboard where it would attract his immediate attention, on return.

Knowing Kirkwood would never read the contents joined a myriad of other regrets. A return address, only a PO box number, headed the upper left of the envelope but no identifying name gave a clue to the sender. Out of curiosity, Damien opened the long brown envelope with a letter opener, slitting it neatly as his diligent partner would have done.

The information within confirmed and expanded details of family connections. Damien resealed the envelope and wept: If only Kirkwood hadn't followed obscure hints and clues trying to find his ancestry. Had he received this further information in time, he may have chosen another path rather than taking that fatal trip.

Although Damien understood Kirkwood's need to know his true bloodline he had worried the knowledge might open a can of worms, making life difficult for his sensitive partner and himself. Yet he agonised over not having been more supportive.

Surely the business could have closed temporarily. It was not as if they were short of money. Damien beat himself up over the idea that if he had accompanied Kirkwood they'd now be home safely together.

Damien searched his own motives and knew he'd privately been against Kirkwood's trip and quest. He preferred keeping Kirkwood to himself without interfering relatives since they had already escaped family interventions by moving to the far north.

Like Damien, Kirkwood had been raised in the Catholic religion by strict older parents. Damien had known Kirkwood since school days and his own parents, the senior Cresswicks, were church members in the same parish as the Bonns.

Kirkwood had never suspected nor been told the Bonns were his adoptive parents until the flack hit the fan over his homosexuality. His parents' fondest wish had been for their adopted son to study theology and enter the noble halls of priesthood. Damien and Kirkwood eventually laughed in sarcasm with the paradox they saw in that.

Damien and Kirkwood had first met as twelve year old boys in boarding school. They were the same age, even shared the same birthday and been innocently attracted to each other from the start.

After Damien and Kirkwood each experienced sexual interference from a priest, they explored their own intimacy, at night, in the shared dormitory. They were not the only boys who went to other beds after lights out, but they remained exclusively true to each other. The young relationship between Damien and Kirkwood grew into an enduring bond.

During a sleepover in the Bonn's home, Kirkwood's parents caught the pair sharing a bed and cuddling each other. Damien's parents had been called in the middle of the night, to come and take their filthy boy home. In defending Damien, Kirkwood had declared his love and the situation escalated to name calling and laying blame.

So Kirkwood learnt he had been adopted at birth. The disclosure was allowed to him in the cruellest and worst possible way, in a blazing row that had his adoptive parents disown him.

The god-fearing senior Bonns feared what other people would think. They could not understand how Kirkwood could be a 'deviant' after they had raised him properly in the Catholic religion and given him the best of everything.

Kirkwood's adoptive parents ranted and raved, saying his condition must be genetic but it did not come from them. They told the boy his birth mother had been a wanton woman, a harlot, adding that explained his woeful life choice, made with no regard for themselves.

The Bonns insisted Kirkwood could have overcome that flawed bloodline if he possessed a shred of moral courage and given more thought to the sacrifices they had made for him.

Damien's parents had also been very disappointed in their only son. Sending him away to a different boarding school, swept the issue under the carpet. Out of sight, out of mind.

Their respective parents separated Kirkwood and Damien physically, in vain and misguided hopes they'd grow out of their predilections and come to their senses. Time would prove, the combined parents' efforts only served to bond their sons more closely. Kirkwood and Damien turned ever more loyally to each other for comfort. The young men kept in touch by phone and online.

"Life is so bland without you Damien." Kirkwood declared during one chat.

"Bland you say?" Damien fished for endearments.

"Insipid. Lacklustre. You must know what I mean, my friend."

"I do know. I feel the same way. I have an idea for a business venture we might do together.   A fresh start far away from our parents. We don't need their negativity."

Kirkwood embraced Damien's suggestion for a wellness clinic awarding the idea with his favourite accolade of brilliant. Both chose study courses towards the plan for a happy future.

After leaving college and university, where they achieved diplomas in physiotherapy, naturopathy and related subjects, the pair cemented their relationship with the decision to move far away, eventually land-ing in a thriving country community south of Darwin.

Being well off financially, Damien and Kirkwood devoted their com-bined efforts and energies into establishing their upmarket Brilliant Health Clinic and Wellness Centre.

The venture filled their days with purpose and a great sense of achievement. The proprietors' homosexuality did not deter custom, if anything, women were attracted by the neutrality.

With Kirkwood dead and gone forever, Damien did not know is he could go on. Yet he automatically stuck to routine as a tentative grasp on sanity. He forced himself to put one foot in front of the other, and took life one day at a time. He gracefully accepted condolences from customers and cried out his heartbreak in private.

The police officer consigned to chaperone Damien in his first shock and grief, had left his house before the funeral. With the goodbyes and burial all over and finalised, Damien wandered about the empty house that no longer felt like home. Eventually the grieving man gravitated to the office where Kirkwood had spent much of his free time.

Damien sat in his partner's office chair facing the desktop computer. Ever methodical albeit rather naïve, Kirkwood kept a notebook, clearly labelled 'passwords' in full view. The notebook was aligned exactly at right angles to the keyboard. Pens and pencils were set out in parallel lines, equidistant apart. Orderliness had been one of Kirkwood's many little quirks. He could not abide anything being askew.

Booting up Kirkwood's computer, Damien accessed his files with the password: Damien4ever which brought a lump to his throat.

Kirkwood's adoptive parents spitefully refused to give away any information regarding how they'd acquired him as a baby. Scrolling through past activities online, Damien realised his partner had gone to extensive efforts to discover his true beginnings.

The Bonns had lived at their current address since before Kirkwood's birth and had been involved with the local Catholic church the entire time.

Damien saw from search history, Kirkwood discovered there had once been a Catholic home for unmarried mothers in the near vicinity. That home had long since been repurposed but he had obviously used logic in thinking he might have been born at that place.

Kirkwood had pursued that line of enquiry. He had searched archives to find names of nursing staff who may have worked at the church baby home. Since the birthing facility had been discontinued twenty years before his search, from what Damien could make out, nothing useful arose from those efforts.

Doggedly persistent, Kirkwood applied to The Freedom of Information Team at the Department of Child Protection South Australia, and been tremendously excited to receive a pre-adoption birth certificate. Damien did not share the joy and only pretended to be pleased. Faking now felt like cowardly deception as Damien mentally beat himself up.

Kirkwood learnt his birth mother's name and the place where he was born was indeed the old Catholic home. The father, listed as unknown, had been no surprise since the Bonn's had declared her to be a lowly type of woman and probably a prostitute.

Kirkwood had been christened for some distant forebear of his adoptive father so there was no clue to be found in his name.

Paperwork with the pre-adoption certificate, noted that the birth mother departed leaving no forwarding address and had not given her newborn baby any name.

The disclosure greatly saddened Kirkwood. Deep sorrow felt for his friend, fuelled Damien's negative attitude to the ancestry search.

Yet, Kirkwood strove to find the woman who had given him life. Generous and forgiving in his sentiments, he decided her sad lifestyle gave valid reasons for secretive behaviour.

Ultimately, Kirkwood had his DNA analysed to seek possible matches. At some expense, he engaged expert assistance in tracking genetic links. The exercise depended on any close relatives also having their DNA recorded. Tired of awaiting results, Kirkwood jumped the gun to undergo his fateful trip on the thin threads of evidence gleaned thus far.

Further information within the brown envelope, uncovered two more close relatives and their home address. If only that letter had arrived sooner and if only Kirkwood had waited.

Damien agonised over the injustice of it all. Life seemed so unfair.

24

Escape

At the same time as Damien lamented over the brown envelope arriving before Kirkwood could read it, The Bruiser stepped around the fleshy lump of Amelia's bloodied corpse.

Her head, turned aside, showed one piggy eye that accused him in a glassy marbled squint.

He went to the balcony and yelled at Mortimer:

"Shut up for Christ's sake you bloody stinking mongrel. You'll get yours in my good time."

Mortimer quit howling. Growling deeply, the dog fixed the man with a burning hatred, laming in an unblinking glare. The Bruiser became unnerved and had to look away. He knew that dog had it in for him, more than ever before.

Dry mouthed, Bruce Luck revisited his childhood self, less brave and more vulnerable than his prison persona, The Bruiser. Terribly afraid of the predatory dog that now kept him imprisoned, Bruce could hardly raise enough spit to swallow.

Trapped in the house, he searched everywhere to see what might be available to help himself out of the dire situation. He doubted Amelia would have any firearms. If he did find a gun and ammunition, he would happily riddle Mortimer with bullets.

Amelia's spacious bedroom, decorated in a purple, orange and black colour scheme more ghastly than the garish guest room, assaulted even his vulgar senses.

A glass dish on Amelia's dressing table held her car keys. The key ring also had another few keys. He thought one could be the shed key but he had no wish to see what horrors that revealed. The others looked like door keys.

Running downstairs, he tried the keys. With relief, he found one opened the door leading to the carport where the car sat parked only a few steps away. Perhaps Amelia had even left the car unlocked, if his good luck came to the rescue.

About to exit and check this possibility, only lightening quick re-action saved him from Mortimer. The enraged dog had tracked the man through the house and, on hearing the click of the key, made an aggressive headlong rush at the door.

Bruce managed to slam the door shut in the nick of time, coughing on a whiff of the dog's fetid breath as it bayed like a demon from hell. The man collapsed onto the floor. He sat in terror with his back bearing the rattle of the solid door as the heavy dog threw its weight against it, growling and snarling.

The Bruiser in Bruce knew he must somehow kill, maim or at least distract the dog long enough to gain the safety of the car. He still didn't know if the car was unlocked. Unlocking it would cost precious seconds if Mortimer was still able to attack.

Bruce Luck got up from the floor. He found an unopened bottle of rum and swigged a mouthful to settle his nerves. Then he gathered an arsenal of knives and boiled a kettle of water as another weapon in case the dog managed to get inside the house.

After a while, all was quiet. Bruce went back upstairs and saw that Mortimer continued his vigil below the balcony where the scent of his mistress would be strongest.

The Bruiser tried throwing kitchen knives at the dog but Mortimer easily avoided them, only to become more aggravated. Every miss gave the dog another victory and the man suffered another loss. The exercise became demoralising. Bruce gave up. He'd have to think up another strategy.

The killer looked through Amelia's bedroom more thoroughly. Her handbag, on the floor of one of the wardrobes, held a handy three hundred dollars in cash. Encouraged, he searched the other wardrobes and chests of drawers.

He found no fire arms but one wardrobe held a lot of mens clothing. If the garments had all been taken from Amelia's victims, she must have finished off quite a few unfortunate blokes.

Looking more closely, Bruce found the mens' clothes to be in a variety of sizes, supporting his belief they'd been taken from different victims. He went through all the pockets and found a four year old petrol receipt but no more money, not even small change or credit cards.

He surmised Amelia must have spent or hoarded the money. She would probably get rid of any incriminating items like plastic cards and anything else that identified the owners.

The Bruiser selected a sleeveless denim jacket from the mix of clothing. He put it on and stuffed the three hundred dollars in an inside zippered pocket. From now on he'd keep all his money on his body and never again in the backpack. The weather might become too hot for wearing the heavy denim jerkin, but he meant to keep it on, regardless.

The style of jacket could have belonged to bikie. It looked like typical biker gear. The Bruiser thought, with a sleeve of tattoos inked on at least one arm, the previous owner could have been Mortimer's latest snack.

That made him wonder if there might be a motorbike in that locked shed. He would be able to make good time on a bike if it still started. But there was no way of telling how long the tattooed victim had been packed in there. His dismembered body could have been kept frozen in pieces for months.

The Bruiser took a last look around Amelia's bedroom wondering if he'd missed anything. Almost as an afterthought, he decided to look under the queen sized bed mattress. It was a thick innerspring that proved very heavy. He pulled the quilt and bedding off onto the floor to lighten the weight and pushed the mattress off the edge of the bed.

There appeared to be nothing underneath anyway. He bent down to look further under the bed and from that position, noticed a zippered insert attached to the underside of the mattress.

Turning the heavy innerspring over, to access the insert, he discovered a flat vinyl case within. The Bruiser pulled the vinyl case out, opened it and emptied the contents onto the floor.

"Wow! Oh wow! Fuck me dead!" he exclaimed in glee.

He had hit the jackpot! Bundles of money, no less than seven driving licences and a bunch of plastic debit or credit cards fell out onto the garish purple and orange carpet. Each were encased in separate plastic bags with various pieces of jewellery, watches, rings, earrings and chains.

Bruce sat on the side of the bed frame and went through the wonderful find, counting five thousand and five dollars in cash which he pocketed with the other three hundred found in Amelia's handbag. With over fifty-three hundred dollars in his pocket, he was now richer than before Fred, the rotten van driver, stole his roll.

The seven driving licences included one for a Reverend somebody. His photo showed he wore an earring and had a tattoo on his face. If that was the tattooed guy Mortimer had been eating, he hadn't been shown much reverence by the lost lamb who might have sought the poor guy's blessing, before murdering him for dog food.

Bruce Luck closely scrutinised the other licences. They had all been owned by men within age groups that could fit his own. He discarded two that had belonged to dark skinned men.

One of the others had a photo that might be passed off as himself as the man had a moustache and beard. Matching his own clean shaven face would be more of a challenge to any inspection so he decided to keep that one. The name, Boris Larssen sounded foreign but the initials BL seemed to be a good omen.

Larssen's plastic packet included a gold cross on a chain. The Bruiser slipped the chain over his head and admired his reflection in the dressing table mirror. Wearing the Christian symbol was a good touch, he thought. It lent him a certain aura of honesty and integrity.

He raised his right hand, mocking a blessing over the people as he'd seen done on TV by The Pope. He intoned a pun: "Let us 'prey'....hee hee." It seemed so funny he rolled about on the floor laughing in buoyant euphoria in the wake of his windfall.

Amelia's dog barked and howled in frustration on hearing the man's laughter. The animal's mourning had a sobering effect on The Bruiser who pulled himself together to reassess his situation.

A change of ID would be a boon at this juncture. It meant the Kirk-wood Bonn persona that was associated with that person's murder and the Calenda Farm incident, could be ditched.

Mortimer remained the problem to be overcome if Bruce Luck was ever to escape. He was desperate to get back to his father's house and seek medical help for the festering of his penis which now itched and oozed a slight viscous discharge. A rancid odour emanating from that cherished member was particularly worrisome.

The Bruiser was desperate for antibiotics and rummaged through all Amelia's cabinets and drawers to no avail. He knew he must not delay any longer in getting away. The best and only distraction The Bruiser could think of to keep the dog busy, was to drop Amelia's body over the balcony onto the ground, where Mortimer held his vigil. The man fantasied it would be amazing if her bulk squashed the bastard dog. But that was wishful thinking and he had to focus on reality.

The Bruiser dragged the naked body of Amelia by her arms, out to the balcony, leaving a long smear of blood on the plush pink carpet. Her dead weight was almost more than he could heft, but with great difficulty and determination, he managed to drape the pudgy corpse head first over the balcony railings, ready for her final dive.

Having got blood on his hands again, he took another shower and dressed in jeans and t-shirt, donning the denim jerkin containing the money and Boris Larssen's drivers licence. His BL pocket knife went into its leather pouch attached inside his jeans pocket as always.

The knapsack containing Kirkwood Bonn's ID, was replenished with the almost full bottle of rum he'd opened earlier and some fruit. The Bruiser wasn't game to take any other food stuffs, not knowing what the crazy woman might have laced with drugs.

He planned to get rid of anything linked to Kirkwood Bonn somewhere down the track so there should be no link to his ever being there.

Jewellery from Amelia's past victims went into the knapsack as well, since he could pawn it later on. One of the gold wedding rings fitted perfectly so he wore it as part of his new disguise.

The Bruiser left the knapsack by the carport escape door with the keys and the killing knife in case Mortimer happened by to visit him again. He supposed Amelia's blood on the knife might be useful in distracting the dog momentarily, if that became necessary.

Lastly, he had to dump Amelia over the balcony and pray Mortimer spent time with her instead of stalking him to the car.

The weighty Amelia landed head first with a satisfying crack as her neck snapped, followed by a meaty thud as the rest of her body somersaulted over onto the hard ground. Mortimer yelped and immediately ran to inspect his mistress and lick blood from her wounds.

With no time to spare, and with a thumping heart, the man ran down the stairs three at a time, shouldered the knapsack, unlocked the door and fled to the car. Thankfully the car was not locked but The Bruiser barely got into the passenger side door, which was nearest, before the massive dog was onto him.

Mortimer ripped the bottom left leg of The Bruiser's jeans, scraping vicious teeth down his ankle before the man could slam the door shut, using the knapsack to ward off the attack.

Both the knife and the knapsack were dropped in the frantic struggle. It was impossible to retrieve the backpack with the savage dog hunting him. Kirkwood Bonn's credentials would be found and most likely traced back to Calenda Farm and the burnt Landcruiser incidents.

The Bruiser was certain those sisters would have reported his attack on Nova. Couldn't be helped. The greatest pity was losing another bottle of rum. It was almost full as well.

Mortimer gripped the knapsack in his powerful jaws, ripping and shaking it about, spilling some jewellery out, before switching his attention back to the car.

The Bruiser struggled over the handbrake and across the gap between the bucket seats, to get behind the steering wheel. Fumbling the car keys into the ignition with a shaking hand, he cried with relief as the car started first go.

All the while, Mortimer jumped up snarling at the window, only inches from the man's ashen face. Bruce prayed the glass wouldn't break. It held, and once again, the devil took care of his own.

Night was falling as the man reversed the car around and aimed it for the sturdy entry gates. At the last second, he reconsidered trying to bash those heavy metal gates apart. He worried such a solid collision might damage the vehicle enough to disable it.

The side fencing panels were wooden pickets that should be weaker to crash through. He backed up again. Mortimer still raged, barking and slavering at the car window. Bruce Luck swerved the car towards the dog, hoping Mortimer would get run over and be crushed under the wheels, but the dog proved too smart.

The Bruiser accelerated and rammed through the nearest fence panel, shattering the wooden pickets and cracking a headlight. The small sedan bounced drunkenly over a drain on the footpath, jarring the driver, who managed to steer it, in a swerving path, onto the road. The jolt, however painful, did not hinder the man from speeding off, his foot flat to the floor as he headed for the highway.

Mortimer tried to follow, but his heavy build prevented him from keeping up. Dejected, the dog had no recourse but to limp home and stand guard over the body of his mistress.

As the day cooled the dog vaguely acknowledged his own many aches and soreness from his failed efforts to bring the man down. Hungry, and in abject grief, Mortimer lay his head on Amelia's stiffening form and whimpered sadly.

The Bruiser experienced a high of elated relief in escaping the house of death at long last. However, the killer only drew a deep breath once he'd made it to the highway and left the hellish dog far behind.

The man checked over the crime in his mind and saw no link to his true identity as Bruce Luck. He counted himself lucky to have gotten away with the money, a new ID as Boris Larssen and his own BL pocket knife.

The Bruiser's next move had to include dumping the car before police began looking for it. He figured to have at least five hours grace before the car became too hot to keep. He drove carefully through the night, obeying all road rules, not wanting to attract attention. Although one headlamp had cracked during his escape, it still worked.

He anticipated that neighbours in Amelia's street might soon report the broken fence since it freed her savage dog. The most rudimentary inspection would find Amelia's naked and bloodied body in the back yard.

The Bruiser laughed to himself thinking *good luck with the dog from Hell.* He celebrated the fact that Mortimer was no longer his problem.

Only Amelia and the devil knew what or who else might be discovered in that locked shed. *Oh to be a fly on the wall for that one.* The Bruiser sniggered.

It occurred to him that Mortimer might get hungry enough to eat parts of Amelia and that would be supreme justice. Even better: Maybe the police would shoot Mortimer. He would dearly love to see that happen.

Having heard nothing in the news on the car radio, The Bruiser wondered if he had gotten away with the Calenda Market Gardens attack as well. Surely they realised he had not been the real Kirkwood Bonn but he felt confident nothing linked that character to himself, the handsome and oh so lucky Bruce Luck.

Certainly, Kirkwood Bonn's ID would now be found in the bag dropped in the carport, as well as the several others left scattered on the bedroom floor of Amelia's bedroom.

The Bruiser imagined police might conclude Kirkwood Bonn's impostor somehow became another victim butchered by Amelia and devoured by her man-eating dog. He smirked with the thought of it being be an ideal way to solve all his niggling little problems.

Assuming traces of various bodies remained in the shed, shreds of flesh, hair or blood stains, the task of identifying and matching a hodge podge of DNA would slow investigations down. The killer planned to be long gone, safe and sound in his father's house, before all Amelia's victims were ever sorted out.

Once more, The Bruiser congratulated himself for outsmarting authorities. He wasn't giving any clues away for free either.

He drove carefully within the speed limits heading southbound into Brisbane, where he ditched the vehicle.

Amelia's car was abandoned unlocked, with the keys in the ignition and parked in a dark back street, nowhere near the railway station where her killer planned to begin his long trip home to his father's house, by train.

Hitchhiking had definitely lost its appeal for The Bruiser.

25

Rum Results

Just hours before The Bruiser boarded a train as Boris Larssen, The Australian Criminal Intelligence System database returned a match for the fingerprints lifted from Alba Jenkins' Christmas rum bottle.

Dulcy Vestige excitedly shared the results with Dougall Grimslade:

"We've got a match to an ex-prisoner named Bruce Luck. He was recently released after serving two years for abetting a robbery. His residential address is in suburban Adelaide." "He's strayed a long way from home then."

"He has. Local officers were sent to the address but only his aged and demented father is currently in residence. The old man told them Bruce probably took off with someone called Greta. He said you couldn't trust either of them and apparently went off into some rant that made no sense."

They wondered who Greta could be:

"Maybe Greta is Bruce's girlfriend?"

"Possibly. But we're still trying to resolve it. But whoever Greta is, she wasn't with him when he got to Alba Jenkins' place."

"True. He seems to have acted alone in every case."

"That we know of. We can safely assume this Bruce Luck is the one who murdered Kirkwood Bonn since he's in possession of the stolen ID." Dougall replied.

"Absolutely. He's easily gotten away with that. Looking at his mug shots, he actually bears a striking resemblance to his victim. I'll send the Bruce Luck images over to you for a look."

"Thanks Dulcy. I will have a good look at it. What now, for you, going forward?"

Dougall Grimslade felt otherwise distracted having just been alerted to a bizarre crime scene he had been called upon to help investigate.

Dulcy stated her position: "I still don't want to make the murder public. This Bruce Luck suspect could still be using Kirkwood's ID. If he's stupid enough. Also I should let Kirkwood's partner know of any developments before he sees anything on the news."

"That's right of course. Let me know how you go Dulcy. Right now I'm on my way to inspect what could be another murder."

"They're keeping us busy. Thanks for your time. Talk later Dougall."

After ringing off, Dulcy visited Damien Cresswick and was shown into his spacious and tidy living room.

"Damien. Early days in this investigation, but we have identified Kirkwood's hitchhiker who called himself Richie."

"Will he be arrested and charged?"

"He will be. When we get him, Damien. But we haven't caught up with him yet."

"So we keep details confidential because he might still pretend to be Kirkwood?"

"Exactly. We're throwing everything at finding him but at this stage, our best chance of nailing him is if he misuses Kirkwood's ID."

"I see. Well thanks for the update. And good luck."

Damien appreciated the news and hoped they'd catch Kirkwood's killer but the love of his life remained forever cold in the ground and nothing could change that. Even catching the murderer would be a hollow victory since no amount of punishment seemed adequate.

While Damien lamented the situation, Dougall Grimslade attended the scene of Amelia Boole's death. Her naked body lay where it landed headfirst, twisted awkwardly over her broken neck.

Discovery of the dead body was made after neighbours reported Amelia's savage dog on the loose, to the RSPCA.

In due course, an RSPCA officer, a middle aged woman named Pamela Burn, arrived at the address. Finding the double gates locked, Pamela entered on foot, negotiating the overgrown drain to go through the broken fence panel. She called out asking if anybody were home. Of course no one answered and neither did the dog bark.

The place seemed deserted. No vehicle occupied the car space but Pamela noted the house door ajar and a bag on the ground with pieces of jewellery strewing from its ripped seams. It looked like a robbery gone wrong.

The RSPCA officer called police while cautiously creeping around to the back of the house.

Thinking perhaps the alleged savage dog had chased the robbers and gone off further afield, Pamela was ill prepared for what she next witnessed.

Turning a corner, she came across the massive dog sitting on top of Amelia's twisted naked body. Mortimer raised his big wide head and seriously regarded the intruder.

Nerves jangling, Pamela Burn backed off slowly and did not draw breath until regaining the safety of her vehicle. It first looked to her as if the dog might have killed the woman. She rang police again with the update which triggered a speedier response from that quarter. A death had priority over robbery and a loose dog.

Sitting in her car, the RSPCA officer realised she could well be mistaken about the dog killing the woman. For all she knew, the dog might be completely innocent. It hadn't gone for her so perhaps it was actually standing guard over the dead woman.

Pamela imagined the police might shoot the dog out of hand which did not sit well with her personal ethics to rescue animals.

So Pamela Burn of the RSPCA risked going back to face the dog, armed with a Dan-Inject Tranquiliser gun. The experienced officer was qualified and well trained in using the humane sedation method. The dog had not moved so she efficiently darted Mortimer and rendered him harmless.

Pamela knew not to unnecessarily contaminate a crime scene but phoned for backup from colleagues to help her cage the huge dog as she would never be able to lift him on her own.

By the time Dougall Grimslade arrived, RSPCA personnel had managed to move the subdued dog on a stretcher and contain him in the back of Pamela Burn's van.

Incarcerated at the shelter, Mortimer had been carried in between two strong men and placed into a cubicle before he became aware. After coming out of sedation over the following says, kennel staff noted the dog always slumped against a wall, unresponsive to anyone or anything. It seemed his future would not be rosy.

Amelia's small ponies, also taken into RSPCA custody, were easily placed in alternative homes.

Despite a housing shortage, Amelia's desirable acreage home retained a ghastly stigma that had it sitting empty for many years.

Eventually an enterprising real estate agent sold it to Asian immigrants, who, blissfully unaware of its macabre past, celebrated a bargain buy.

26

Remains To Be Seen

At the crime scene, the coroner in charge put Amelia's time of death occurring at between ten and fifteen hours ago.

"Sexual assault?" Grimslade asked.

"Definitely. I'm afraid this is a particularly grisly one." he said, "Looks certain she's been pushed over from the landing above, sustaining a broken neck. Also a lot of other body bruising consistent with sexual assault. Can't say more until I get her on the slab. But looks like she's been knifed in a frenzied sex attack."

"What's with all the other knives on the ground around her I wonder."

"Could be ritualistic."

"Are you thinking satanic?"

"Can't rule it out. Something unholy definitely went on here, that's for sure."

Grimslade donned protective clothing and entered the house with forensic investigators and photographers. He noted the bloody drag marks on the pink carpet of one bedroom. The other bedroom looked to have been trashed as if it had been searched for something.

This type of frantic search, in his experience, often involved drugs. Toilet cisterns being a popular hiding place, led Dougall to check them, where he discovered the black warning scrawl: *Run for your life. Don't drink the juice.*

He ordered any juice be taken in for analysis, along with other likely substances. This case was proving to be a puzzler.

The ripped bag with the spilt jewellery remained where it had fallen. It seemed the person or persons responsible may have dropped it in a hurry to get away. The RSPCA officer told the detective that although the big guard dog had been deemed aggressive, it looked more like its priority was guarding the woman's body.

"He made no move to attack me. Even though I was trespassing on his home territory. So I decided to tranquillise him for his own safety."

"His own safety?" Dougall echoed.

"In case anyone saw fit to shoot him. He is a large scary looking dog and it could have been taken that he killed the victim. But it seemed obvious to me that he was mourning over the body. I'm sure he was guarding it." Pamela replied, in defence of her own actions.

"Yes. Well you are the expert there. Good call." Dougall said.

The dog was the least of Dougall's concerns. After photographs had been taken from all angles, he searched through the ripped knapsack. Lo and behold, it held Kirkwood Bonn's credentials.

"Aha!" the detective couldn't help exclaiming in triumph. He lived for these eureka moments.

"You've had a find?" another officer asked.

"I certainly have. This is gold. And I don't mean the bling jewels." Dougall replied.

Less senior officers, tasked with surveying the outbuildings, gained entry to the garden shed, soon to exit gasping and gagging. One of them vomited loudly and colourfully.

The senior detective was called over. *What now? Can this get any worse?* Grimslade thought. On inspection, he soon acknowledged the event, as it unfolded, to be indeed a lot worse.

Discovery of human body parts, crudely dismembered and stored in freezers and refrigerators would never be forgotten. Various knives, meat cleavers nd a butchers block furnished the space.

Investigators at the Amelia Boole crime scene, theorised the human remains had been fed to her dog. But by then, realising the dog would not have been fed since his owner's demise, too much time had elapsed to examine the dogs actual stomach contents.

Amelia had always picked up and buried Mortimer's faeces. However, viable samples found in the pony paddock retained enough evidence to confirm the theory. No one was surprised that the dead had been fed to the dog for there seemed no other reason to store the body parts. Speculation had it that Amelia's dog possibly consumed several people over the years.

That night, Dougall couldn't wait to phone Dulcy: "You're never going to believe this…"

"You're kidding! And how likely is it that our man has joined the others in the freezers?"

"Remains to be seen. No pun intended." Dougall replied.

"Well I guess since Kirkwood Bonn's credentials have been found and can't be misused any more, it wouldn't hurt to put out a general all-points bulletin to see if any information turns up on the whereabouts of our Bruce Luck."

"If he wasn't turned into dog food." Dougall said.

"But assuming he might still be at large." Dulcy replied.

The Bruiser was indeed still at large and his luck held. He needn't have worried over Amelia's car being found anywhere near his Brisbane departure point. A group of five tearaway youths, ranging in ages from thirteen to seventeen, stole it for a long joyride, driving it back up the coast highway.

The tearaways had visions of making it to one of the Sunshine Coast beaches but ran out of fuel just an hours drive North of Amelia Boole's location. Thwarted, the young yobs skulked away, leaving the car precariously perched on the shoulder of the busy highway. Faced with having to hitch back home or steal another car, they argued amongst themselves, blaming the designated driver for not keeping an eye on the fuel gauge. In a fit of pique, the young hoon ditched Amelia's full key ring into swampy bushland beside the highway.

When Amelia Boole's car was found, police guessed the thief or thieves had driven it from the murder crime scene. It seemed a northward escape route had been intended, but the vehicle had run out of petrol. Service stations are known to have CCTV so rather than risk being caught on camera refuelling, the car had been abandoned.

Going by the amount of fresh cigarette butts and lolly wrappers left in the car, police determined more than one perpetrator had to be involved.

A hypothetical scenario emerged with three or more killer thieves, who dropped their loot and fled on being confronted by the guard dog.

Grimslade tried to tie the Kirkwood Bonn find into the equation. He was sure Bruce Luck had always acted alone so did not discount that the man had fallen victim himself.

Brainstorming scenarios, the possibility that Amelia's car had been dumped and by chance, subsequently stolen, also arose. Yet the case was no closer to being solved.

Bruce Luck's guardian devil of good fortune still looked out for him up to that point.

27

Last Trip

After dumping Amelia's car in the dark side street, Bruce Luck continued on foot into Brisbane city, arriving at Roma Street Station to peruse travel options.

Having lost the knapsack, he had nothing to carry. The money was safely zipped into the inside jacket pocket with Boris Larssen's ID and his BL pocket knife remained in its leather holster in his jeans pocket.

The Bruiser peeled off a few fifty dollar notes to keep separately in a front pocket, so no one ever glimpsed his substantial main roll of cash. He planned to wear the denim jerkin like a second skin, at all times.

Bruce Luck walked to an all night Maccas in the city mall and sat over coffee and breakfast, planning the next few days.

He needed a change of clothes and a disposable shaver. Once shops opened, he needed to buy another bag and some new jeans. He would change in a toilet cubicle and leave the pair torn by Mortimer on the floor there. New socks were another must, the ones he had worn since his escape were smelly and the left one, crusted with dried blood. His old boots were coming apart so a new pair were well overdue.

An airline bag would represent his only luggage for the long haul, to be stocked with basic items for his train journey.

Resisting the urge to rub his irritated penis in public, reminded the man to add some sort of soothing ointment to his shopping list as well.

Fronting to buy his train ticket, Bruce Luck found he had another day to kill before the next departure. He hired a taxi to take him to the nearest backpacker hostel where he booked in using the Boris Larssen ID. He had no way of knowing how long Boris Larssen had been missing and could only hope there were no current alerts out for him.

In fact, Boris Larssen had been missing for four years. He had broken up with his fiance and been between jobs. With a free break of several weeks, Boris decided to hitch up to Queensland and soak up some sunshine, only to become another hapless traveller who mooched a ride with Amelia Boolie.

Before taking off to the Sunshine State, Boris Larssen had resided in Canberra with his parents, who, having no contact for weeks, reported their son as a missing person. Police did rudimentary checks to find Boris. Given the circumstances of his broken engagement, it was decided he probably dropped out from society and did not want to be found. His case remained open but buried under a similar stack on the back burner.

Bruce Luck's one-way train trip to take him from Roma Street in Brisbane to Adelaide's Parkland would take almost three days with a lengthy stopover in Sydney. The fare option he chose set him back by the best part of five hundred dollars.

At last seated in the carriage and underway on the first leg of his home journey that would land him in Sydney, Bruce Luck found he could not get comfortable. He attributed a stiff and sore neck from the jolt of driving Amelia's car through the fence and over the deep drain.

Antiseptic cream applied often and liberally soothed his irritated penis somewhat, though that affliction became the least of his ailments.

Try as he might to relax, The Bruiser's heart began to beat so rapidly he worried he might be experiencing coronary failure. He put heightened anxiety over the tempo of his heartbeat as a cause to breathing difficulties that added to his suffering.

Clearly, the prolonged ordeal at Amelia's hands had not done his health any good and he cursed the woman anew. If only he had finished her off sooner. *Live and learn.*

Bruce couldn't stand watching the scenery reeling by the windows of the speeding train. The motion made him feel nauseous. The man tried to decompress and sit back, closing his eyes against the light and willing the debilitating symptoms to settle down.

Travel time to Sydney took over fourteen hours followed by a long stop over between 8pm and 1pm the next day but the man had failed to make prior arrangements for over night accommodation.

By the time the train arrived at Sydney Central Station, Bruce Luck began to suffer from painful cramp like spasms in his face and neck. He blamed the infection from Amelia's enforced duration of intercourse. He bought a pack of Ibuprofen from an all night chemist and took three. He felt a little better after the medication kicked in.

Bruce hired a taxi whose helpful driver recommended an economical backpacker hostel with free breakfast and not far to walk back to Central Railway Station. He used the Boris Larssen ID again.

Complimentary cups of tea were supplied in the hostel kitchen. Bruce tried to eat a sandwich he'd gotten earlier from a vending machine. The sandwich was quite awful but he was past caring. He just wanted to get home.

The stricken man collapsed to sleep in the hostel bunk, only to be disturbed by more painful cramps. He got up at 3am to swallow three more Ibuprofen tablets.

After a terribly restless night, not feeling up to the short walk, The Bruiser took another taxi to the station for the Sydney to Adelaide Parklands leg of his journey.

Aboard the trains and about to turn his back on a talkative passenger, his ears pricked up when some bizarre crimes were mentioned involving dismembered human parts fed to dogs. Bruce knew of only one dog but was not about to offer any correction to the story. Suffering a throbbing ankle from Mortimer's gnashing teeth, he didn't want to think about dogs at all.

The annoying chatterer seemed amused by the story:

"Could only happen in Queensland hey?"

"Did they catch who did it?" Bruce asked.

He smiled to himself despite his ailments.

"I don't think so. Not yet anyway. But they found a car that was stolen from the property."

Of more interest was the good news that Amelia's car had been found abandoned on the North Coast road. *Chalk another one up for The Bruiser*, he crowed to himself, the victory, balm to his wretched condition.

The false trail lain couldn't have worked out better in sending police in the wrong direction. Sore and annoyed by the blabbering passenger, Bruce at least felt his old 'Luck' luck still held him in good stead. The gabby informer rabbited on:

"I wouldn't live in Queensland, myself. They're a wild bunch up there. Heat affects their brains of course. You never know what some maniacs can be capable of."

"No. That's a fact." The Bruiser replied.

Despite feeling unwell, The Bruiser entertained his imagination with dropping a bombshell on the chatty nuisance, by admitting his leading role in the freaky news story. It was a shame in a way that he couldn't do that. The idiot would probably think he was joking anyway.

The irksome talker liked the sound of his own voice and jabbered more:

"Now doesn't it make you wonder? Why would the dogs want to eat human remains? I reckon they might get the taste from commercial dog foods. I mean, you never know what goes into that processed stuff."

With three months having elapsed since he murdered Kirkwood Bonn, Bruce Luck felt himself to be safe from any connection to that crime. Now, speeding away free and clear of Amelia Boole's death as well, he once again revelled in outsmarting the law.

The irritating passenger kept on and on until his captive audience feigned sleep.

28

The Beat Goes On

Three weeks after Kirkwood Bonn's funeral, Alba Jenkins went into the bank to withdraw her fortnightly allowance, and by chance, ran into Dulcy Vestige.

The detective had been meaning to tell Alba that her Christmas rum bottle fingerprints had provided a useful case break through, but until now, had been too busy with work to do so.

With the opportunity at hand, Dulcy suggested they grab a quick cuppa together in cafe.

"I might have coffee and raisin toast. You want the same?" Dulcy asked.

"No thanks. I'll have tea and just plain toast. For some reason coffee has been making me feel sick lately."

"Oh that's no good. But look Alba, I have to thank you for saving that rum bottle. The fingerprints have identified who your hitchhiker actually is."

Alba's eyes widened, she had thought of little except that Kirk man ever since he left.

"And you think he really must have killed the poor person named Kirkwood Bonn?"

"Personally, yes I do. But it is only alleged at this stage." Dulcy replied.

"Alleged?"

"Not absolutely proven. I can say your hitchhiker thief is wanted to assist with our enquiries. As they say. But we're still working on it."

"I can't bear thinking about it. I took that murderer in and all."

Although Alba was beginning to see Dulcy as a friend, she could never admit to what the *and all* entailed. The hitchhiker had been the best sex Alba had known in her life, so it was a great pity to her, that he turned out to be such a bad egg.

The detective had to get back to work but kindly assured Alba she could contact her at anytime for updates or if she had more questions. At the same time, Dulcy hoped Alba did not become a nuisance. She felt sorry for the back-country woman but found Alba to be slow and tiresome. Still, mingling with all sorts of people was unavoidable in her job.

Dulcy told herself the beat must go on.

Bob Bartleigh bobbed up again, continuing his regular visits to Alba. She was glad of the meat he supplied, most of which went to her dogs. The rum was also always welcome, though she'd gone off it lately.

Alba cooked a nice meal of braised steak and vegetables for Bob, who stored the new bottle of rum in her pantry and began to pour from the opened one. Alba put a hand over her glass.

"None for me, thanks Bob."

Alba had for the first time ever, turned down a rum and cola although she put a new can of Coke out for her guest.

"What? No rum and Coke for you? Am I to drink alone then?" Bob exclaimed.

"Just hasn't sat well on my tummy lately. I might just have a cup of herbal tea." Alba said.

Bob had a disquieting thought as he scrutinised his fun partner and noticed minute changes in her bodily appearance. Her face looked rather flushed and fuller too.

"Have you been feeling unwell Alba?"

"I have, to be honest. And you know me, I'm never sick."

"You need to see a doctor." He told her.

"No. It's not that bad. And I hate doctors."

"You at least should go to the health clinic and see the matron. You never know but you might be having some female type of problem. Like your dear mother did. Bless her soul."

"Do you think? That's a worry. Yes. I see. Maybe I'll drop in next time I go to town."

What Bob Bartleigh imagined had nothing to do with what finished the long departed Mrs. Jenkins. He thought Alba might be pregnant. Bob couldn't buy a test kit himself, not without the whole town knowing.

In due course, Alba tested positively pregnant at the women's health clinic. The matron shook her head at the woman's ignorance of her own reproductive system.

"Truly? I am having a baby? Oh my God." Alba didn't know whether to laugh or cry.

A couple of young nurses tittered behind her back:

"She probably doesn't know what caused it. Hee hee hee."

Alba was instructed to attend antenatal classes at the clinic and given a leaflet with some information and the session schedule, which she could not read.

"It is very important that you learn what is going to happen to your body and how to care for your baby, Alba." The matron tried her best to impress the message on the simple woman.

"Have you got a friend or a partner to help you?"

"Not really anyone I could ask."

"Perhaps I will find a case worker to visit you then Alba. How would that do?"

"Thank you." Alba replied politely although she certainly did not want anyone visiting.

The very thought of some nosy home nurse butting in on her privacy appalled her.

Alba thought of asking either Bob or Dulcy to nominate as her partner, just to stop the threatened home visits. In the end, she shied off asking either because it seemed like such a personal problem.

Driving home, Alba cried as she did not know who had fathered her child. Going by the dates the matron explained on a calendar, it could be the murdering hitchhiker's child. Otherwise it could only be old Bob Bartleigh's. But he was married. Oh it was a disaster! Alba wished she could down some rum but even the smell of it now made her retch.

Nothing was sacred in the small town. By the next time Bob called on Alba, he'd heard enough critical whispering on the grapevine to know she must indeed be pregnant.

It came as no surprise to Bob when he copped flack on the domestic front. His skinny wife had not been even slightly amused to hear the scandal:

"I've had to field cheap hints and innuendo that you are the culprit, Bob." His wife cried.

"Me? You know very well I had a vasectomy years ago."

"I do know. And now so does the whole town." She replied caustically.

"Crikey. Is nothing private." Bob exclaimed, taking umbrage.

"You should thank me Bob. Did you know they were taking bets down at the pub? You were the favourite."

"Is that right? Who else were they tipping?"

"Someone in the bank. They reckon Alba often presses her face to the glass doors to catch a glimpse of whoever it is. I reckon on it being that sleazy looking bank manager, myself. And he is a married man as well."

The upshot was, only Bob Bartleigh knew the obvious contender, and he wasn't about to share the information with anyone apart from Alba:

"So Alba. You are going to be a Mum." Bob said mildly and without preamble.

"I am. So they say."

"I have to tell you Alba, my dear, I am not the child's father." Bob said gently.

"How do you know?"

"I had the snip long ago."

"The what?" Alba had no idea what he meant.

"It's like getting neutered but you can still perform the deed but just not make babies."

The information slowly processed through Alba Jenkins' mind: So, not the old married man. It had to be Kirk, the mysterious handsome visitor who emerged from a red dust storm.

Alba decided it was far better being her Kirk because he need never know. Yes. She thought that was much better and could be her own secret forever, until Bob piped up:

"You must have had sex with that stranger Alba. Did you? Did he force you?"

Bob asked the question, not for a moment believing she had been forced. He was giving her a way out to let her save face. Alba took the convenient excuse and ran with it, fibbing:

"Well. I was asleep and he just crept in. You know. At first I thought it was you Bob."

"Of course. That explains it. Oh well these things happen." Bob smiled and shrugged.

He held fond feelings for the silly woman. She'd always done right by him. Bob knew himself to be no prize and counted himself fortunate to have the ongoing affair as a sideline.

Alba felt tremendously relieved to learn Bob didn't mind. Perhaps it would all work out.

Having a handsome, macho and mysterious man father her child, appealed to Alba. The criminal aspect of that donor faded from her memory as she imbued Kirk with desirable qualities, in optimistic fantasies.

Looking forward with happiness and excitement, Alba decided she was going to love having a little baby to look after. She could tell it stories and teach it everything she knew.

29

Can't Trust Anyone

Meanwhile, back at the Calenda Market Gardens, Marcha, July and Nova were busy weighing and packing their melons and pumpkins ready to go to the wholesale distribution centre in the city.

Their work took a little longer than usual, hampered somewhat by a couple of recently acquired farm pups. Following the fright of Kirk's attack on Nova, the girls had gone to the nearby town to check out some young whelps. Unanimously deciding it was high time to populate the farm with dogs again, they called on the old church gardener after hearing his blue cattle bitch had produced a litter. The pups were almost certainly crossbred with dingo blood, he said, and assured them they would make good loyal watch dogs. That was exactly what they wanted. They chose a blue with black ears and a red with brown ears, both speckled like the mother. The old gardener had chatted on about the latest news:

"Did you hear of that man the police are looking for? They reckon he might have stayed at the evacuation centre during the floods. Right here under our very noses!"

"Did he? We think he might be a man who worked at our farm for a while."

"What did you make of him?" The old man asked.

"We didn't get a good impression." Marcha said in understatement.

"Glad to see the back of him." Nova added.

"The CWA ladies thought he was some bloke who called himself Richie. But they liked him a helluva lot. Seemed to think he was the ants pants. A good looker they reckon. Rare in these parts. Ha ha."

"He could lay on the charm if it suited him," July said, "if it's the same man."

On their way home they discussed the news. They had no doubts the Richie fellow at the evacuation centre would have been Nova's attacker who called himself Kirk.

"So Kirk wasn't his real name anyway. Then he changed his name to Richie after he left us. I guess the detective was on to that." Marcha mused. "So we don't need to tell him."

July and Nova agreed. None of them were keen to talk to that grumpy lawman again. As they discussed Kirk or Richie or whoever he was, their transporter arrived in his Isuzu fridge van bearing the distinctive market logo and map of Australia on the side. The van driver, Fred, was agog with startling news he'd just listened to on the radio, on his way in, and he couldn't wait to tell someone.

"Have you heard this girls? Some maniac sheila lured men to her parlour for years and chopped them up for dog food."

"Now there's an idea. We've got two new dogs to feed now." July replied.

Fred gave July an old fashioned look, before going on:

"Well that sheila got murdered anyway. And they're looking for a bloke connected to her death, going under a false name belonging to somebody who turned up dead in the outback. Kirkwood something. Funny name hey. I reckon he did that poor bugger in too."

"What? We had a Kirkwood working here temporarily," July said, "if it's the same man."

"Oh my god! Kirk might have murdered people?" Nova exclaimed.

"To be exact, the Kirk we knew wasn't using his real name." Marcha corrected.

Exchanging troubled expressions, the possibilities of what could have happened, sunk in. They harboured a murderer! Their consternation wasn't lost on the van driver.

"You should tell the police," Fred advised, "in case it is him."

"Reckon they already knew. We had a visit from a detective a while ago." Marcha replied.

"Police were already looking for him." July added.

"We heard Kirk changed his name to Richie and hitchhiked out of the next town." Nova said.

Fred's jaw dropped. *Richie! Cripes.* He robbed a dangerous criminal? While the guy took a shit? Now it was Fred's turn to be dismayed. That bloke Richie had seemed completely harmless apart from being tone deaf. He absolutely murdered Me And Bobby McGee. Subsequently, Fred left Richie busted flat in a far worse place than Baton Rouge. Thank God he dumped him at that bog stop.

"What did you make of that man then?"

Fred asked the sisters the same question the church gardener had done.

"Not much. We didn't like him. Glad to see the back of him to be honest." July replied.

"Why was that?" Fred asked.

"He was untrustworthy." Marcha replied. She conveyed a look to her sisters to keep quiet.

"You can't trust anyone these days." Fred commiserated.

Marcha, hands on hips, fixed Fred with cold accusation in her ice blue eyes:

"That's right Fred. You can't trust anyone. And if our goods come up underweight at market again, we will want to know why."

Fred squirmed. He didn't think the young women would miss the odd box of vegetables and fruits occasionally, but guilt was written all over his face. He said something about shrinkage that didn't wash with the three girls who stared him down until he had to drop his gaze. Marcha had no real proof Fred had been robbing them but went by her gut instincts. His reaction confirmed her suspicions. July and Nova agreed. Fred was guilty as hell.

So this would be the last consignment the old thief would ever get from Calenda Market Gardens. The current lot was sure to come up perfectly correct and all accounted for, now that the van driver had been caught out. Fred knew he deserved to be fired, never dreaming the girls would actually do it. He sorely underestimated Marcha who enforced the clause that voided his contract.

Losing one of his better scams rankled and shrunk Fred's household income, and his nagging wife gave him grief for the lack of produce to sell on her weekend market stall.

30

Brutus

While the Calenda girls adored and played with their new farm pups, another dog's life teetered precariously on the brink of termination.

Mortimer languished depressed and forlorn at the RSPCA shelter. His days were spent hiding his massive head in the bare corner of a concrete walled enclosure.

Having no appetite, and unaccustomed to the cheap dried kibble offered, he lost weight, worsening his unlovely appearance.

The huge ugly scrawny dog did not endear himself for adoption and had no hope of attracting any new owner. He did not respond to voices and shrunk from any attention.

Scheduled to be euthanized as a matter of course, his rescuer, the RSPCA officer, Pamela Burn, opted to spare him at the eleventh hour.

Some workmates advised against taking on such a problem dog, reminding that RSPCA personnel were not supposed to become emotionally involved.

Nevertheless, the woman felt a certain affinity with this particular miserable animal. Pamela felt the ugly dog's despair and hopelessness. She had known those same feelings herself, during and after her failed marriage.

Pamela told her workmates a lie, claiming she was not emotionally involved but just being practical. Her parents had retired to the city and she'd taken over their property. She considered this inmate would make a good watch dog.

Privately Pamela had her fingers crossed, praying the ugly dog would work out well.

The dog understood death and having mourned over Amelia's body, knew his beloved first owner could never come back to him.

Head and tail down, Mortimer meekly allowed himself to be loaded into Pamela's van. Having no microchip or any clue to the dog's original name, Mortimer was renamed Brutus.

On first being released in the green acres of his new home, the dog just stood, blinked and heaved a sigh. It seemed he had no will to live.

It took Pamela three whole weeks of patient perseverance to bring Amelia's dog out of depression and begin to regain self confidence.

Pamela addressed him as Brutus often and always when offering food, so he responded to the new name. It might have helped if his original name had been known.

Slowly but surely Brutus transferred his loyal devotion to his rescuer. Free to roam wide paddocks and sleep in a comfortable bed, Brutus aka Mortimer enjoyed a new lease on life.

It became apparent that Brutus disliked most men but was trustworthy with women. Pamela was okay with that. She had suffered domestic violence at the hands of an abusive partner in the past, an ordeal ending in divorce.

Pamela Burn's beauty was limited to a kind heart and caring nature. A pock marked face and rodent-like overbite vied for worst feature with her crooked nose. She defied a bad hair life by shaving her head, and dying the stubble in green and magenta polka dots.

Brutus and Pamela understood each other.

The plain woman was smart enough to realise her main attraction to men lay in her potential to inherit valuable family property.

Nevertheless, Pamela fell in love and been grateful for a marriage proposal. Keen for motherhood, she prepared to give it her best shot.

Sadly, her husband soon defaulted to his misogynistic nature. Pamela became thankful no pregnancy resulted from their union, as she no longer wanted children by him.

Although Pamela had brought more to the marriage than her spouse had, he had considered his assets were all his, and hers should be all his as well.

The poor excuse for a man even objected to his wife having her own bank account that he could not access. He was unable to prevent his wife having that modicum of privacy and independence, so bled her income by refusing to contribute to necessary household expenses.

Any new purchase made for herself, without his consent, angered him.

After most disagreements, Pamela would find some item of hers broken. He favoured breaking off windshield wipers, which could be blamed on hoons. Damaged shoes and handbags in her wardrobe, however, could only be attributed to his fits of retribution.

Averse to failure and aware of her own shortcomings in the looks department, the abused woman worked at saving the disappointing marriage. Pamela's good intentions turned against her as the situation became intolerable.

The first time her husband punched her, Pamela retaliated. Unable to get out of a dinner scheduled that night with friends, she let everyone know he had struck her.

A true coward, her partner denied it and made it seem like a joke. He was a popular character and everyone laughed thinking the couple were pulling their legs over an accidental broken nose.

The second time, careful not to leave evidence, he only slapped her face, but hard. The red mark faded before she could show it to anyone.

Pamela felt that a third time would not end well. She reported his physical attacks to police. Although the law did nothing, at least her husband's violent actions were on file.

The RSPCA officer almost wished her ex would show up again to meet her big new dog.

When Pamela Burn learnt of the dog's macabre diet in his previous home, she did not blame Brutus for it. The experienced handler knew dogs. As carnivores, canines instinctively relished raw meat as a main source of protein needed for survival. With no other choice, Pamela reasoned Amelia Boole's dog accepted what he trusted his owner to feed him.

Some concerned people, including her own vet, advised that her chosen dog could never be trusted, having gained 'the taste'. Fortunately time proved them all wrong.

In his new home, Brutus still enjoyed a diet containing plenty of raw meat and bones, just not the human kind. Pamela varied his diet to cover prey species likely for a big dog in the wild, finding he had a preference for kangaroo and lamb.

Introduced to fetching a ball to keep him fit, Brutus satisfied a natural urge to chase and hunt. The playful activity was new to him, but he took to it joyfully.

Pamela Burn had a guilty secret: She hoped all the men eaten by her big ugly dog, had been guilty of domestic violence.

31

Not Our Boy

Before Mortimer became known as Brutus, Amelia's killer embarked on the last leg of his journey, heading for Adelaide in South Australia.

Feeling very unwell, the man longed to get home. His condition and symptoms worsened significantly before the train reached its destination.

Bruce Luck began to perspire profusely as spasms racked his jaw and neck. Gripping seizures lasted for minutes at a time, forcing grimaces of agony. Gluey strings of spittle dribbled from froth forming in the corners of his mouth. He could do nothing about it.

The talkative person who'd sat beside Bruce, vacated the seat in haste when he noticed the man appeared terribly sick. Fearing the affliction could be contagious, the once amiable chatty passenger called out along the carriage to ask if there were a doctor on board.

A retired nursing matron who answered the call, acknowledged Bruce's distress and assessed him. The elderly nurse noted healed over claw marks on the man's face. The able lady thought she recognised Bruce's affliction but had never actually seen a case before. Clinical interest went hand in hand with dire concerns she held for a happy outcome.

"Young man. Listen to me. You are very ill. I am a nurse not a doctor but I believe you must go into hospital as soon as possible. Can you tell me your name?"

"Br. Br. Bruce." He mumbled.

"Bruce?"

"No. Not Bruce. Boris." The Bruiser caught his own mistake.

"Okay Boris. I will take the responsibility of ringing ahead for an ambulance to meet the train. It is not up to me to diagnose anything but I will describe your state to the medical staff. Is that alright with you?"

"Th...thanks. Yes." Bruce managed the words in a lull between spasms.

"Have you cut yourself anywhere? Had any animal bites?"

"Dog...ankle." He groaned.

Rolling his sock down, the nurse saw what she suspected as tetanus infection, otherwise known as lock jaw, judging by his classic symptoms. The man's ankle had a recent deep laceration surrounded by angry reddened flesh. The nurse tried to learn more about the man:

"What is your surname Boris?" The good nurse asked.

"Um. Er. Br..no..Rich...no...um Boris. Yes that's it. Boris."

"Yes Boris. I know Boris is your first name. But can you tell me your last name?"

"I'm lucky. The good old....you know...whatsit."

"Boris Lucky?"

"Nope. His luck ran out."

The Bruiser became incoherent, addled with distress as cramping progressed down his back, he could no longer think straight.

The nurse took note of the man's confusion but it seemed quite understandable in the circumstances. She made sure his luggage, one airline bag, went with him in the ambulance and told the attendants his name was Boris something or other.

Despite being hot with fever, the patient objected to having his denim jerkin removed. Rather than upset the man more, the heavy jacket stayed on. They understood it probably held his valuables.

A doctor anaesthetised the patient as initial treatment for painful muscle spasms. After Bruce succumbed to sedation, hospital staff removed his clothing. Finding Boris Larssen's ID in his pocket, Bruce Luck was formally admitted to hospital under Larssen's name.

Valuables including the money, wedding ring, gold cross and chain were duly itemised and stored safely, along with Boris Larssen's drivers licence.

The ankle bite wound was cleaned out and the sweaty unconscious man given a sponge bath. A nurse wrote 'rash penis' on his chart, having no idea of the apt double entendre.

Older wounds to his face, delivered by Nova's double pronged hay tool, were assessed as claw marks possibly inflicted by the dog that bit him, or some other animal.

Doctors confirmed the nurse's first suspicions and administered antitoxin and antibiotics. Symptomatic spasms could be treated with medications that could also clear up his penal infection. While it is possible to survive tetanus, there is no cure.

Childhood neglect left Bruce Luck susceptible to every preventable disease as he had never been vaccinated. The legacy of bad parents came to be bestowed upon him, escalated by his own hostility to decent social conventions. His breathing faltered. Ventilation support failed to sustain life. It was too little too late.

Bruce Luck aka The Bruiser, died before reaching his thirty-second birthday.

So ended a useless and misguided life of crime. The body went to the morgue tagged as Boris Larssen late of Canberra ACT.

Searches disclosed that a Boris Larssen had been reported as a missing person, by his parents. However, nothing had been done on the case for three years.

Officers visited the Canberra address on Boris Larssen's driving licence. That man's parent's still resided there and were bereft at being informed of their son's passing.

"But Boris was vaccinated. How could he die of tetanus?"

The Larssen parents wanted to see their son for the last time. This suited authorities who needed the body to be positively identified to sign off on the paperwork.

The old couple flew down to Adelaide and arrived to view the deceased man. Firstly, an officer showed them the gold cross and chain, the gold wedding ring and the pocket knife bearing initials BL to see if they recognised the items.

"We gave him that gold crucifix on his twenty-first birthday." Mrs. Larssen sobbed. "It's engraved on the back: *Love Mum & Dad*."

The officer checked and saw the gold cross was so engraved, as the mother claimed.

"But is this a wedding ring? We did not know Boris had married." Mr. Larssen added.

"How about the pocket knife?"

"I don't remember it. Although it looks quite old."

"No. I don't remember the knife. I never knew Boris to carry a knife."

The traumatised parents clung to each other in dreadful anticipation as the sheet was removed and the face uncovered. Nothing was said for ten fraught seconds of silence.

Mrs. Larssen almost collapsed but her husband held her up. Suddenly, both spoke at once:

"That is not our boy."

"It isn't Boris." They cried.

The presiding officers were taken aback. Identifying the body seemed only a formality.

"Are you sure? He may look different....this way."

"Of course we are sure. We know our own son."

"Boris has a birthmark across his lower face. It is why he grew a beard as soon as he was old enough."

"True. And he never wanted to shave it off. It is why he argued with his fiance."

"She was studying psychology and said it would do him good to face the world and show his birthmark. Otherwise he was hiding from reality. The uppity...b...thing."

"Now now. That is over now."

"Even if he changed a lot in four years, this poor person is definitely not our boy."

"But may God rest his soul whoever he is."

Tears were shed in emotional relief. The residing coroner had to believe the parents.

The inconvenient result meant the body became a John Doe, however, fingerprinting and DNA analysis would spearhead attempts to verify the deceased.

"I knew Boris should not get tetanus, he was vaccinated and he had that booster the time he stood on a rusty nail. Remember dear? That was not long before he went away."

"Yes, and the antibodies were supposed to be good for ten years."

It was not all good news. The Larssens were again captive to the waiting game. Not knowing what had become of their son was the worst torture and it aged them prematurely.

Certain their son would never pawn the gold crucifix, it occurred that the dead man could have stolen it. Afraid to tempt fate, they shied away from discussing any possibility that Boris met with foul play. Yet in their heart of hearts, hope faded that Boris might still be alive. Neither parent expected to ever see their boy again.

The gold chain and crucifix were given to the Larssens. However, the substantial amount of cash and other items were withheld pending further investigation.

Fingerprints taken from the alleged Boris Larssen corpse, turned up a match on the system with the wanted man: Bruce Luck. Detectives Grimslade and Vestige were duly informed.

"So not eaten by the dog." Dulcy commented.

"But the dog killed him in the long run." Dougall said.

"Karma?"

"Tetanus."

32

Brothers

Dulcy Vestige made sure to inform Damien Cresswick of latest events before he perceived any inkling from media.

"It might be cold comfort but I can confirm Kirkwood Bonn's killer has died." Dulcy said.

Damien's feelings were mixed. He attempted a rational reply as his head reeled.

"Oh. God. I do appreciate being told. Thanks for making the time. What happened?"

"He contracted tetanus after being bitten by a dog. We believe he also murdered the dog's female owner. Perhaps you've seen the horrific story?"

"Not the woman who slaughtered men to feed her dogs? It was hard not to see that. It was all over everything."

Dulcy nodded: "That's the one. We found Kirkwood's ID at the scene. That gave us the definite link."

Damien had to sit down. Dulcy fetched a glass of water for him as the news hit home.

"And I saw something about a wanted man. Was he the person of interest named as somebody Luck?" Damien asked.

"Yes. Bruce Luck. We firmly believe he is our culprit. Almost a shame he will never face court. Though perhaps he was justly punished by the awful way he met his death."

Damien believed no amount of punishment made up for killing Kirkwood. He could only offer a compromise:

"Perhaps. At least he can't hurt anyone else now."

"Thankfully. At least there is that, when all is said and done. Even given a long prison sentence, Bruce Luck might have been released eventually." Dulcy added.

"It might sound savage, but I still feel he got off lightly." Damien admitted.

"I fully understand. I would feel the same." Dulcy commiserated.

Damien had a niggling feeling he had seen the name Luck somewhere, even before the sensational news story came to public notice.

"For some reason the name Luck rings a bell. I've been wracking my brain to place it."

"Sometimes when you hear a name mentioned often enough, it feels like you've known it."

"Maybe." Damien was not convinced.

Damien had been about to make lunch and invited Dulcy to share a sandwich and cup of coffee. He took the opportunity to credit the good work done by the detectives:

"I really must acknowledge the exceptional job you and the force have done on this case."

"Thanks Damien. It doesn't bring Kirkwood back but I hope it helps with closure. The memorial funeral was amazing by the way. He touched so many people."

Damien looked surprised as he hadn't seen Dulcy there.

"Were you at the funeral Dulcy? Sorry I can't recall. There were so many well wishers there. I hope I thanked you at the time." He said.

"That's ok. You wouldn't have seen me. I was standing up at the back. Then I saw a woman I'd interviewed right back at the beginning of the missing person case. She left at the end of the service so I followed her out. You see, she would have had to travel a long way and stay overnight so I was curious about her attendance."

"Oh? Did this woman know Kirkwood?"

"No. That's the issue. She thought she did and was confused by events."

Dulcy didn't want to mention the ghost story but had to offer some explanation:

"You already know Kirkwood's ID had been stolen. A man calling himself Kirk arrived out of the blue and asked for water at the woman's isolated homestead. She felt obliged to put this stranger up at her house overnight because he was on foot and miles from anywhere. So, when the funeral notice for Kirkwood came out in the newspaper, the woman thought he had been the stranger she took in."

Damien digested the implication.

"But that stranger must have been Kirkwood's killer?" Damien asked.

"Yes. And by the way I must tell you, that led to getting Bruce Luck's fingerprints."

"How so?"

"I had an informal chat with the woman after the funeral and found out the man had handled a rum bottle that could still have his prints. And it did of course. It was an absolute fluke."

Damien topped up Dulcy's coffee and congratulated her again on her persistence.

"Kirkwood didn't even drink rum or any alcohol at all." Damien added as an aside.

"Well, we know it wasn't Kirkwood the woman helped anyway. Between you and me, this woman is mentally challenged. Actually very slow. To put it bluntly, as thick as two short planks. She was upset and confused about Kirkwood because she liked the stranger she took in. Only later she found out he had robbed her."

"Oh my goodness. The woman was lucky he only robbed her."

"Exactly what I told her. So that's what led to the chat about the rum bottle with his fingerprints."

"Does she still think it was Kirkwood?"

"Oh no. I explained to her that it was a bad man who only pretended to be Kirkwood. She was happy to help catch him. I followed her home, and she gave me the rum bottle."

The detective's visit and news brought the subject back to the forefront of Damien's mind. Puzzling over where he'd seen the name Luck as he went to bed, had his brain churn up a latent clue while he slept.

Damien awoke in the witching hour with a start and a sudden recollection.

Rolling out of bed, he went into Kirkwood's den and retrieved that brown envelope with info on his partner's birth origins. Quickly he scanned the letter and the name Luck jumped out from the page. Aha! He knew he'd seen it somewhere.

Damien read the letter more slowly, taking in the gist. Kirkwood had already learnt his birth mother's name was Greta Vossberg. Knowing he might have to drive around chasing up obscure clues, Kirkwood treated the Adelaide journey as a camping trip. Damien opted to stay behind to keep their business operating, a decision he would always regret. Now, in the dead of night, Damien scrolled through Kirkwood's data.

Kirkwood updated a diary on his computer from time to time. Damien read he had found a distant Vossberg relative through social media. Soon Damien accessed that thread.

The Vossberg second cousin in South Australia had purportedly been out of touch with Greta for years but told Kirkwood she had an idea Greta had gone to live in Coober Pedy.

Subsequently, Kirkwood followed the thin trail to the opal mining town with the thought that with a population less than 1500, he had a good chance of finding his natural blood mother, yet with no idea what he would say to her if she were found.

What Kirkwood didn't know was that his birth mother did not want to see him. Greta Vossberg had dreaded either of her sons ever finding her. She asked that the young man be given a bum steer, with some long winded story to justify it.

So the Vossberg contact suggested Greta might have moved to the opal mining town, a vague hint with no foundation in truth, just to put Kirkwood off and send him far away.

The small town of Coober Pedy, known for its underground homes dug out in caves, sits on the edge of the Stuart Ranges. Being approximately halfway between Adelaide and Alice Springs, the location at least wasn't far too off Kirkwood's way home.

He had been sorely disappointed in finding no trace of his birth mother and Damien relived the disappointment shared with Kirkwood, in sorrow.

Reading the latest information, within the brown envelope, Damien discovered that Greta Vossberg was not an unmarried mother when Kirkwood was born, as they had assumed. Her married name had been Luck.

Archives showed Greta had born another son seven years prior to having Kirkwood. For some inexplicable reason, she had reverted to her maiden name at the Catholic home where her second child had been put up for adoption.

Further research took Damien away from his work for the next several days. The shocker emerged that Kirkwood's older sibling had been named Bruce. *Bruce Luck!*

The name Bruce Luck smote a stinging slap across Damien's face. Chilled to the core, Damien had to know if Kirkwood had been murdered by his own blood brother.

Damien got straight onto Dulcy Vestige to ask if greater access to records might be sourced through police channels. He told Dulcy he had Kirkwood's DNA analysis on hand and asked if it might be matched to the that of the deceased, Bruce Luck.

Dulcy phoned Dougall Grimslade: "You're never going to believe this..." she began.

In time, Damien received the dreaded phone call:

"Damien. Dulcy here. Pathology had already extracted Bruce Luck's DNA to identify any link to the previous man-eating dog case. And yes.

It confirms a very close match for Kirkwood's. They were almost certain-ly full brothers."

"My God. This is not the outcome I hoped for. How could this be? Do you think Kirkwood was stalked by Bruce Luck on purpose?" Damien exclaimed. "Maybe out of jealousy. Or was he afraid he'd inherit a share of his own entitlement?"

"I thought of that. But since Kirkwood was legally adopted as the Bonn's son, he would not be eligible to inherit from the Luck estate. From what I can gather, Bruce Luck had no idea he had a brother. He couldn't have known Kirkwood existed." Dulcy explained.

Grimslade agreed the coincidence seemed improbable. Yet there it was. They delved into it as far as possible but every incursion returned the same assumption: Bruce Luck had unknowingly killed his own blood brother, his younger sibling named Kirkwood Bonn.

Dulcy added:

"And there is no record of Greta ever trying to contact her children or husband, Dougall."

"So she is the Greta the old man ranted over, saying you couldn't trust either of them."

"Of course. The mother. Not the girlfriend. No love lost there either."

The coincidence seemed too unlikely. Damien held onto his scepti-cism:

"Are you sure? I have trouble getting my head around it."

"Damien, we have turned this inside out. This is what I know: Their mother, Greta, abandoned her first born, Bruce, before he turned seven. She went back to her maiden name of Vossberg and gave birth to her second son in a home for single mothers and immediately signed him over for adoption. As you know, the Bonn's adopted the boy and named him Kirkwood."

"Okay." Damien accepted it for the time being. "I can only add that Kirkwood didn't know he had been adopted until later in life. However, he came to be relieved that the Bonns were not his genetic parents. Long story. Kirkwood's adoptive parents were notably absent from his funeral by the way. Although they had been informed in plenty of time."

Dulcy theorised homosexuality would be a factor. Privately, she attributed the tragedy of both brothers to two sets of failed parents. Damien had seemed the only happy connection in Kirkwood's short life.

As for Bruce Luck, who knew how he might have turned out, given a stable childhood. Dulcy doubted if anyone was actually born bad but knew better than to offer any excuses for murderous behaviour to Damien. Dulcy continued:

"In any case, Greta seemed careful not to leave any clues to her whereabouts. We don't know if her husband looked for her but if so, it is assumed he couldn't find her and never knew a second child existed."

"Yes. I can see that. It had been a long road even for Kirkwood to find anything about his birth mother." Damien concurred.

"Admittedly, it is a very odd. A strange twist of fate."

"It is more than strange to me. I find it haunting." Damien concluded.

Bruce Luck's DNA had also been separated from Amelia Boole's body, confirming he definitely had sexual intercourse with that woman. Due to the knife attack, it was believed he had committed rape before the murder.

In wrapping up the case, the stash of money and the BL pocketknife were given to Bruce Luck's father, the senior Bruce Luck. The old man used the unexpected windfall to binge on rich foods, cigarettes and strong alcohol, bought at his request by his doting day care nurse. Those excesses killed him inside of six months.

The neglectful cold hearted mother, Greta Luck nee Vossberg, successfully contested her husband's will and was granted unencumbered ownership of the nice house in suburban Adelaide.

The elder Bruce Luck had willed everything to his devoted home help, who fully expected to benefit after all the extra services she'd provided. The entire episode left her with a bad taste in her mouth, nevertheless, she sought another well heeled lone old man as her next patient.

Greta's claim held enough truth to be validated. Her plea of being in an abusive relationship held and was indeed true. Authorities deemed leaving the marital home was understandable and noted the woman had fled, penniless.

Greta emerged as the victim, saying her destitution and homelessness forced her to leave her son, Bruce, with his father. Circumstances prevented attempts at gaining custody and her low esteem as a mother subsequently had her put a second child up for adoption.

Greta Vossberg turned the house into a suburban brothel. It became particularly convenient working from home during the pandemic.

33

Alba's Baby

Concerned that Alba Jenkins might fear the killer hitchhiker returning someday, Dulcy Vestige took time out to let her know that man had died.

On hearing the news, Alba seemed to go into a trance, staring off into the distance, a dreamy smile on her face. Dulcy was not easily unnerved, but she felt disturbed by the slow woman's unusual reaction.

"Alba, did you hear what I said?" Dulcy asked gently.

"Yes and thank you for letting me know. Now I know my baby is extra special."

That garbled response confirmed what Dulcy suspected all along: Since Alba apparently believed herself to be pregnant to the killer, she had definitely taken Kirkwood's impostor to her bed. Dulcy privately congratulation herself on her own accurate intuition at the time.

"Are you sure about being pregnant to that man, Alba?"

"Oh yes. I have been to the clinic. They worked it out on a calendar. He is the only one it could be. Old Bob agrees because he had...um...anyway the traveller is the only one it could be." Alba tripped a little on her words. Dulcy did not miss her near slip.

"What will you do Alba?"

"Do? Well the clinic are telling me what I will need to do."

"Are you happy about the baby Alba?"

"Oh I am. Very happy. I can't wait." Alba hugged her expanding waistline.

To Dulcy's amazement, the simple woman managed a positive twist to her predicament.

Learning her hitchhiker had died, Alba fantasied angels took him to live in the forever after, in heaven, once he had accomplished his very special mission at her lonely homestead.

The handsome stranger calling himself Kirk evolved in Alba's memory to embody a plundering pirate, a swashbuckling rogue. Nevermind that he had robbed her and probably killed someone, it only added to his adventuresome mystique.

In her simple mind, Alba entertained the romantic notion that 'her Kirk' had been mysteriously ordained to drift into her life, amid a cloud of red dust, leaving her with a precious baby to love. She imagined herself to be especially chosen for the mysterious role of motherhood, and coyly let Dulcy in on the secret.

Alba's account, related seriously, left the pragmatic detective speechless. Dulcy Vestige did not deign to discourage Alba's beliefs. If Alba's dreamy ideas were coping mechanisms against aversions to the child she carried, such delusions served her well.

High blood pressure towards the final months of pregnancy, meant Alba had to be admitted into hospital early, to monitor risks to both the mother and baby.

Bob Bartleigh moved into Alba's house temporarily to take care of the dogs, chooks and to keep the house appearing occupied against squatters.

He brought an old cot and highchair down from the attic and cleaned them up. The baby furniture had been hand-made for Alba by her father, before she was born.

During her months in waiting, Alba had opened an old trunk of her own old baby clothes and rugs that had been carefully packed in camphor by her own mother. For the age of the items, all were in remarkably good and usable condition.

Alba lovingly hand washed everything and pegged the tiny garments and bunny rugs on the clothesline to air in sunshine. Seeing the little outfits fluttering in the breeze, had made the imminent arrival very real and even more exciting.

Alba imagined 'her Kirk' admiring the preparations. In her minds eye, the child's father stood amongst fluffy white clouds, sometimes proudly holding a sceptre and wearing an ermine fur across his shoulder. Other times he just donned his wide brimmed hat and gave her a wink, as he did when they'd parted at the bus depot. That seemed a lifetime ago now.

In other preparations, the baby clinic recommended disposable nappies. Alba pretended to heed their advice but instead, opted for towelling ones. Bob agreed, saying disposal would be a problem since they could expect to use around a dozen a day.

Prior to the birth, while Bob stayed in the Jenkins place for three weeks, his skinny wife cleaned out their joint bank account, hired a moving van and shifted everything of value from their home.

Bob's frequent absences allowed plenty of opportunity for his wife to pursue a torrid affair with a local used car salesman. The amorous couple absconded joyfully to relocate in Cairns, leaving no forwarding address.

Bob only found out his wife had left him when he returned to his almost bare house. A neighbour told him there had been a large removal van in the driveway for most of one day.

At first Bob thought they'd been robbed and reported it to police. When his debit card was declined for having insufficient funds, he finally twigged: His skinny wife had outfoxed him at his own game of deceit.

Bob might have laughed at the irony. But he did not.

Alba gave birth to a small but healthy baby boy close to the estimated due date. Beguiled by her romantic idealised version of his conception, she insisted on naming her son Kirk.

By the time Alba returned home with the newborn Bob Bartleigh had moved what scanty possessions he still owned, into her large farmhouse.

In the long run, the cohabitation worked out well. The man was always on hand to help out and more than pulled his own weight.

So it came to pass that Bob Bartleigh, who had made a useful convenience of the slow-witted landowner, became a surrogate parent and father figure for her illegitimate son.

Between Alba and Bob, they had no experience of a new baby in the house, but somehow fumbled by, managing to raise the boy with little mishap. Although underweight for his age, the child thrived.

Bob revelled in having a boy to raise. He took his role as guardian seriously. Against Alba's better judgement, Bob made sure the child started primary school at the proper age and kept attending regularly through to finishing high school.

Kirk Jenkins' amiable nature won friends. He proved to be clever, studious and disciplined. Blessed with an enquiring mind, Alba's son enjoyed learning and did well.

Neither Alba nor Bob proved much use in helping young Kirk with school homework. Most times, the smart student kindly humoured their efforts, only to apply corrections in secret later.

A sentient being, the lad benefited from greater intelligence then the sum of his genes could have thrown out, in the roll of the genetic dice.

Bruce Luck's mother Greta was never to know her eldest had sown that wild oat, whose existence made her a grandmother. She'd have been horrified.

34

Eighteen Years Later...

Tropical Cyclone Kirrily affected East Australia and the Northern Territory in the early months of 2024, lasting for three and a half weeks.

As the rain poured down and drummed on the iron farmhouse roof, the three adult Calenda sisters chatted over morning tea, around the familiar and well worn kitchen table. They reflected on events that had shaped their lives since Cyclone Larry flooded the farm in 2006:

Four years after The Bruiser, masquerading as Kirk, fled the farm, Nova reached her nineteenth year. She become enraptured with a budding agricultural student, who signed on to undergo six weeks work experience at Calenda Market Gardens.

Nova's beau, Alec, an outgoing trendy dresser, could and would expound on a variety of subjects. He liked holding the floor and hearing the sound of his own vice. More than once, the scholarly Marcha bit her tongue on calling him out on points of accuracy, not wishing to burst Nova's bubble of happiness.

Other temporary male workers shared the quarters at the time, but Nova only had eyes for Alec, who seemed to her, very sharp and worldly wise.

Although Nova reached maturity with no lasting trauma from being set upon at fifteen years old, Marcha and July remained protective. They would never forget the horror of the attack on their innocent young sister.

For Nova's sake, her older sisters broke their own stringent rule by allowing Alec to stay in the farmhouse. Comfortably billeted, the uni student remained for a further three months.

Marcha and July regretted letting Alec into their home. They'd expected the novelty of his presence would wear thin for Nova long before his initial six weeks duty had expired.

Thankfully, Alec outstayed his welcome by voicing ambitious plans to re-develop Calenda Market Gardens to his own plans. Perhaps he assumed taking Nova came with entitlements, though he had never hinted at marriage.

They'd all just finished a meal in the kitchen when Alec gave them further benefit of his sterling wisdom. The three sisters listened politely but dismissed his favourite suggestion of replacing their drip irrigation with an automatic overhead system. Alec demanded to know one good reason why they rejected his idea.

"Downy mildew." Marcha clipped in reply.

"Cucurbits." July expanded the reason.

"Three generations of experience." Nova offered with a frown to Alec.

Alec was put out. He muttered something inadvisable about the female mind not being wired to process scientific innovations. He'd have dropped dead on the spot if looks could kill. The sisters silently stared daggers at the student. Marcha and July resisted calling him an opinionated upstart but only out of respect for Nova's feelings.

Alec felt a cooling undercurrent yet did not possess the nous to shut up or concede defeat. Instead, he attempted to change the subject:

"Why must you all persevere with the old fashioned braided hair? I mean it has a certain country charm but surely you'd do better to be more individual. You look like clones, dare I say?"

"Have you missed your true calling Alec?" July hooted.

"Are you a hairdresser at heart?" Marcha toned in a quiet and precise reply, which might have warned Alec to lay off. Yet it did not.

"Just saying. Have you even seen any modern styles?" Alec laughed scornfully.

"We're happy. Why does it bother you?" Nova added, bristling at last.

Alec took offence at being ticked off by his girlfriend. He dug himself deeper:

"Furthermore, is it actually hygienic to be doing your hair in the kitchen? Or for that matter, allowing animals in the kitchen?"

As Alec's voice rose an octave on the final word, Nova suddenly recognised a whiner.

"Foot in mouth disease." uly declared into the chilled atmosphere.

"Foot AND mouth disease." Alec contradicted too quickly, a split instant before he twigged to the put down.

"Rare on a farm with no cloven hoofed animals, Alec." Nova snapped.

Alec pontificated that sarcasm was the lowest form of wit. Marcha and July tactfully vacated the kitchen so Nova could indulge in a ding dong row with her boyfriend. Alec warned her she was destined to end up an old maid like her sisters, if she wasn't careful.

That hit the final nail in the coffin. Nova's attraction to Alec shrivelled and died as she saw his true colours and ulterior motives.

Marcha and July breathed deep sighs of relief when Nova sent Alec packing, forthwith.

The family of three independent females had all resented the student's presumptions and his uncalled for opinions.

Nova knew she'd escaped a bullet. Alec would have been an overbearing and controlling life partner or husband, had they married.

By the time Severe Tropical Cyclone Kirrily visited, enough years had passed for the 'Smart Alec' episode to no longer be taboo for discussion. Nova had gained her thirty-third year and had long ago written Alec off as a misguided youthful error.

Kirrily brought welcomed rain that cooled the house and freshened the air. Half a dozen slumbering dogs and cats shared the warm and cosy ambience in the farmhouse kitchen. Marcha carefully stepped over two furry bodies as she took a fresh batch of raisin scones from the oven for the morning tea break. The tight knit trio of Calenda sisters remained happily single and content as they listened to rain lashing against the windows. Tea was poured and hot buttered scones slathered with home-made fig jam while conversation replayed over reminisces:

"This reminds me of that time we thought we'd drowned Nova's attacker." July said.

"I was just thinking the exact same thing." Marcha marvelled.

"That damned Kirk seemed so nice at first. You can never tell." Nova added.

"Are you thinking of your Smart Alec now?" July asked gently.

"Yes he did come to mind. As I said, you can never tell. Live and learn." Nova shrugged.

"Plenty more fish in the sea little sister." Marcha remarked matter-of-factly.

"Yep. Just kiss the tempting ones and throw them back. That's my motto." July laughed.

"Perhaps it should be our family motto." Nova replied.

Marcha thought about a family motto:

"Yes maybe so. We could make up a logo for Calenda Market Gardens. I see some fancy script in Latin on a family crest." She daydreamed how it might be.

"You'd have to pick Latin." Nova rolled her eyes.

"Dictum Factum?" July suggested.

"Do you actually know what that means July?" Marcha asked.

"Nope, but it sounds really appropriate. Dictum Factum has a ring to it."

Nova spluttered a mouthful of tea across the table and their sudden loud shrieks of mirth startled the dogs into barking and the cats spitting. Marcha, whose interest in Latin sayings prevailed, translated:

"Dictum Factum means: What is said is done."

"And it is said and done." July laughed. "I stand by my suggestion."

"Do you think we share the same warped sense of humour?" Nova asked, wiping tears of laughter from her eyes.

"Ipso Facto." Marcha replied. "By the fact itself."

"Here's to us. The old maids." Nova toasted.

Forever pedantic, Marcha amended that:

"Not exactly old and not exactly maids. Though Tempus Fugit."

"Yeah. That's what I reckon too. Tempus Fugit. Then throw it back."
July enjoyed her own Latin interpretations.

"Tempus Fugit - Time flies." Marcha translated.

"When you're having fun." Nova added.

Happy with their lot, the sisters drank to having fun while all the pets resettled around the warm stove.

Meanwhile, in the Northern Territory: Damien Cresswick had endured alone in the long grey eighteen-year aftermath of losing his beloved Kirkwood.

Singly running The Brilliant Health Clinic and Wellness Centre had kept Damien sane, but after his partner's demise, the light and enthusiasm had gone out it for Damien. The enterprise started so enthusiastically with the pair as a team, waned ever more over the years. Increasingly bored and dissatisfied with his venture and chosen career path, the lonesome man felt himself sinking, mentally and financially.

Damien made a supreme effort to rally himself out of chronic depression. He imagined Kirkwood giving him a pep talk, telling him he must never give up.

"Alright just for you Kirkwood. I will make a last ditch attempt at making changes. If I fail, I will pack it in." Damien meant the whispered promise.

Having read about crystal therapy being a popular alternative medicine practice, Damien looked into incorporating the novelty into his business. Although, the belief that any gems, such as semi-precious stones had healing powers, he considered to be complete balderdash. Yet crystal therapy drew custom where the desperate and the gullible clutched at straws. Damien justified offering the method of relaxation by the fact that positive vibes, even from a placebo effect, could benefit people. Furthermore, he had not heard of anyone ever being harmed by it.

"What say you Kirkwood? If it doesn't cure them, it won't kill them at least? My thoughts exactly." Whispered Damien, aware he should stop thinking aloud, though he was alone.

So Damien went ahead and incorporated crystal therapy as an alternative to traditional care offered at The Brilliant Health Clinic and Wellness Centre.

Two conventional treatment rooms gained water features and softer lighting. A collection of opals, agates, amethysts and quartz gems decorated a front window display, beside a placard purporting alleged benefits of crystal therapy. Ethically, since Damien knew there to be no scientific proof, he included a disclaimer in smaller print at the bottom of the promotional spiel.

Apparently no one read the small print or took any notice of it. Damien's health clinic enjoyed a trendy revival with an influx of eager customers seeking the mysterious but dubious benefits of crystal therapy.

The business bank balance grew healthier as no further overheads had to be added and the gem stones used in crystal therapy, were reusable.

A local hobbyist who made jewellery incorporating gemstones, asked to display her wares in the reception area. Damien agreed to take fifteen percent on any sales. The glass display cabinet enhanced the waiting room that previously relied on an antique hat stand and potted plant as points of interest.

For crystal therapy sessions, Damien changed from wearing his usual pristine white clinic coat. Instead, he self consciously donned a long batik printed kaftan. A local newspaper blurb described him as a new age guru. Adding to his bemusement, that free advertisement generated even more custom and income.

Damien knew Kirkwood would have chuckled over the crystal therapy phenomenon and probably labelled it bling hoodoo. Remembering their shared sense of values and humour, Damien smiled.

Still, every reminder of Kirkwood sobered Damien's day, despite it being eighteen years since the loss.

Rushed off his feet with avid demand for crystal therapy, Damien decided it was time to take on a junior as a general dogsbody assistant. As it stood, alone, he had to close the front doors to prevent interruptions while treating clients.

A small classified advertisement in the local rag simply asked for well presented juniors interested in assisting at The Brilliant Health Clinic and Wellness Centre, to apply in person at 7am the following Saturday.

The early start allowed two and a half hours before the first customer appointment. Damien miscalculated it to be ample time for job interviews, if indeed anyone showed up at all.

Damien awoke on the interview morning with an old feeling of regret, it was not only his own forty-second birthday but would also have been Kirkwood's, had his loved one and soul mate survived past twenty-four years old.

"Happy heavenly birthday Kirkwood. Here's me leaping energetically out of bed to see if anyone applied for the job." Damien yawned and dragged himself to the bathroom.

In astonishment, Damien found that the job vacancy ad attracted a room full of applicants, many more than anticipated. No fewer than nine young hopefuls sat or stood in a row in Damien's waiting room. His eyes skimmed over them in a blur, as he poked his head around the office door.

Overwhelmed, he told the group he would interview each in turn but give them a general warts and all idea of the position, in case anyone chose to back out.

Obviously so many single interviews would take too much time. If they all chose to compete for the job, some would need to be rescheduled, as he had appointments booked starting at 9.30am.

Damien addressed the group:

"Ahem. I will give you the bad news first."

Feeling inhibited with the nine pairs of eyes riveted upon him, Damien held a clipboard as a prop and pretended to read from it.

Up front he told the applicants the extent of remuneration, which met the legal award yet was minimal. Despite it being a full time permanent position, the prospect of advancement would also be minimal, unless having or achieving relevant qualifications. Damien honestly told the job seekers, the position was not glamorous, it entailed cleaning, fetching and interaction with customers who may not always be polite.

"The good news is... most people are polite. I hope that didn't give you a wrong impression.

There is variety and it is a tranquil workplace environment. I could facilitate if an employee needed time off to further studies pursuant to this position, further down the track. Any questions?"

"Is there a company car?" one dared to ask.

"No."

The disclosures thinned the applicants down to just three. Some grumbled that their time had been wasted. Damien wished the disgruntled drop outs good luck in finding a junior position where they started at the top. One of them flipped him the bird and tried in vain to slam the door, which only closed slowly and softly by its hydraulic arm. Caught on CCTV, Damien entertained himself with the notion of posting that frustrated dummy spit online.

Only after the majority vacated the reception area, did Damien closely regard the hopeful faces of the remaining three teenagers. With an electric jolt to his heart, Damien beheld that the last in line, who had stood partially hidden by the hat stand, was the spitting image of his long-lost partner, Kirkwood Bonn.

The boy's even features, wavy brown hair and clear green almond shaped eyes were identical to Kirkwood's. In that instance, Damien acknowledged the existence of Doppelgangers. He made an effort to clench his jaw, aware his mouth had gaped open in shocked surprise.

Shakily, he handed out clipboards with application forms to the three teens and they began filling out their names, addresses and relevant information. Before the individual interviews, Damien thanked the trio as a group and told them they would be informed of the outcome no later than the next day.

Somehow, Damien got through the first two interviews, leaving the Kirkwood lookalike till last. The lad entered the office and sat where he was told in front of Damien's desk.

The aspiring assistant placed his clipboard down, aligning it exactly square to the edge of the desk and the biro precisely parallel to it. Such fastidious neatness was another stark reminder of Kirkwood. Damien experienced a warp in time and tried not to stare at the lad, but the man's hands began to tremble when he read the boy's name: Kirk Jenkins.

Kirk! He stalled on reading the rest of the application. It took Damien a dizzying moment to pull himself together. He had to take some very deep breaths before continuing.

The boy waited patiently. He was aware of being closely scrutinised but had never attended a job interview before and did not know what to expect.

"Kirk. That is a name I don't hear very often." Damien smiled. "Ah...is it a family name?"

"No. I think my mother just liked the name."

"I see. It is a very nice name too. May I ask who your mother is?"

"Alba Jenkins. We have a place way out of town but I've got my own car now."

"And your father..?" Damien held his breath.

The boy appeared a little discomforted by this question though he squared his shoulders and replied stoutly:

"Mr. Cresswick, sir. If you met my mother, you might understand. Mum has some fanciful ideas. So, here's the thing: My Mum reckons I came about after a handsome ghost visited her and gave her a baby. Me of course. I am an only child. Obviously illegitimate."

The lad rolled his eyes. The eye roll was another of Kirkwood Bonn's traits. To Damien, he boy's catlike jade coloured eyes held an echo of Kirkwood's soul.

Kirk Jenkins knew the prospective employer might as well be told about his simple minded mother. He would find out soon enough. Alba had only become more ingenuous with age as she neared her half century. Young Kirk loved his mother but she could be embarrassing.

Old Bob Bartleigh the cattleman, occupied the back sleep out of the Jenkins homestead and thankfully still had his wits at almost eighty. The old man looked after necessities as Alba sank further into her dream world. Losing touch with reality, Alba spent more and more time living in her own glamorised version of La La land. Kirk Jenkins had once imagined old Bob Bartleigh could be his father. Bob only laughed and denied the possibility when it was put to him. Yet, the old man offered no further suggestion or hazarded any clue.

As a youngster, Kirk realised Santa Claus and the Easter Bunny were myths and that he hadn't been sired by a ghost nor found under a cabbage leaf. He knew himself to be a mistake and realised his elders strove to shield him from whatever ignoble truth brought about his existence.

Kirk Jenkins long ago accepted he qualified for the bastard label. Nevertheless, he had to swallow sudden shame in front of the genteel Mr. Cresswick.

"A handsome ghost?" Damien had goose bumps.

"I know how strange that sounds. I am afraid my mother seems to believe it completely."

Kirk blushed as Damien struggled to make sense of it and come up with some reasonable response:

"We can't discount what others believe in, Kirk. Um...Take crystal therapy for instance. To be honest, I'm surprised so many resort to that fantasy. There is no scientific proof behind the healing power of crystals or gems although I see the beauty in them."

Encouraged by the reply, Kirk spoke up:

"I am led to agree, Mr. Cresswick. Logically I cannot see how crystals can direct healing energies into a person. Except that if people really believe it is helping them, perhaps that is the key to it. Mind over matter, if you will."

"So you can see a compromise? You think it may not all be complete mumbo jumbo?"

"I do. Yes. And if crystal therapy has a placebo effect, it can be somewhat validated."

"That is a creditable observation, Kirk. Perhaps I can use it if ever I'm accused of chicanery."

Kirk Jenkins smiled, enjoying the high quality of communication. He felt drawn to this nice Mr. Cresswick even if the man gave him some odd looks.

"I must say, Mr. Cresswick, I have missed this." Young Kirk said.
"Missed this?"

Once more, Damien shivered. They had only just met. Hadn't they?

"Stimulating discussion. Since I left school, I have only Mum and Bob to talk to. Bless them both, but their conversations are bland."

"Bland you say?" Damien recognised one of Kirkwood's favoured adjectives.

"Insipid. Lacklustre. I realise that sounds disloyal, but I am not complaining. I love Mum and Bob of course."

The counter held a few small glass jars of opal chips. Damien selected one and held it up to catch the light. He felt perplexed and needed time to regroup.

The encounter with the Kirkwood double seemed surreal. It felt so dreamlike, Damien almost expected to wake up at any moment.

"Are they opals? I believe a lot of those are mined at Coober Pedy." Remarked young Kirk.

"That is correct. Have you been to that town?" Damien asked, almost afraid of the reply.

"No. I have not Mr. Cresswick. I've read a lot about it though. I did some research on gem therapy before applying here. I'd love to visit Coober Pedy someday. It seems absolutely fascinating."

As the boy expounded on research done towards his application, Damien's mind reeled back over the years, to a conversation had with the good lady detective, Dulcy Vestige:

Damien recalled mention of a mentally challenged woman who had taken in a hiker calling himself Kirk. Dulcy had said her curiosity stirred by seeing that simple country woman at Kirkwood's funeral. The slow woman had been confused. Dulcy explained to her that the visitor to her homestead had been an impostor, not the real Kirkwood. At the time, Dulcy and Damien both realised the unknown hiker must have been Kirkwood's killer.

Damien remembered the important breakthrough enabled by fingerprints on a rum bottle. History and DNA proved Bruce Luck and Kirkwood Bonn to be genetic brothers although neither could have known of the other's existence.

Reality dawned on Damien with an avalanche of mixed feelings that included crushing disappointment. The young job applicant was not a miracle rebirth of his beloved Kirkwood after all.

Kirk Jenkins had to be sired by the worst possible donor, the deceased and despised Bruce Luck. The embodiment of evil who had murdered Kirkwood, lived through this young man.

Alba Jenkins, with her fanciful ideas of a ghost giving her a baby, fitted with the lad's age. Kirk Jenkins' unmistakable similarity to Kirkwood in appearance and mannerisms fully supported the close family connection.

Damien experienced a frisson of dismay that he had the son of Kirkwood's murderer sitting before him, breathing the same air, sharing the space he and Kirkwood had made theirs.

While Kirk Jenkins enthused over his research towards the job vacancy, Kirkwood's lonesome partner agonised over a myriad of conflicting emotions.

Damien might have loathed the boy for his paternity. Briefly, he wondered if he should do so out of loyalty to Kirkwood. That unworthy idea evaporated quickly.

Natural integrity raised Damien above hating the innocent offspring. Rather, it seemed a blessing to have some part of Kirkwood returned, the definite connection surely a wondrous gift to be treasured.

Kirk Jenkins disbelieved the fairytale of how he'd come to be born. He would never learn the sorrowful truth from Damien, who vowed to protect Kirkwood's kin.

"When can you start Kirk?" Damien asked.

"Do I get the job then?"

"You do."

"That's brilliant. Thanks so much. Would Monday be alright? I'd start today but it's actually my birthday and Mum is doing something special."

Damien felt his hair stand on end and his heart rate increase. He wondered if his conjecture to clarify Kirk Jenkins' creation as being fathered by Bruce Luck really held true. The shared birthday fitted perfectly and young Kirk's appearance, voice and turn of phrase were pure Kirkwood. Damien could not shake off the notion of reincarnation.

"Happy birthday Kirk. It's actually my birthday as well." Damien managed to choke out.

"Happy birthday to you too." The young Kirk smiled Kirkwood's melting smile.

Damien's aching heart found peace at last.

To his great surprise, in the far distant future, Kirk Jenkins became the sole beneficiary of Damien's estate.

35

Rotten Luck

Bruce Luck had been a victim of toxic parents. Arguably his unforgivable crimes could be partly contributed to them. As The Bruiser, he had felt justified and empowered to exact retribution against society. Accustomed to being the aggressor, he credited a faithful belief in his own luck for any successes.

Generosity of the slow-witted homesteader had been abused without giving her a second thought. Yet he found those who seemed weakest may not be complete pushovers like Alba Jenkins. The Calenda sisters had him soil his pants.

The Bruiser's foray into a crime spree across Australia, broadened his horizons in a variety of ways. During his journey, the felon met few entirely good human beings. Mildly surprised at how many people carried latent rogue streaks lurking beneath benign facades, he nonetheless understood the game in a dog-eat-dog world. Amelia Boole and her man-eating dog, however, had pushed the boundaries even for The Bruiser.

An old grey pony taught the embittered man that nurturing another living creature could be a worthwhile and uplifting experience. The Bruiser had been lucky only for never realising Bouncer had not been stolen, but the pony chose to abandon him. A kindly old Welshman made Bruce regret his life of crime and long for plain normality. Yet the beautiful country home bequeathed to him as Jonesy, was always destined to be lost through The Bruiser's own deceptions.

The Bruiser had been fortunate in meeting the Kombi surfers although he viewed his foreign feelings of thankful indebtedness to them as weakness. Had he known those guys would commit arson on his behalf, he'd have warned them off a life of crime. Caring for others, another alien emotion, he'd no doubt see as a lapse of strength on his own part.

The Bruiser did not expect to fall victim to others. The conniving cafe owners, the thieving van driver and the psychopathic Amelia Boole, all dealt hard lessons.

Unable to undo his crimes or change his ways, Bruce Luck's chances of a better life spiralled ever downwards to his own destruction. Fate created contradictions that mocked Bruce Luck's belief in his own luckiness: He was never to know he sired an admirable child. Such a good son could have been a source of great pride for a man resentfully disappointed with his own parents.

Eluding capture before meeting his end favoured Bruce Luck with one stroke of good fortune: It spared him ever hearing he murdered his own brother.

So, in the end, shuffling off the mortal coil early, handed a lucky break to the bedevilled individual known as The Bruiser.

The End